COMING HOME TO THE SUNFLOWER CLIFFS

BOOK 4 OF THE SUNFLOWER CLIFFS SERIES

GEORGINA TROY

Boldwood

First published in 2016. This edition first published in Great Britain in 2024 by Boldwood Books Ltd.

Copyright © Georgina Troy, 2016

Cover Design by Alexandra Allen

Cover Illustration: Shutterstock

A CIP catalogue record for this book is available from the British Library.

Paperback ISBN 978-1-80426-137-8

Large Print ISBN 978-1-80426-139-2

Hardback ISBN 978-1-80426-138-5

Ebook ISBN 978-1-80426-135-4

Kindle ISBN 978-1-80426-136-1

Audio CD ISBN 978-1-80426-144-6

MP3 CD ISBN 978-1-80426-143-9

Digital audio download ISBN 978-1-80426-141-5

Boldwood Books Ltd
23 Bowerdean Street
London SW6 3TN
www.boldwoodbooks.com

My grandmother, Mary Troy, was a beautiful woman, both inside and out, and it's to her that I dedicate Coming Home to the Sunflower Cliffs.

Mary was a finalist in The Most Beautiful Girl in the World pageant in the 1920s. She qualified for the finals at the Albert Hall with the winner being awarded £1,000 and a film contract with Alfred Hitchcock. However, her mother had other plans and to soften the blow when refusing to let her attend, took her on holiday to Jersey instead, determined to keep her close by.

Unfortunately for her mother, it was there that Mary met her future husband, George, a larger-than-life character, who was smitten the instant he saw her.

1

DAISY

'It's true, chocolate can kill you.'

Daisy shook her head as she stood outside, trying not to take any notice of Fi's chatter. She waved goodbye to two of their guests as the taxi drove them away, cheered as she always was by the pristine white building that her boss had referred to as looking like a block of ice cream. To her it looked like a softly curved ship standing proudly at the top of the driveway. It spoke to her of history and Jersey between the wars and happy days filled with sunshine like the old 1930s posters she'd seen hanging up in the back office.

She smiled, taking in the elegant white building with its marine blue thick stripe painted across the entire length of the frontage just above the second-floor windows and its narrower triple stripes at either end. She loved this place with its history and what it meant to so many people in the island and those that visited.

'I promise you, I'm right. Daisy, are you listening to me?'

She held back a groan and walked back inside, returning to sit at her desk. Daisy glanced at the large, geometric clock behind

her at the minimalist reception in the hotel. She was determined
to finish reconciling the hotel bookings before the end of her
shift. Her boss needed to know where the hotel stood so alterna-
tive plans could be made. The unexpected fire in the orangery
had come at the worst possible time, losing the owners money at
the height of the season when they'd had to pass several parties
out to other establishments.

'You don't believe me, do you?' Fi added.

Daisy frowned. 'Sorry?' She tried not to ask her young,
bubbly colleague what she was going on about and focused on
the screen in front of her. Her resolve lasted all of ninety seconds.
'Oh, go on then, tell me.'

Fi giggled. 'I knew you couldn't resist any mention of
chocolate.'

Daisy laughed. 'You can talk. At least I only eat one bar at a
time; you buy a family pack and wolf the lot down,' she said,
looking in amazement at girl who must be at least five feet ten in
height but remained skinny. She'd heard from other members of
staff that Fi's brother, Sebastian Fielding, was a hugely successful
local businessman, who was also very tall, so height obviously
ran in their family.

'So?'

Daisy turned her gaze on her assistant. 'It must be in your
genes, because you should be stones heavier than you are, with
what you consume in a day.'

Fi opened her mouth to speak, when a whirlwind in the form
of Mrs Grey, the eighty-something co-owner of the hotel, pushed
back the double black lacquered front doors and raced in. Daisy
had grown very fond of Lydia since she'd begun working at the
Encore. Although the huge white ship-like hotel was mostly run
by Lydia's daughter, Francesca, and son-in-law, Rick, both of them
spent several months a year working away and Lydia always

stepped in to oversee things in their absence. Despite her age, Mrs Grey had more energy than most people Daisy knew, and the older lady never ceased to amaze her.

'Has he arrived yet?'

Daisy and Fi exchanged confused glances.

'Who, Mrs Grey?' Daisy asked, hoping she hadn't missed a booking. She was usually vigilant about these things. She studied her computer screen, trying not to panic.

Lydia Grey rested her fine bejewelled fingers on top of the reception desk. 'My grandson Gabriel, dear,' she said. 'He was supposed to be arriving in Jersey just after lunchtime, but he hasn't been to the house yet.'

'Gabriel? Coming home?' Fi smiled so widely that Daisy could see every tooth in her mouth. 'He hasn't been home for ages.'

Hearing the unusual name Daisy had to focus on not conjuring up the image of a man with the same name she'd met and fallen in love with in Vietnam when she'd been travelling two years before. She knew he was from Jersey, but his work kept him well away from the island. It was why she'd felt comfortable coming to work at this beautiful place two months before.

Lydia sighed. 'Ten months, just over,' she said, twisting her gold watch around her slim wrist to check the time. 'We've spoken on the laptop he bought me a few times and he sends me postcards and the occasional letter, but now the hotel's had this fire trouble, and his parents have to go away on tour, Francesca has asked him to come home for a few months and help out.'

Daisy tried to picture her flamboyant actress boss, Francesca Fiore, as the mother of the Gabriel she knew. No, they didn't look alike at all. She thought of Francesca's equally extrovert American husband, Rick Malone, but his bright blue eyes were nothing like those of the man she'd loved in Vietnam. Anyway, she consoled herself, her Gabe's last name was Wilson.

'Where has he been, Mrs Grey?' Daisy asked, relieved that the two couldn't be connected or that she hadn't messed up any bookings. She'd heard the older lady talking several times about her grandson but knew nothing about him other than that his grandmother doted on him and when he was in Jersey he stayed with her.

'He's a marine explorer,' Mrs Grey said, her eyes shining with barely concealed pride.

'A...' Daisy couldn't manage to say the words. The name Gabriel was unusual enough, but surely there couldn't be many of them who were also marine explorers? Her heart pounded and her ears rang.

Mrs Grey must have misunderstood her confusion and said, 'Essentially he identifies and collects new species of corals, fish, or whatever their current project is in aid of, in different waters around the world and works to secure protection of them. It's a very worthwhile job.'

'Oh,' Daisy said, unable to think of anything more intelligent to say.

Fi gasped and clamped her left hand on Daisy's wrist, squeezing so tightly Daisy felt it growing numb. 'He's here, Mrs Grey,' Fi squealed, pointing outside. 'Look. He's getting out of the pool.'

Mrs Grey's ice-blue eyes widened, and she turned and hurried outside. 'Darling, darling boy,' they heard her calling, as both girls stared after her.

Fi let go of Daisy's wrist and ran to the door to watch. 'Look, Daisy,' she whispered. 'Isn't he gorgeous? My friends and I used to call him Angel Gabriel, because he's so lush. And to think he'll be working here, with us.' She waved Daisy over to join her without taking her eyes off the figure in the pool.

Daisy watched, her breathing shallow, as the swimmer spotted his grandmother walking towards him and his mouth drew back into a wide smile. He grabbed a towel from a nearby sun lounger and shook his head, sending a shower of droplets around him as he walked towards her.

'I've seen him in the pool before,' Fi said breathlessly. 'Those tight muscles, that gorgeous bum. He's so hot.'

Daisy clenched her pencil so tightly she snapped it in half. He looked like some sort of Greek god with the sun shining on his tanned shoulders. This wasn't happening. She heard the unmistakable deep voice that had pleaded with her to stay with him in Hội An. She would have given almost anything to say yes. Now he was here and she was totally unprepared. She took a deep breath and looked up from the remains of her pencil to see the unmistakeable face of the man she'd fallen desperately in love with in Vietnam and whom she thought she'd never see again.

As she watched him hugging his tiny grandmother, her brain slowly processed the realisation that not only was he here at the Encore hotel, but he was also the son of her employers, Francesca and her singer husband. No wonder she hadn't connected them with Gabe; they had different last names to him. She couldn't believe her stupidity. Of course, actors and musicians usually had pseudonyms! Well, it was too late to leave now – she'd just have to face him and any resentment he still held for what she did to him.

His dark hair was much shorter than when she'd last seen him, she noticed, as he bent his head down to listen to something his grandmother was saying. Throwing his head back in delight, he laughed loudly; it was a sound Daisy remembered only too well. Her heart was in her mouth.

She didn't want him to see her here. What could she do? She saw him kiss his grandmother's cheek.

Daisy stared in horror as Lydia looked over her shoulder towards her and pointed into the reception area. The next thing she knew he was following his grandmother inside. Willing herself to become invisible, she closed her eyes briefly, opening them as he stepped into the hotel. He stopped suddenly, a wide-eyed look of shock on his face as he registered who was standing in front of him. Apparently, she was very much recognised and probably looking more gormless than professional. It wasn't the best impression she would have liked him to have of her after all this time.

'Daisy?' He shook his head slowly as if he couldn't believe what he was seeing. 'Daisy Woods,' he whispered, almost to himself.

She sympathised with his shock. She still couldn't believe he was in front of her and she'd had a few moments to get used to the idea of seeing him again. She cleared her throat, reaching out to shake his hand.

He brushed it away gently, hesitated a moment, then said. 'You're not going to greet me like that. Come here.'

Now it was his grandmother and Fi's turn to look surprised.

He lifted the barrier and joined her behind the reception desk, holding out his arms. 'It's good to see you.'

She automatically walked towards him, breathing in the chlorine smell from his T-shirt-encased chest as he wrapped his arms around her. She'd missed this so much. 'It's good to see you too, Gabe,' she said honestly, barely able to force the words out.

If Lydia or Fi spoke she didn't hear them. It dawned on her that he was speaking. She leant back slightly and looked up into those unforgettable eyes, the colour of the richest chocolate. She forced herself to speak. 'Sorry?'

He looked down at her and smiled. 'I can't believe it's you. Here in Jersey and at the Encore, too. How come?'

'Never mind that,' Lydia said, interrupting their closeness. 'How do you two know each other? Fi and I are intrigued.'

Daisy stepped back from Gabriel and shrugged. 'We met in Vietnam,' she explained, trying her best to sound calm. 'Almost two years ago.'

Lydia clapped her hands together. 'How perfectly lovely,' she said. 'You must come to supper tonight then, Daisy. It'll give you and Gabriel a chance to catch up.' She grinned. 'And I can discover more about my grandson. I didn't know you'd been away travelling too.'

Daisy nodded. 'Yes. We met when I was finishing my year away and just as Gabe was beginning his trip to Asia.'

Lydia narrowed her eyes. 'Well, you can have all the time in the world to catch up now you're both here,' she said, looking, Daisy thought, very pleased with herself.

'Gabriel will collect you at six-thirty. That will give you a bit of time after your shift ends to freshen up.'

Knowing Lydia well enough to be aware that she wasn't asking as much as telling Daisy what her evening arrangements would be, she nodded. 'Lovely.' She looked at Gabe, realising he was still staring at her in amazement, and smiled. 'I'll be waiting for you at the back of the hotel.'

He nodded. 'I'll look forward to it.'

'Right,' Lydia said, waving her grandson over to join her. 'Come along; I was expecting you earlier and there's a few things I need to show you.'

'Of course, the fire.'

Daisy watched them walk down the corridor together. Gabe followed in silence as his grandmother spoke excitedly, telling him about the night a week before when they'd all been woken by the alarms sounding off throughout the hotel. He glanced over his shoulder at Daisy, who gasped and sat back down in her chair. She reached out to take a new pencil from the tub on her desk and spotted the time on her computer screen. She didn't have long if she was going to get this lot to balance before her shift ended.

'He's gorgeous,' Fi murmured, staring after him. She sat down next to Daisy. 'So, tell me, then?'

'Tell you what?' Daisy asked, having no intention of doing any such thing.

'I'm not blind; you two were clearly much more than just friends.' She nudged Daisy. 'Oh, go on, Daiz, tell me.'

'Don't call me that,' she said, hating the nickname that her ex, Aaron, had given her. 'There's nothing to tell,' she lied, pushing away any thoughts of the man who'd controlled two years of her life. 'Now let me get on with this or Francesca is going to go mad. You know she leaves tomorrow for that shoot and she wanted to see this lot reconciled. I want her to go away relaxed and not worried about how things are carrying on while she's away.'

'Jobsworth.'

'Nosy cow.' Daisy couldn't help smiling at her annoying colleague and pointed at Fi's keyboard. 'You have letters to type. Now would be a good time to do them, ready for Francesca to sign in the morning.'

Fi groaned. 'Fine, but I will be asking about you and Gabriel again, so don't think I'll forget.'

Daisy didn't doubt for a minute that Fi would bring up the subject again, but for now she needed a little time to get used to the idea of seeing him here. She stared at the spreadsheet in front of her, pretending to be absorbed by it, but all she could think of was Gabriel.

2

DAISY

It was hard to know what to wear for dinner. Daisy wanted to be respectful and dress smartly, but at the same time she didn't want Gabe to think she was trying too hard. Seeing him again was bittersweet. She hoped his initial cheerful reaction to seeing her continued, though he had every right to be angry with the way she'd left things between them.

Trying to remain positive, she took a quick shower and stared at the floral cotton dress she'd decided to wear. Wrapping her arms around herself, she thought back to Gabe holding her, if only briefly, back in reception. She couldn't deny it had felt good.

'Gabe,' she whispered, sitting down at the fitted dressing table and pulling a brush through her damp hair.

She stared into space, remembering meeting him in Vietnam on a sun terrace in Ho Chi Minh City. She'd taken a seat at his small metal table because it was the only one available. He'd been laughing when she sat down.

'What's so funny?' she asked, trying her best to sound self-assured after taking a sip of her drink. She couldn't help noticing how good looking he was, but knew her lack of confidence meant that if there had been any other seats free she'd have rather taken one of those instead of trying to make small-talk with this intimidating stranger.

'I've just messaged my dad to say where I am and he was shocked,' he said. 'I know the Vietnam War ended back in the seventies, but in my dad's mind this is still a dangerous place, a war zone even. He was quite concerned to think I was in Saigon, as it was back then.'

Daisy understood his father's reaction. 'My mum said the same when I told her I planned to visit here. She said she remembers her parents listening daily to the news bulletins about the dreadful losses.'

They gazed down at the busy streets and cheerful faces around them.

'It's hard to imagine the chaos happening here back when the city fell, isn't it?' he asked, staring at her.

'It is.' She recalled a documentary she'd seen recently of grainy film showing an Air America helicopter resting on the top of a building with people crowding up a roof ladder, trying desperately to reach it.

That hot evening in the bar had been the first of many evenings spent in each other's company. She'd readily agreed when Gabriel suggested she travel with him to see a few towns on their way to Hội An, where they'd both planned to stay for a while. By the time they reached their destination they were besotted with each other, but unfortunately her mother's health had taken a nasty turn and she had to hurriedly return to England. Everything had disintegrated after that.

Now though, seeing him back here and giving up all that he loved to assist his family, she could see he'd meant it when he'd told her, 'Family is the most important thing you'll ever have, Daisy. If you need to go to your mum, then we'll just have to deal

with it. We'll make a plan to meet up again when she's settled.'
She'd reluctantly agreed with him, but things hadn't turned out
as either of them initially hoped.

The landline in her room rang, making her jump. She
glanced at her bedside clock and saw she was late to meet him
downstairs. Picking up the phone, she heard Fi's stammering
attempt at professionalism and could tell Gabe must be standing
in front of her.

'Thanks Fi,' she said. 'Please tell Gabriel I'm on my way.' It
seemed odd referring to him by his full name. She pushed the
thought aside and hurriedly dressed, picking up her bag with
one hand and running the other through her long, wavy fair hair.
She hoped it would be dry by the time they arrived at Lydia's
house.

She pushed open the door leading from the staff quarters to
the reception area and hesitated when she saw him leaning
against the counter, laughing at something Fi was saying. He
looked so relaxed and at home here. As he should do, she
thought, but it was still strange seeing someone she associated so
much with her travels and the heady colours and scents of Asia,
standing at her workplace in Jersey.

He looked up, and seeing her at the doorway held up a set of
car keys. 'I've got transport and have been instructed not to
dawdle, so we'd better get a move on.' He waited for her to reach
him, then smiled at Fi. 'It's great to see you again, Fi,' he said. 'Tell
that brother of yours that I'll take him up on his offer to go
kayaking with him and his mate Ed one of these days.'

'Will do,' Fi said, winking slyly at Daisy as soon as Gabe
turned his back to hold the door open for her. 'Have fun,' she
mouthed.

Daisy pulled a face at her and followed him to the red sports
car. 'Wow, you must be special to Mrs Grey if she allows you to

drive her car,' she teased as she got in, happy that the roof was down and her hair would have a chance to dry during their drive.

Gabriel took his seat in the car next to her and started it. He put the car into gear and turned to her, smiling. 'It's not hers, it's mine. You're looking very lovely,' he said. 'Your hair's grown a lot.'

'Thank you. It probably needs a trim, but I haven't got around to finding a hairdresser in Jersey yet.'

'It's small, but there's a lot to discover here,' he said, steering the car down the driveway. Checking nothing was coming, he pulled out onto the main road. 'Does it feel strange seeing me here?'

She was relieved she wasn't the only one experiencing that surreal sensation. 'Yes, very.'

He drove in silence for a couple of minutes. 'I hope you don't mind me asking, but how come you ended up working at the Encore?'

Gabe had never been one to hold back from facing anything awkward, so his question didn't surprise her. 'I'd never been here before, and after...' She hesitated, not ready to share her story with him. 'Well, after I decided to leave Devon, I remembered you mentioning how beautiful it was here. I needed somewhere to work and have experience working as a receptionist in a hotel back home. The Encore provided me with a job and somewhere to live.'

'I can tell by the look on your face when I arrived at the hotel that you didn't know it was run by my family.' He studied her face briefly, then turning back to focus on the road ahead, added, 'You wouldn't have come to the Encore if you'd known I was connected to it, would you?'

'No,' she said honestly.

'Then I'm glad you didn't know,' he said, turning the car into a small lane. 'Why didn't you answer any of my messages?'

As soon as she'd see him standing outside the hotel Daisy knew he would ask her this question. It didn't help her come up with an acceptable answer for him though, and she certainly wasn't ready to tell him about her issues with Aaron. 'I'm not sure what to say, really,' she said, racking her brains to come up with something that didn't divulge her true story.

'It's OK,' he said, giving her one of his smiles she remembered only too well. 'I understand if you've moved on. It was two years ago after all, but our time away together was pretty amazing.'

'It was,' she said wistfully. 'But our lives were going in opposite directions.' She hoped he wasn't going to question her too much, although he had every right to expect a few answers. She recalled the promises they'd made to each other to stay in touch and meet up again as soon as they could manage to, but she'd left him in Hội An and believed their relationship to be a beautiful memory from her past.

'So, what have you been doing since I last saw you? I mean, after you returned home to Devon. You seemed so happy in Vietnam, it was hard to imagine you staying back in England.'

'It wasn't easy,' she said truthfully. 'But I haven't been doing much,' she fibbed. 'I've been here in Jersey since April to help set up for the season and I'm loving it. Your grandmother is incredible,' she said, hoping to divert his attention away from her. 'I really like her.'

'She is,' he nodded. 'I spent a huge amount of my childhood staying with her.'

'Was that because Francesca and Rick were away working?'

'Yes.'

'You never told me your family had a hotel,' she said, trying not to sound accusatory. 'I never connected you with Francesca and Rick. You said your last name was Wilson.'

'It is.' He laughed. 'It's a little complicated. You see, my dad's real surname is Wilson, but there was another Rick Wilson with an Equity Card, so he uses his mother's maiden name of Malone. Mum uses her maiden name, Fiore. Nan used to be an actress back in the fifties and she reverted to her maiden name, Grey, the one she used for her acting career after she split up with her husband.'

Daisy followed what he was telling her until he reached the bit about Lydia. 'I never knew your grandmother was an actress too!'

He gave her a wide smile. 'You didn't realise she was *the* Lydia Grey, fifties blonde bombshell and Jersey's answer to Marilyn Monroe?'

Daisy laughed at his teasing. 'My mum was a huge fan of hers and had all her films.' She conjured up a picture of the actress at the height of her fame. He wasn't joking – his grandmother was the Lydia Grey. 'How did I not realise that before? I love her work.' She stared at him, trying to recall what had happened to end Lydia's career at the height of her success. 'But she disappeared suddenly after only a few years. What on earth happened?'

Gabe slowed the car to turn into a long driveway. He sighed. 'It's a bit of a mystery, I'm afraid, and one she refuses to discuss,' he said. 'She fell in love with my grandfather, but things didn't work out; that much I do know. She has said that I look very much like him.'

Daisy wished she could see a picture of Gabe's mysterious grandfather and hoped she'd be able to find out more about Lydia's past. She recalled her mother talking about the actress's disappearance from the public eye and much had been speculated about it. At least she knew Lydia was OK now. 'It's exciting to finally have met her,' she said eventually.

He shrugged. 'She's always seemed happy. I think whatever

did happen was life-changing. Her marriage didn't last all that long, but she's never encouraged any of us to ask about it, always changing the subject if we do get a little curious.'

Daisy opened her mouth to ask him what Lydia had done next, but he parked the car and got out, holding her door open for her. 'She'll be waiting for us around the back on the terrace.'

They hurried round along the stone pathway and Gabriel raised his hand and waved at his grandmother, sitting at a table. Her step faltered as she was confronted by the exquisite view in front of her. She presumed Lydia's home had been built sometime in the fifties and the garden, which looked as if it led straight out onto a beach, was awe-inspiring.

'See, I told you I'd get her here safely,' Gabriel called.

She hurried to catch up with him. She straightened her dress and tried to tidy up her unruly hair before greeting her hostess. 'Hello, Mrs Grey,' she said, looking around her at the perfectly manicured lawn that dipped gently towards a view of the bay, framed on two sides by two enormous pine trees. 'What a spectacular view.'

Lydia stood up and gave Gabriel a hug, then motioned for Daisy to take a seat at the table. 'I'm glad you like it.' She stared out to the rolling waves on the navy sea out in the bay. 'I've lived here for decades and still think I must be dreaming for the first few seconds that I'm awake.'

'I can see why,' Daisy said, imagining how idyllic it would be to wake up at this house every morning surrounded by the vivid colours from the garden and going to sleep with the sounds of the waves all around.

'Darling, go and pour Daisy a Bellini, and get yourself a cool drink.' She turned her attention back to Daisy. 'I hope you like them. I make excellent Bellinis, so I'm told.'

She thought she spotted a hint of sadness in Lydia's eyes. 'I love them,' Daisy said.

Gabe was soon back with her drink, which was delicious.

'Good?' Gabriel asked. 'Nan only uses the best white peach juice,' he said. 'She insists that's the difference between a perfect Bellini and an average one, don't you, Nan?'

'It's heavenly,' Daisy said, before taking another sip.

'I'm glad you like it, Daisy,' Lydia said, raising her glass to them.

'So,' Gabriel said. 'What are you treating us to for dinner tonight?' He leant forward slightly and in a mock whisper to Daisy, said, 'Nan is an excellent cook and likes to try out different recipes, so be prepared.'

Daisy laughed. 'You look perfectly healthy on Mrs Grey's cooking,' she teased.

'Please call me Lydia,' she said. 'Being called Mrs Grey in my home is making me feel old.' She rested a hand on Daisy's forearm. 'I don't do all the cooking. I have Anna – she's my housekeeper and cooks for me, as well as keeping everything in order. I mainly potter around my garden and take long walks on the beach.' She laughed. 'Gabriel doesn't enjoy much of my cooking. He wasn't impressed with the chocolate chilli sauce I concocted the last time he was staying.'

Daisy wasn't surprised. She hoped she wasn't being treated to a similar combination. 'Oh?'

Gabriel laughed. 'I think Daisy is a bit more of a traditionalist when it comes to food, Nan.'

'Not necessarily,' Daisy said, not wishing to offend Lydia.

'You like the idea of chocolate and chilli in a dish?' Lydia asked. 'I can't help thinking of it as rather an unnecessary combination.'

Daisy couldn't help smiling. 'No,' she said.

'I have to admit, I didn't much like it either,' Lydia laughed. 'But it was worth a try. I haven't made anything too unfamiliar for us tonight though.'

Daisy smiled, then sat back in the cushioned metal chair and looked out across the well-kept garden to the sea once again. 'It's very peaceful here, isn't it?'

Lydia nodded. 'It can be a little too peaceful when Gabriel is away. Sometimes, in the summer, I rent out rooms to Francesca and Rick's acting friends who've come over on tour to the Arts Trust or the Opera House. I like the company and it's good to talk to new people in the business.'

Daisy was delighted Lydia had brought up the subject of acting. 'Gabriel and I were only just discussing your fascinating career on the way here in the car,' she said. 'I grew up looking at books on film and actors that my mum collected. There were loads of pictures of you.' She hesitated before adding, 'Do you miss that life at all?'

Lydia took a sip of her drink and stared at her thoughtfully before answering. 'Sometimes.' She placed her drink back down on table. 'I'm far too old for all that now, but I loved it when I was filming and even the initial struggle to be discovered.'

'I think my mum dreamed of being an actress and when she didn't realise her dream she tried to encourage me to act,' Daisy admitted. It wasn't something she'd shared with anyone else. 'She made me go to dance and acting lessons and even took extra jobs to pay for them all.'

'What happened?' Gabriel asked, resting back in his chair, his long legs stretched out in front of him.

Daisy smiled at the memory. 'I was hopeless and so shy the last thing I wanted to do was perform in front of anyone. I hated the lessons.' She thought back to that first time in the class with twenty other children, all of whom seemed to love what they were doing. 'We had to be ants wading through honey, or some-thing. I didn't see the point and would have much rather been out with my best friend riding her pony.'

'I don't blame you,' Gabriel laughed. 'I was always in a swim-ming pool.'

Lydia turned her attention to her grandson. 'I remember when your father was certain you had the voice of an angel and should audition for one of those church choirs on the mainland.'

Gabriel nodded. 'Until Mum told him that if I was going to be an entertainer I should be an actor. That was when I decided to go into something far removed from their business.'

'Marine exploration?' Daisy asked. 'That's quite a different route to go down on the career front.'

Lydia got up. 'He was in the water at every opportunity, this boy.' She rested a hand on Gabriel's shoulder. 'I'll go inside and sort out the food and leave you two here to chat for a few minutes.'

'Call me when you want me to come and carry out the plates,' Gabriel said, before turning his attention back to Daisy. 'Nan doesn't often talk about her acting, you know. I think she misses it more than she lets on. I also believe it's why she's always been so supportive of Mum and Dad by taking over at the hotel and looking after me, so they could take on work.'

Daisy wondered how it must feel to have someone willing to do that whenever you needed them to. She envied Francesca and Rick their freedom. 'She's a wonderful lady.'

He looked towards the doorway through which his grand-mother had just walked. 'She is. I'm very lucky to have her.'

'It must have been wonderful to spend so much time here when you were growing up.'

'Yes, I always loved it. Nan is very relaxed and great fun to be with. If I'm honest, I used to look forward to my parents going away. They were always happier to be doing something they loved, and Nan was pleased to have me here with her. How about you, what was your childhood like?'

Daisy thought back to lonely days in Devon with her mum working long hours trying to make enough for them to live on, and the occasional visits from her father. She'd learnt from experience that lies hurt. Her mother had been let down by him before she was born and despite him running away then coming back after Daisy's birth, insisting he wanted to make a go of their relationship, her mother had been so hurt by his initial cowardice that she'd said no. He'd gone off and married another woman within months, and her mother had never got over losing him.

Daisy recalled the humiliation of only being allowed to see her father when his family didn't expect him to be around. She hated that she was his secret child, despite her mother trying to make her accept that being a 'love child' was in some way romantic. It wasn't. She refused to be anyone's second best ever again.

When she'd grown into a teenager her dream had been for her art to be good enough to hold her own exhibition, and that ambition had been on the point of realisation until Aaron had made life so impossible for her that she'd had to leave everything behind at barely a moment's notice.

'I lived in a pretty village near the sea,' she said finally, not wishing him to know the full extent of her story. 'So I spent most of my time on the beach, or wandering around the cliff paths, finding places to sketch or paint.'

'Do you still paint?'

'Sometimes,' she said, not wishing to think about how much she missed those days.

There was a brief silence before Gabe asked, 'Do you think that's where you got your travel bug?'

'Maybe. There were always so many holidaymakers around and I always wondered where they'd come from.'

Gabe stared at her in silence for a bit. 'How come we spent so much time together in Vietnam and never talked about our pasts? What did we talk about?'

She shook her head, allowing herself to think back to those perfect weeks where she'd been happiest. 'Probably the places we'd been to and what we'd seen.' She had spent two years trying not to think too much about those blissful days and nights with him. 'I should think Jersey and Devon were farthest from our minds when we were so far away.'

He nodded. 'Yes, you're probably right. And art, of course.'

Daisy smiled. Gabe had been a keen sketcher in Vietnam and they'd had many conversations about it and about how the light was different there to at home, making the colours of the earth and sky seem more vibrant somehow.

She twisted the ring on her finger.

'You kept it then?'

She frowned, unsure what he meant. Then following his line of vision realised he was referring to the interlaced triple rings he'd bought her at a tiny jewellery shop they'd come across during the last week of their time together. The ring, with its yellow, gold and white bands. 'Oh, yes, I wear it all the time.' She didn't add that it comforted her when she was feeling especially vulnerable. The thought made her glance down the garden towards the beach. She was being silly. She was safe here. No one knew her, so who could let him know where to find her?

'I'm pleased,' Gabe said, bringing her back to the present. He frowned. 'You OK?'

She forced a smile. 'Yes, I was just thinking.'

'You looked troubled for a moment,' he said. 'Are you sure there's nothing bothering you?'

'Nothing,' she lied. Aaron had ruined far too much of her life already; she was determined to overcome her fear of him, somehow.

She really must learn to hide her feelings if she didn't want anyone to start questioning her about her past, she decided. If she was going to make a new life for herself then she needed to push aside her memories of Aaron and what he'd done to her. He'd ruined her life in Devon but she had a chance to make a life for herself here in Jersey. She placed her hand on the table, letting the sun glint on her ring. 'I didn't think there was a reason to take it off,' she said, awkwardly bringing the subject back to happier memories. 'It's a beautiful ring.'

'I'm glad you like it; I wasn't sure if you were just being polite when I bought it for you, but when you told me you had to leave it seemed the perfect sentiment.'

She stared at the three intertwined bands. 'They met, they fell in love, they parted,' she said, thinking how sad they'd both been when she discovered she had to cut her trip short.

He raised his glass. 'Come on, let's not think about the past. Nan will go mad if she thinks I've ruined your evening. We're here to enjoy her food.' He laughed. 'I hope.'

Relieved he'd lightened the mood, Daisy joined him. She was enjoying herself, not only because of seeing him again, but also for the chance to get to know Lydia a bit better and spend an evening away from the hotel and the constant noise that went with living on-site.

'Gabriel, can you come and help me please?' Lydia shouted from inside the house.

He gave Daisy a smile and got up. 'It's good to have you here,' he said simply, before walking off to help his grandmother.

Daisy breathed in the rose-scented air in the pretty garden. She didn't think she'd ever spent time in any private garden as beautiful as this one. She looked at the herb border and longed to smell a sprig of the abundant rosemary growing along the back. She would love to paint it sometime.

'Here we are,' Gabriel said, placing a plate of penne pasta in front of her and another on his grandmother's place. He took the plate his grandmother was holding for himself. 'I'll go and fetch the salad and bread.'

'It's arrabbiata,' Lydia said. 'I hope you like it.'

Daisy did. In fact she thoroughly enjoyed the entire evening with one old friend and another newer one. Lydia asked Gabriel more about his latest project and Daisy could see how proud Lydia was of her grandson from the sparkle in her eyes.

'I love it, but it's very intense, which is why I can't afford to be here for too long,' he said, between mouthfuls. 'I need to get back to the others and do my bit as soon as possible. We're hoping for approval from a new sponsor to keep the project going.'

'Where is it,' Daisy asked, 'and what does the project involve?'

'It's in South Africa. Down the south coast from Durban, just outside Umkomaas,' he added. 'We're looking at newly discovered marine life and why it's chosen that habitat to breed in.'

'When will you find out if you've been successful?' she asked.

'Any day now,' he said. 'It's taken months to get this far with it. We had enough to start the process and to take part in initial tests, which have come back with interesting results, so we're hoping they don't back out. They've assured us everything is almost in place, but I'll believe it when the money's in our account.'

'I hope you get the funding you need,' she said, acutely aware that for him to obtain the funding would also mean he'd be leaving again.

'Thanks. We've all worked very hard for this, so it would be a shame for it to fall through at this stage.'

'Let's not discuss that now,' Lydia said. 'I've only just got you back here. Let's eat this delicious meal and talk about something else.'

After they'd finished, Daisy asked if she could go to the bathroom and Lydia showed her into the house. They stepped into the kitchen, the scent of tea roses and jasmine wafting in with them as they passed the huge tubs on either side of open sliding doors. As they walked through the house Daisy noticed that the back of the building curved around a stone tower. 'What's that?' she asked, intrigued.

'That's a Martello tower,' Lydia said. 'They were built here in the early nineteenth century to guard the island against an invasion from France. That was in Napoleon's time, you see.'

Daisy had seen a few dotted along the coast of the island but had never been sure what they were. 'You own it?'

'I do,' Lydia said. 'Some are owned by the States of Jersey, I believe, or Jersey Heritage, but some are privately owned. That's where Gabriel lives when he's in the island; he has a bedroom and a bathroom and kitchen in there.'

Daisy couldn't imagine what it must be like to live in a tower. 'It's amazing.'

'I'm sure he'll show you around after dinner, if you'd like him to. Although you'll probably have to step over a few surfboards and things. Gabriel has a lot of stuff and there's never enough storage in these places.'

Daisy wouldn't know, but she nodded. 'I'd like that very much,' she said. The Gabriel she'd spent time with in Vietnam had had nothing more than a rucksack with a few changes of clothes inside, along with his sketchpad and pencils. It was strange to try to associate this clean-cut man who was obviously used to living in luxury with the long-haired, bearded one who'd shared cheap hostels with her.

She re-joined them at the table. He did look happy to see her back. The thought pleased her.

Lydia placed a plate with a cheesecake and a few small red berries in front of Daisy. 'Leave what you don't want,' she said. 'This is lighter than it looks. Anna made it for us.'

'It's New York cheesecake with raspberry sauce running through it,' Gabriel said. 'It's her speciality and she always makes it when I come home.'

Daisy pushed her small cake fork into the dessert and tasted it. 'It's delicious,' she said, licking her lips to clean off the dusting of icing sugar delicately coating the top of the sweet treat.

'Have you been painting much since you got to Jersey?' Gabe asked.

'Painting?' Lydia placed her knife and fork down on the sides of her plate, narrowing her eyes thoughtfully. 'Tell me a bit more about your painting, Daisy. And your time in Vietnam. Gabriel didn't tell us much about it, really.'

'Do you want to tell her?' Gabe asked.

Daisy shook her head. 'No, you go ahead,' she said, wanting to know how he'd describe their time away to his grandmother.

'Daisy and I met up on my first day in Ho Chi Minh City. We bumped into each other at a bar, got chatting and then discovered we were staying in hostels very near to each other. I spotted her in the street a couple of days later, so I shouted out and she was so surprised to hear someone calling her name that she dropped her artists' pad on the floor.' He looked over at her. 'Do you remember, Daisy?'

She forced a smile on her face. She remembered only too well. She had never expected to hear anyone calling out for her so far away from her home. 'I do,' she said, still a little embarrassed.

'Anyway, we went for something to eat after that.'

Daisy listened to his deep voice, tinged with a slight American accent. They hadn't spoken much about their lives when they'd met previously but she did recall him telling her that he'd spent most of his childhood living in California with his mother and father, but now she realised it must have been while they pursued their careers in the entertainment world.

'Yes,' she said. 'And you told me all about the wonderful holidays you'd spent staying with your grandmother whose house was next to the beach in Jersey. I can't believe I'm there now.'

'I'm glad you are,' he said.

She closed her eyes and he did sound just like the Gabe she recalled from her halcyon days in Vietnam, when anything seemed possible and she felt more in control of her life than ever before. Lydia was asking her something. She opened her eyes. 'Sorry, I was miles away.'

Lydia smiled at her sweetly and Daisy could see that she had picked up that there was more to her story than she was letting on.

'I was asking if you had any paintings that you could show to me?'

She shook her head. 'I haven't painted since I left Vietnam,' she admitted quietly.

Gabe frowned. 'Why not?' he asked, leaning slightly closer to her, his concern obvious.

She shrugged. Now wasn't the time to confide her private family matters. 'Too much going on,' she said, forcing a laugh. It wasn't exactly a lie.

'If you've got talent you should make the most of it,' Lydia said, taking a sip of her wine. 'I'd love to see what you can do. I used to paint but I was hopeless.'

Gabe laughed. 'It didn't stop you though, did it?'

'Of course not,' she said, a determined twinkle in her blue eyes. She looked at Daisy. 'You can come here and paint any time you want to make the most of these views – if it's landscapes you like, that is. You'll be left in peace.' She smiled at Gabe. 'Won't she, Gabriel?'

He nodded. 'Yes, of course. If that's what you want.'

She saw Lydia raise an eyebrow at him and had to struggle not to let them see how amused she was. If there was one person in the world Daisy wouldn't mind disturbing her it was Gabe.

'I'm so pleased you two know each other,' Lydia said smiling. 'Why haven't I heard anything about Daisy before?'

'Because I don't report back to you on my private life, Nan,' Gabriel teased.

Daisy could see an unmistakeable glimpse of pain in his eyes and had to look away, but then felt his hand brush hers as he took it. 'We spent a couple of months together and travelled around a bit, but then Daisy had to return home.'

Did she hear an accusatory tone in his voice? Daisy wondered. Determined to keep the mood light, she ignored her suspicions. 'Yes, my mum was unwell.'

Daisy pulled her hand slowly from his. He released his hold on her but kept up the eye contact.

Lydia looked from Daisy to Gabriel and back to her again. 'You didn't keep in touch?' she asked. Daisy shook her head. 'Oh. I hope I haven't made things difficult for you, inviting you to dinner here with Gabriel tonight. I can be rather impulsive, but I thought it would be nice if we all had a catch up.'

Daisy shook her head. 'Not at all,' she said. 'I think it's a bit of a shock for both of us to see each other again after nearly two years.'

'I'd say it was more of a surprise,' Gabe said. 'It was fantastic to find Daisy at the Encore this afternoon.'

Daisy couldn't help relaxing in his company. 'Thanks, Gabe,' she said. 'It was great to see you again too.'

Lydia straightened her place mat. 'Sorry to harp on, but I'm intrigued. You both say you're happy to see each other here and it sounds to me as if you had a splendid time in Vietnam together, so why haven't you kept in contact?'

Daisy was astounded by Lydia's directness, and when she glanced at Gabe she saw he too was struggling to answer. 'I'd really wanted to continue travelling,' she said, 'but I heard from back home that my mum had had a stroke, and I had... um... a few issues that needed to be faced. I ended up having to make an emergency trip back home. It cost me the rest of my travel funds.'

Gabe's dark eyebrows lowered. 'What issues? Why didn't you tell me about those?'

She took a deep breath. Now was not the time to try and explain her dramas with Aaron. She didn't want to have to think about his nastiness on this perfect evening. 'Mum has always been intensely private, so I wasn't used to sharing any information about her, or our life. I suppose it never occurred to me to say anything,' she said. 'She had another stroke before I arrived home and from then on needed constant care.'

He took hold of Daisy's hand. 'I would have come back to help you, if I'd known.'

She believed him, but couldn't tell him how mortified she'd have been for him to come to their home and be turned away by her highly defensive mum. She placed her hand on the top of his. He was still the same Gabe, caring and adorable. 'I know you would and that's exactly why I didn't tell you. You'd only just begun your adventures. I couldn't expect you to give everything up and come to Devon.'

'Yes, you could.'

She shook her head. 'Thank you, that's really sweet.' It wasn't something worth debating, not now.

'How is your mother now, Daisy?' Lydia's soft voice drew her attention from Gabe's stricken face.

Daisy shrugged. 'She died, Mrs Grey. Six months ago.' She cleared her throat to push away the tears that were threatening to take over.

Focusing her attention back to Gabe once more, she said. 'I thought I'd been distant from you for too long by the time she died and knew you'd either have met someone or were involved in a project somewhere exotic. I didn't think it would be fair of me to interrupt your life.'

Lydia stood up. 'I'm going to clear this table and leave you two to catch up. You obviously have a lot to talk about and you don't need me sitting here hindering your conversation.'

Daisy was horrified at the thought of pushing Lydia away from her meal. 'No, please. Gabe is in Jersey now and I'm sure we'll have plenty of chances to say all we need to.' She gave him a pointed stare. 'Won't we, Gabe?'

He nodded. 'Yes, Nan, we will. Now, please sit down and let me clear these plates.'

Daisy suspected Lydia was referring to her own experiences. She couldn't help wondering what Lydia's story must be.

Lydia smiled. 'Daisy,' she said, when Gabriel had collected their plates and left them alone at the table. 'I can see by the way you're studying me that you've got questions you'd like to ask.'

Daisy opened her mouth to disagree, then realising Lydia had seen straight through her, smiled. 'I do. My mum was a huge fan of yours.'

Lydia tapped the side of her nose with one of her bejewelled fingers. 'I do have my own story to tell and maybe one day I'll let you in on everything.'

'I thought you might,' Daisy said, desperate to get to know this fascinating lady even a little bit. She couldn't help being sad that her mum hadn't lived long enough to know her daughter had met this famous actress. She thought back to the iconic images of Marilyn Monroe that she'd been fascinated by growing up, and then to the more regal version that Lydia Grey had been. 'Was it fun being the Jersey Bombshell?' she asked, unable to resist one question.

Lydia relaxed back into her chair and smiled. 'It was the best fun a young woman could hope for. Sometimes it seems like only last year.'

'My mum said that growing up she wished she could look like you.' Lydia smiled.

They turned when they heard Gabriel's footsteps crossing the terrace. 'I'm hoping this pavlova was meant for us,' he said, placing the largest meringue pudding Daisy had ever seen down the table.

'Well, I didn't intend keeping it all for myself.' Lydia laughed as she served up the messy but delicious treat. 'Gabe loves pavlova,' she said, smiling at him as she handed Daisy a bowl. 'I hope you do too.'

'Love it,' Daisy said with relish, not sure why they were being served with a second pudding. 'My mum used to make me a meringue covered with chocolate and cream for my birthdays instead of a cake.'

Lydia seemed to like this idea. 'Then I'm delighted I made it for us. I couldn't choose between this or a cheesecake, so I thought we could have a little of both.'

They chatted a bit more, mostly about incidents at the hotel and the garden Lydia had spent the past twenty years designing. Then, when they'd finished eating, Lydia suggested she show Daisy around it. 'It's especially beautifully at this time of year.'

Lydia stood up and Daisy and Gabriel stepped down from the

terrace after her onto her lawn. They walked slowly in the direction of the beach.

'Where exactly are we?' Daisy asked, aware that although she knew they'd driven east, she wasn't entirely sure where this place was.

'Near La Motte – Green Island, that is,' Lydia said. 'I used to come here as a child and spend hours by the sea looking out at that tiny island.'

Daisy followed Lydia's direction to see something that wasn't much bigger than a grassy knoll sticking out of the sea metres from the shore. 'It's very close. I suppose you can walk there when the tide is out?'

'Oh yes,' Lydia said. 'But you have to be careful not to get caught by the rip tide when the tide comes in. It's much faster than people assume and occasionally visitors get marooned and need to be rescued.'

'I hope you have a good rescue team over here with all these beaches,' Daisy asked.

'We do.' Lydia slipped off her shoes when they reached the steps down to the beach. 'You can leave your shoes here, if you like.'

'Luke, the guy who's been working on the orangery at the hotel, he's in the RNLI. There are two lifeboat crews over here,' Gabe said, kicking off his loafers. 'One over that way in St Catherine's and another in St Helier. They're out a lot over the year. Most of the call outs are for tourists who've sailed to the island, don't know the waters and underestimate the currents.'

'I know they have their work cut out for them near where I lived in Devon,' Daisy said, recalling her mother once being upset about someone she'd known drowning when they'd gone to save a crew in distress. She'd always had a strong respect of the sea and never understood when others took chances.

'The tides in Jersey can rise by forty metres in twenty-four hours, so it can be pretty dodgy here,' Gabe said, picking up a shell and inspecting it.

'Why did you choose Jersey to come and work in, Daisy?' Lydia asked. 'I would have thought you'd want to stay somewhere familiar, especially growing up in Devon. It's beautiful there.'

Daisy shrugged. She couldn't tell them she was hiding from someone. 'Jersey is more like Devon than I expected,' she said.

'You mean the narrow lanes and high banks,' Gabe teased.

'Well, you also have lovely Jersey cream over here, too,' she said. 'But I meant the rocky headlands and the pretty little bays and coves. Not that I've seen too many yet.'

'Most people come here to work because they were brought here on holidays as children and liked the idea of returning to work for a season or two,' Lydia said, bending to pick up a string of seaweed. 'I love putting this stuff on my garden; it's the best thing for the soil.'

Daisy didn't like to admit she'd never had any holidays when she was growing up. Her mum had never managed to earn enough to have the luxury of spare cash in her pocket. 'No, I came here because Gabriel mentioned it was where he was from. I'd never been before and knew nothing about it, so I looked it up at our local library and discovered a Jersey-based jobsite. I applied for a few things and ended up being offered a job at the Encore.'

'So, you didn't particularly aim to work with us?' Lydia asked, linking arms with Daisy as they walked across the soft creamy sand.

Daisy shook her head. 'No, but I've always loved Art Deco and the architecture fascinates me. I wasn't aware Gabriel had any connection to the place. We only ever spoke about his ambitions as a marine explorer, didn't we, Gabe?' He nodded. 'It was only him describing the pretty beaches and coves and the clifftop

walks and the happy, relaxed lifestyle that made me intrigued
enough to find out more. When Mum died I needed somewhere
to live, so I left Devon and came here.'

She could see both Gabe and his grandmother were saddened
by her mentioning the loss of her mother, so smiled at them.
'Please, it's fine. Don't be concerned for me, I'm very happy here. I
love it. Mum had come here as a girl and she told me once how
pretty it was and how she'd loved it. So, the connection of Gabe
and my mum gave me the impetus to come here and see for
myself what this place has to offer.'

'Good, I'm glad you did,' Lydia said, giving her arm a gentle
squeeze. 'You're an asset to the Encore. Many people have said so,
and I'm enjoying getting to know you.'

'Thank you,' Daisy said. 'That means a lot to me.'

They returned to the table and Lydia served them coffee.
Daisy could feel a yawn trying to escape and held her hand up to
try and hide it from the others, but Gabriel had noticed. 'You're
tired,' he said. 'We should be going.'

'No, really, I'm having a lovely time,' Daisy argued. She wasn't
ready to go back to her small bedroom at the back of the hotel.

'He's right,' Lydia said, standing up. 'I forget you youngsters
have been hard at work all day. Well, *you* have, Daisy,' she said,
resting a hand on Gabriel's muscular shoulder. 'Gabriel has that
pleasure to look forward to from tomorrow when his parents go
on their way to their various contracts.'

Daisy had forgotten to consider what it was going to be like
working in the same building as Gabe. She realised she was
feeling happy, truly happy, for the first time since she was last
with him in Vietnam.

She hadn't expected to recover from the trauma of witnessing
her mother's rapid decline and those seemingly endless days at
her hospital bedside. For someone as desperately ill as her

mother had been, it had shocked Daisy when she'd taken eight long days to die. Now though, she was beginning to see a hint of colour in her own life once again. She'd made the right decision coming here. It wasn't as far away from Devon as she'd meant to go. It was far enough away to be a fresh start, somewhere where no one knew her, except Gabe. This was a place where she could feel safe and start her life again. Here she could be the person she'd always wanted to be, the one she'd tried out when she was in Vietnam. It was a pleasure to return to that version of Daisy, rather than the frightened version of herself she'd lived with for most of her life.

She picked up her bag from the chair and slipped the cloth handle over her shoulder. 'Thank you very much for inviting me to your beautiful home, Lydia,' she said. 'I've had an incredible evening.'

'I'll take you back to the Encore,' Gabriel said, bending to kiss his grandmother.

'There's no need,' she said, not wishing to disturb him, fully aware his grandmother hadn't seen him much in the last few months. 'I can catch a bus.'

He shook his head. 'Nan wouldn't dream of letting you go back to the hotel by bus when I'm perfectly capable of driving you there, would you, Nan?' Daisy could see the mischievous twinkle in his eyes as he smiled at his grandmother.

'No, I wouldn't,' Lydia said, giving Daisy a hug. 'It's been wonderful having you here and I meant what I said about coming to paint. I'll be offended if I don't see you in my garden with your easel sometime soon.'

Daisy appreciated her invitation and said so.

'Good, then it's settled,' Lydia said.

They began walking over to Gabriel's car. 'Maybe I'll tell you a little more about my past,' Lydia whispered. 'But I'll choose a time when we're alone and my grandson isn't nearby to overhear.'

Daisy giggled. 'I'll look forward to it.'

* * *

Gabriel drove down the curved driveway and they both waved to Lydia who stood with a wide grin on her face on her front steps.

'She's a very special lady,' Daisy said. 'You're very lucky to have her as a grandmother.'

'I am,' he said, winding down the window of his red vintage Triumph Stag. 'I miss seeing her when I'm away.'

'I'll bet she misses you too, although I'm told she keeps herself very busy helping run the Encore when your parents aren't here.'

He indicated to turn left and nodded. 'I think it's keeping busy and being such a positive person that keeps her looking so young.'

'You must be very proud of her.'

'I am.' He drove in silence for a while, then glanced at her and said. 'I'm sorry about your mum, Daisy. I had no idea she was so ill. I see now why you didn't contact me again after you left.'

'At first I was too wrapped up with everything to think of anyone else, although I did miss you, of course. There wasn't an internet connection at Mum's house and I lost my phone on the way to the airport in Delhi,' she lied. 'I panicked at first about trying to keep in contact with you but then when I arrived home and saw how bad Mum was, I didn't have a chance to think about much else.'

She thought back to those black days and nights trying to resign herself to this utter change in her circumstances. 'My world went from one of happiness, vitality and colour to one of misery and sickness. I kept going while she was ill, but fell apart a bit when she died. My doctor said it was exhaustion as well as grief.'

He reached his hand across to hers and gave it a squeeze. 'I'm so sorry. You shouldn't have had to go through that alone.'

She sighed. 'I was glad to be there for Mum. I would have hated being away knowing I hadn't kept her company for the last months of her life.' She shook her head, hoping to obliterate the picture of her skeletal mother lying in her once-pristine bedroom, now with medicine bottles and boxes spilling over each surface. 'I did think about going to a nearby internet café to see if you'd emailed me, but by the time I thought about it, I was sure it must be too late to contact you.'

'It was never too late,' he said quietly. They didn't speak for a few minutes while they reflected on his words. 'Do you mind if I pull over for a bit?' he asked after a while.

'Not at all,' she said.

He drew into a small car park by a bigger, more open beach than the one where Lydia lived. Unclipping his seatbelt, Gabriel turned to her. 'There are so many things I need to tell you, Daisy. I have to admit being crushed when I didn't hear from you again. I'm so sorry I wasn't there for you.'

'I don't know why you're apologising to me, Gabe. I completely understand why you would be hurt, and let's face it, it's not as if you've been horrible to me at all.' She stared transfixed at his beautiful face, every inch so familiar to her. Raising her right hand, she rested the palm against his cheek. 'I've missed you so much and can't quite believe you're here with me now.'

'Would you mind if I kissed you?' he asked.

It seemed like the most natural thing in the world. 'Not at all,' she said.

He hesitated briefly, then, pulling her into his arms, kissed her with all the passion she remembered. Daisy seemed to melt into him. He eventually pulled back and smiled at her. 'I've missed you so much.'

'Me too,' she admitted.

He took a deep breath and restarted the ignition. 'I suppose I should be getting you back to the hotel; the last thing we need is Fi sending out a search party for you. The hotel grapevine would go into overdrive by morning.'

3

GABRIEL

Gabe woke the following morning and stretched. He stood up, pulled on a pair of boxer shorts, and grabbed hold of the bottle of water he'd left on his bedside table. Then he climbed the ladder attached to the wall of his bedroom, opened the metal hatch to the roof and breathed in the familiar salty smell of the sea. He loved being able to do this and knew it was a luxury few could enjoy. He stepped up to the roof terrace to breathe in the warm air. Sighing deeply, he gazed out at the rolling waves and took a deep swig from his bottle. He recalled his kiss with Daisy in the car the evening before.

As much as he missed his research, he did relish coming home to Jersey. Even more so this time now that he'd discovered Daisy working at the Encore. He knew he wouldn't have mentioned his parents' names to her when they were away, because he never spoke about his parents by name. Too many years growing up with people changing their attitudes towards him when they discovered that his mother was a renowned beauty and his father a well-known singer had put paid to that before he reached his teens. So it had been an unexpected surprise having Daisy turning up at the hotel.

Daisy. He couldn't help smiling at the thought of her pretty face, so shocked to see him standing there talking to his nan. Then again, he must have looked stunned to see her working there. He suspected he was still in shock. After so many months trying to put her out of his mind and get over his feelings for her, to see her behind the reception area was unexpected to say the least. He rested back in a chair and raised his bare feet on the circular granite wall. Something tickled the side of his heel and he moved to see it was a ladybird. He reached down, waiting for the bug to step onto his finger before holding up his hand to let it fly away. He couldn't help smiling. He hadn't felt this carefree or happy since Vietnam. Daisy, he thought closing his eyes. It was easy to imagine being back in Vietnam with her on a hot morning like this one.

He swatted a fly away from his face and realised that someone was calling his name.

'Gabriel!' his grandmother shouted from the garden.

He peered over the side of the tower, to see her with a hand either side of her mouth. 'Darling, are you coming to join me for breakfast this morning?'

He nodded, happy to be able to share times like these with her. 'Give me five minutes.'

Hurrying back down to his room, he quickly showered and changed into a T-shirt and khaki shorts. Pushing his feet into worn flip flops, he ran outside to join her where he knew she'd be waiting at the table on her terrace.

'Good morning,' he said, bending down to kiss her lined cheek. 'How are you today?'

'All the better knowing you're so close and that I can have you all to myself for a bit.' She lifted the metal cover from his plate to reveal a full English breakfast. 'There's seeded toast under that napkin and I made you a pot of coffee, though why you prefer that when you could have Earl Grey like me, I don't know.'

'I suppose I must have got used to drinking it when I was in LA.'

She shook her head and smiled. 'You do look a bit like one of those beach bums sometimes, Gabriel,' she teased. 'Especially when you let your hair grow longer like it is now.'

'It's easier,' he said, deciding not to bother telling her that he'd actually had it cut recently. He tucked into his breakfast with relish. Nan was a pretty good cook when it came to breakfasts, at least.

'Do you mind terribly having to come back here to work at the hotel, darling?'

He shook his head. 'I've been working without a break for a few months now, so they understand me taking a little time away from the project.' He shrugged. 'It can get too intense if it's all you ever think about. It is important to me, but sometimes it's good to step away and be forced back into the real world.' He swallowed another mouthful of his food and, unable to resist, asked, 'So, what do you think of Daisy, Nan? I could tell by you inviting her here that you like her, but now you know we were—' he hesitated to find the right word '—close in Vietnam, does that change your feelings about her?'

'No, of course not,' she said immediately. 'There's a definite chemistry between you two, probably a little too much.' She rested a hand on his shoulder. 'I don't want either of you to get hurt, though.'

'Why would we?' he asked, knowing exactly why but needing her to voice his concerns so that he couldn't ignore them.

'We don't know how long Daisy will want to stay here. Even if she is happy working at the Encore, how long will it be before you have to return to wherever it was you were last working?'

'South Africa. And I should only be here for a month,' he admitted quietly.

'You see, that's not long at all. You work away for months at a time. Do you think it would be fair on Daisy to expect her to wait here for you each time?'

He could see where she was coming from. 'Maybe she could come with me in some capacity,' he said, although what exactly she would do he wasn't quite sure. 'She's an artist, Nan, she can work anywhere, surely?'

'I don't doubt it, but what if she doesn't want a life following you around the world? How well do you know her, anyway? Would you consider giving everything up for her?'

He shook his head. 'We haven't got to that point, Nan,' he said.

'But you do like her, don't you?' she asked. 'A lot.'

'I really like her. We spent some incredible weeks together in Vietnam and then went our separate ways. I guess I was hoping we could carry on from where we left off.'

He waited for her to agree, or argue, but instead all she did was look down vacantly at the scrambled egg on toast she'd barely touched. 'Not necessarily,' she murmured eventually.

Gabe put down his knife and fork and rested one hand on his grandmother's back. 'Are you all right?' He'd never seen her act like this before. It was out of character for her to appear down; even if she was upset, she always put a brave face on things. 'Why does it matter to you how close Daisy and I are? Are you thinking about something that happened to you? Between you and Grandpa Lorenzo?' He hoped she might finally be opening up to him about her mysterious past.

She nodded slowly. 'I suppose I am. I resented him for something he did, something that I should have forced him to deal with, but instead I stupidly let my pride get the better of me. I ended up missing out on, well, I don't really know, but it was impulsive and short-sighted of me, I know that now.' She grabbed hold of his forearm. 'When you're young you assume you have all the time in the world to put things right, but life isn't that simple sometimes.'

She smiled at him, but he could see it was forced and that she was trying to lighten the mood that had dipped so rapidly between them. 'All I'm saying is, be sure of your feelings for Daisy before making any decisions. Try to remember that she will have her own ambitions for her future that might not fit in with yours, and if you want to be together try to find a compromise that works for you both before giving up on a future you might otherwise miss out on.'

'I will, Nan,' he said. 'I promise.'

She smiled and patted his cheek. 'Enough serious chat for now,' she said. 'Come on, let's eat and make the best of this glorious July morning.'

He nodded. 'Yes, let's do that.' He gave her a quizzical look. It unnerved him to hear her speaking so seriously about something, especially when referring to her past. She never spoke about anything from when she was young.

He could hear the phone ringing inside the house and stood up, but before he could step away from the table, Anna, the housekeeper, came outside holding the phone.

'Madam, it's Mr Rick on the phone. He says Miss Francesca is thinking she might not go away after all.'

His grandmother sighed and held out her hand to take the phone. 'Thank you, Anna.' She pushed her plate away and lifted the phone to her ear. 'Francesca, what is all this nonsense?' There was a silence while she listened to what his mother was telling her. 'Absolutely not. I'm fine, and your son has generously taken the time to come back to Jersey and help me run the hotel. So, you will pack your bags and get on that flight and stop all of this. You do it every time you have to go away on location. It's stage fright, nothing more. You'll be fine once you get there.' She raised her eyes heavenward.

Gabe smiled. He knew this routine by heart; he'd experienced it for as long as he could remember.

'Gabriel will be there to collect you.' She shook her head and pointed at her watch.

'Two-thirty,' he mouthed.

He zoned out from the rest of the call to finish off his meal. Lydia soon rang off and placed the phone down on the table. 'I don't know why she puts herself through this,' she said.

'She loves it when she gets there. And when she comes home after filming has ended and she has something new to entertain her guests with back at the hotel.'

'Yes, she does.' Lydia took a sip of her tea and grimaced. 'That's cold now. I have to feel a bit sorry for your mother though,' she said, laughing.

'Why?'

'Because each time she has one of her turns your father phones me. She knows I've got enough experience in films that she can't argue with me. It always infuriates her.'

'Poor Mum,' Gabe said, smiling. He was relieved someone was able to stop her dramatics. He loved his mum very much, but she could be exhausting and as much as his father could be difficult to live with, with his roving eye and slight excesses with alcohol, Gabe knew that most of the time they had a great relationship, and for that he was very grateful.

'Do you think Mum should have married someone who doted on her and followed her to her locations?'

His grandmother nodded. 'Yes. She needs that hero-worship

more than most and she doesn't get it from your father because he's too busy demanding it for himself. Mind you, I think at times like now that's good for her.' She laughed. 'How you turned out to be so placid and happy with your own company, I don't know.'

'Is that what I am?' he asked. He was different to his parents, that was for certain. 'I'm just relieved I never wanted to go into the acting business too. Can you imagine what it would have been like to have three of us involved in show business in the family?'

'Four,' she said, tapping his arm. 'What about me?'

'But you're not a drama queen, Nan.'

'No, but I probably used to be when I was younger.'

'I have a feeling you would have secretly loved to come from a normal family like Daisy. She must think we're all a little crazy.' Lydia laughed. 'Poor girl.'

'What's normal, though?' he said, realising how little he knew about Daisy's family, or her past. Then again, he thought, he hadn't divulged very much about his own family either. If he had she wouldn't be working at his family's hotel. He was glad they'd mainly stuck to discussing their travels in Vietnam, otherwise he was pretty certain Daisy would have taken a job elsewhere.

Lydia raised her eyebrows. 'I think we're a little less normal than your average family, don't you?'

'Yes, I can't argue with that.'

Lydia ate a little more, then put her fork down with a sigh. 'We have an anniversary party to deal with while your parents are away,' she said. 'I know that the girls from Lapins de Lune took over a wedding reception for us immediately after the fire, but I think that maybe if that young builder... Luke, was it?' Gabe nodded. 'Well, if he completes the work quickly then we could hold the next event at the Encore.'

'Lapins de Lune?' The name rang a bell, but Gabe couldn't quite place it.

She took a sip of her tea. 'You remember, it's that events busi-ness.' When he shook his head, she added, 'They specialise in vintage linen and crockery for weddings and other parties, and they do event planning. The Le Lievre girl, you know, the one whose mother is a sculptor, well it's her and her friend Jessica Moon. They started the business a couple of years ago, and after the fire took over the reception for a couple.'

Gabe could picture them and nodded. 'Did they expect to host this party too?'

'No, but your mum suggested that maybe they might do so, if Luke didn't manage to finish the work on time.'

Gabe was all for helping others, but on this occasion his parents' hotel needed the money. Summer was their most prof-itable time and what they made between May and September had to keep them going for the rest of the year. 'I'll help Luke with the work if I have to,' he said. 'We can't afford to turn away any more business, Nan. These events are worth a lot of money to us.'

'I know. Give Luke a call today then and see if there's anything you can do.'

'I will.'

After they'd finished, he gave his grandmother a lift to the hotel so that she could run through the bookings with his mum before they left. Phoning Luke, he was relieved to discover that with a little extra help from him the work should be completed in time for the couple's big day.

He walked around the back of the hotel through the colourful rose garden to check on the work being done to the orangery. His father had sent him photos of the fire damage and it had shocked Gabe at the time, but now – a couple of weeks later and after quite a bit of hard work from Luke and his team – it didn't look nearly so bad. Burnt wooden frames had been replaced, the walls had been plastered and now just needed a little paint. It was going to be fine, he thought, relieved for his parents' sake.

'Looks much better now, doesn't it?' His dad asked, coming up to stand next to him, a pipe clenched between his teeth. Gabe couldn't help smiling. How the constant puffing on that thing hadn't ruined his father's singing, he couldn't imagine.

'You must have got quite a shock on the night of the fire?' Gabe asked.

'It could have been so much worse,' Rick said. 'Though your mum nearly had hysterics, especially as we were ninety per cent full with guests at the time. It did show us that our fire drills worked though, which was something.'

Rick put his arm around Gabe's shoulders. It was good to be alone with his father for once. Gabe loved his mother but she always demanded so much attention, and if she was with them then his father never got the chance to say his piece.

'We're very grateful to you for coming all the way to Jersey to help your grandmother.'

'I'm happy to spend time with her and I needed to step back from the project, anyway. Hopefully while I'm away I'll come up with ideas to raise more funds to keep it going too.'

They began walking to the back of the hotel along the gravel pathways that meandered through the geometric line of tiny pools, some bridged with a large slab as a way to cross from one side to the other.

'Your grandmother would kill me for saying so, but despite how well she looks, she is getting older and I don't like to think of her being left to run this place on her own. When I signed up to do this tour, I thought your mother would be staying in Jersey and the two of them could work together.'

This was news to Gabe. 'So when did she receive her offer for the part in the film?'

'Only a month ago, when another actress fell ill and had to pull out. Your mum was delighted, of course.'

'You can't blame her,' Gabe said, picturing his mother's joy to be offered the part. 'She's always fretting about work drying up.'

Rick took the pipe from his mouth and nodded. 'I know, but we always agreed that one of us would stay behind if the other had an offer of work.'

Gabriel stopped walking. 'Dad, it's fine. I'm thrilled she's got something to look forward to and Nan and I will be perfectly happy here looking after everything until you both get back home again. Don't worry about it, really.'

Rick pulled Gabriel into a tight hug. 'You're a good boy, Gabe. We're very lucky to have you as a son.'

His father always became sentimental when he was about to go away and Gabe knew how he hated goodbyes. He suspected it was because his father had lost both his parents at an early age. For him, though, his parents going away to work was so much a part of his life that it never worried him at all. 'Everything will be fine. You two go and forget about us. Enjoy your tour, have fun, and we'll have a party to celebrate once you both get back.'

'Great idea, my boy, I'll mention that to your mother.'

4

DAISY

'He's so annoying,' Fi said, slamming down her car keys on the top of the reception desk.

'Who is?' Daisy couldn't help being amused by Fi's drama-queen tendencies. There was never a dull moment when she was around, and Daisy wished she'd had a younger sister like Fi when she was growing up.

'My brother,' she said through clenched teeth. 'He can be such a pig.'

Daisy didn't know Sebastian Fielding, but she'd seen a picture of him in the local paper a few times. She'd heard enough about him from others and doubted very much that he treated Fi badly; in fact, she'd heard he doted on her.

'How come?' Daisy asked, trying to pacify her before any of the guests wondered why their receptionist was flouncing around the marble entrance hall. 'Didn't he buy you that shiny red Fiat 500?'

'Yes,' Fi said, glowering at Daisy. 'That's not what I'm referring to though, is it?'

The phone rang and Daisy held up one finger to indicate Fi

should wait while she took the call. 'Gabe, hi,' she said, unable to help smiling at the sound of his voice. Forcing away the image of him in faded denims, she listened while he explained that he was going to be slightly late to collect his parents.

'I'm giving them a lift to the airport,' he said. 'Please let them know I haven't forgotten them.'

'Of course,' she said. 'I'll tell them straight away.' She put down the receiver.

Fi opened her mouth to continue her rant just as Francesca flounced out of the door linking the staff area of the hotel to the front lobby. She tapped her watch dramatically, before turning to open the door she'd just slammed shut behind her.

'Rick, come along, darling, we're going to miss this blasted flight if we're not careful.' She flicked her long reddish hair from her shoulder and added. 'Why you always leave everything until the last minute I'll never know.'

Daisy could hear him cursing and banging what she assumed to be their cases against the hall walls. 'Bloody hell, Francesca, what crap have you filled your suitcases with this time? You're going to be working on location. You do remember that they have costume and makeup departments there?'

Francesca squeezed her tiny form as far back against the doorframe as she could to let him through while she held open the door.

'And,' he said as he half dragged her suitcase through the hallway, 'I only left things until the last damn minute because I was doing my best to placate you, if you recall.'

'Miss Fiore, Mr Malone,' Jose, the flustered head porter, called, frantically waving over two of his young assistants. 'Please, we will take these to the car for you.'

'Where is Gabriel?' Francesca asked Daisy as she neared the reception area. 'He was supposed to be here half an hour ago.'

Daisy couldn't help noticing that Francesca had forgotten to draw in one of her eyebrows, giving her a lopsided look which made it difficult for Daisy to concentrate. She didn't point out that if he had been on time then he would have had to wait half an hour for them both to be ready, but simply said, 'He's just phoned. He should be here any time now.'

Rick left the cases he'd been struggling with for the porters to handle and stomped outside. Daisy spotted him lighting a cigarette as soon as he was far enough away from the building not to infuriate his wife.

'You'll ruin your beautiful singing voice if you carry on doing that,' Francesca said, spotting him as she stepped outside to peer down the long driveway for Gabriel.

'Why don't they just refer to themselves as Mr and Mrs Wilson?' Fi asked. 'Those are their real names, after all.'

Daisy shrugged. 'I suppose it's because Francesca is an actress and is still referred to in her work and the press as Francesca Fiore, and Rick is known as Rich Malone, his stage name.'

'Weird,' mumbled Fi, sitting down in her chair next to Daisy. She bent down behind the raised desk so Francesca couldn't see her and took her pink lip gloss from her bag and reapplied it to her lips. 'I find life confusing enough with one name, never mind having to listen out for people calling you by several names. I don't know how Gabriel copes with their lifestyle, do you?'

Daisy sat up straighter as she recognised the deep purr of Gabe's car. 'I'm sure he's quite used to it,' she said. 'After all, his grandmother was famous too, wasn't she?'

Fi knitted her eyebrows together in confusion. 'What, Mrs Grey you mean?'

Daisy smiled at Fi's surprise. 'Yes, she was the Jersey Bombshell, didn't you know?'

'The what?' Fi giggled.

Daisy was indignant on Lydia's behalf that Fi found this revelation amusing. 'Mrs Grey was famous in the fifties.' She recalled
pictures of a young Lydia dressed in a red-and-white polka dot
dress with a tiny cinched-in waist. 'She was very glamorous and
incredibly beautiful. She was always photographed looking
immaculate, not like actresses these days,' she said, aware she was
sounding just like her mother. 'I particularly liked one of the
pictures of her with a leopard-print silk scarf over her hair and
wrapped round her neck. All you could see of her face were these
huge dark glasses and perfectly made-up red lips.' Daisy sighed.
'I still can't quite believe I've met her.'

When Fi didn't answer, Daisy turned to her. 'What's the
matter?'

'You're so old for your age sometimes, do you know that?'

Daisy couldn't understand why and said so.

Fi thought for a few seconds. 'I mean, who in their twenties
would know anything about something that happened over sixty
years ago? It's odd.'

Daisy shook her head. 'I don't see why. I don't even come from
here and I know who Lydia Grey is. Maybe it's because my mum
was such a huge fan.'

'Your mum can't have been old enough to remember the
fifties though, surely?'

Daisy sighed. 'No, but she loved fashion and old movies, and I
suppose I inherited that trait from her.'

Fi looked her up and down. 'Even in your uniform it's obvious
there's something a little different about you,' she said.

'Meaning?'

'Your make-up, or what little you use, is like something out of
the fifties. You only put eyeliner on your top eyelid and wear red
lipstick.'

Daisy pictured herself. 'I suppose you're right. I hadn't

thought about that before.' It also hadn't occurred to her how different she must appear to Gabe now. He'd only ever known her with a make-up free face sporting nothing more than a tan.

'Hi there,' he said, as if she'd conjured him up with her thoughts. He was leaning through the doors into reception. 'I can't stop.' He indicated his mother calling him from the back seat of his car. She hadn't noticed them getting in and hoped Francesca hadn't given her any orders she'd missed. 'But I was wondering if you wanted to come out to see a band down at St Ouen tonight?' he added.

Daisy didn't have to consider the proposal. 'I'd love to.'

'Gabriel, will you stop drooling over that girl and drive us to the sodding airport,' his father bellowed from the car.

Gabriel cringed. 'He's so embarrassing sometimes.' He turned to leave. 'I'll pick you up at six-thirty,' he shouted over his shoulder, before he got in the car and they sped off down the driveway.

'So, you've pulled then,' Fi said giggling. 'Lucky cow.'

Daisy frowned at her. 'We're old friends and we're going out for the evening to catch up, if you must know.'

'You keep telling yourself that,' Fi giggled. 'If you're not interested in him then I most certainly would be, so don't go making out that he's nothing to you if he is.'

Daisy admired Fi's honesty and couldn't help liking how direct she always was about everything. She supposed it probably had something to do with never having to worry if you upset someone, and knowing that whatever you did, your brother would be able to sort out any issues you inadvertently caused.

'Fine,' Daisy said. 'I do like Gabe. Rather a lot, in fact. So keep your sticky mitts off him.' She laughed. 'I just know you're going to be more offended by insinuating that you have sticky hands than the thought of you pinching some guy from under my nose.'

Fi held up her immaculate hands. 'Damn right,' she said.

'There's nothing mucky about me.' She hesitated for effect. 'Apart from maybe my imagination – that can be downright filthy.'

Daisy shook her head. 'You're impossible, do you know that?'

* * *

Gabriel was waiting for her outside the front of the hotel when she hurried through to meet him just after six-thirty. He was chatting to two elderly ladies, who came back to stay at the hotel several times each season. She waited for them to finish their conversation, staring out to the rectangular pool with its wooden steamer chairs which Fi told her had been sourced from an old liner and restored. She wondered how many times they'd had to re-order the cushioned covers in their navy and cream piping after they'd been ruined by a visitor getting careless with sun cream.

She breathed in the heady scent of tea roses and jasmine, and rather than looking as if she was impatient for him to finish talking, headed to the back of the hotel and the pretty herb garden. Watching the tall, toned man she'd missed so much made Daisy smile. He was beautiful inside as well as outside and now she knew how he'd left his own project to return to help out his grandmother, she loved him even more.

'There you are,' he said, a few minutes later. 'Sorry to keep you waiting.' He bent down to give her a kiss on the cheek.

'It's no problem at all,' she said. 'It's so tranquil out here, I was happy to wait.'

'Isn't it a perfect evening? You can't beat Jersey on days like these.'

They walked a little further. 'There are so many glorious smells out here,' she said. 'I was just admiring the roses, then the different herbs over there, and now I've got a waft of salty air from the bay.'

'The wind direction probably changed,' he said quietly. 'Come on, let's get going. We don't want to miss the music.'

She walked with him back to where he'd parked. 'I do love it here though,' he said. 'It's a little like going back in time to a more genteel era.'

'It's wonderful,' she agreed.

Gabriel shrugged. 'Mind you, after a couple of months I need to get away and get back into discovering things in the ocean.'

She bent to sniff a dark-red flower; the scent was heady. 'That is incredible,' she said.

'I think that's Nan's favourite,' he said. 'If it is then that one is called "Deep Secret". Nan has a few of those in her rose garden.' They walked a few steps further. 'So, how do you like living in Jersey; is it to your liking?' He grinned at her.

'It is,' she said, trying not to giggle. 'I never thought I could find anywhere I'd be as happy as I was in Vietnam,' she admitted. 'But it's lovely here, if not quite as exotic.'

'Or as hot,' he laughed. Gabriel took her hand in his, lifted it to his lips, and kissed it. 'Meeting you here has made the anticipation of an amazing summer even more special than it usually is,' he said.

Daisy didn't answer; she was unable to trust herself not to fling her arms around his neck and kiss him.

He led her over to his car and they began the short drive to St Ouen's. He sighed. 'I was pretty upset having to leave my team,' he said. 'But I knew I couldn't leave Nan to look after the hotel alone, especially now the high season is nearly upon us.' He shook his head. 'I still can't believe you're living and working here.'

Neither could she sometimes. They continued in silence for a few moments. 'That storm last night woke me up,' she said, recalling the loud clap of thunder that had given her such a fright sometime around two in the morning.

'It was,' he said. 'I could hear Nan's little rescue dog, Jack, yelping and barking the whole time it thundered. I went down to the house to check everything was OK.'

'Poor little thing. Did he calm down in the end?'

Gabriel shook his head and yawned. 'No. Nan took him up to her room. He sleeps in the utility room and is usually perfectly happy. I think I eventually fell asleep around four o'clock.'

'Me too,' she said. 'Poor little dog. How long has she had him?'

'About a year or so. He's a Jack Russell cross about four other breeds. He's a funny-looking thing, but he's sweet and she adores him.'

They drove the rest of the way in silence. Daisy stole glances at him when she thought he wouldn't notice. The last time she did it, he turned and smiled at her.

He turned down a narrow road. 'Look,' he said, pointing across to the beach where a paraglider was circling. 'The tide is up at the moment, but when it goes out there'll be all sorts of flotsam and jetsam dumped on the beach from the rough tides. It always happens after a storm.'

'I'll have to make sure I pop down to the beach later to do a bit of beachcombing,' she said. 'I could do with finding a few bits of faded glass and driftwood for my windowsill. It's a bit bare in there at the moment.'

'Good idea,' he said.

'I can't believe your parents are my bosses,' she giggled. 'They're characters, aren't they?'

'A bit larger than life, would you say?' He smiled, the skin around his dark-brown eyes crinkling in amusement.

Daisy laughed. 'You could say that.'

'Have you been this way before?' he asked, motioning down towards the sea on their right-hand side.

'No,' she said, looking down the cliff face close to the road at the waves crashing against hidden rocks below the surface. 'St Ouen is on the north-west of the island, isn't it?'

'Yes. I love it down on that beach, it's so wild and unspoilt.'

The car meandered its way through the narrow lanes, with grassy banks and flowers leaning precariously over towards the side of the car.

'I'm sure these roads would be wider if the grass wasn't so long,' she said, wishing she could have shown him around the places she loved in Devon. Her emotions dipped as she realised that the chances of her having a reason to return to her home town were minimal. There was no one she wanted to visit there, no one worth the risk of being seen for. She fought her resentment. She realised Gabe was speaking and focused her attention to what he was saying.

'The banks and bushes on the sides of the roads will be cut soon. They call it "the branchage". We'll all be moaning when they're doing it because there will be traffic hold-ups. Even worse are the machines hired to cut the grass; they're slow and a lot of them damage the hedging. It drives me nuts when I see that happening.'

'That's awful.'

Daisy closed her eyes and relished the heat of the evening sun warming her face. This island seemed so similar to her home in some ways, but the use of French road names and words like 'branchage' reminded her that she was on an island off the coast of France and not in south-west England. She'd never experienced anything this glorious when she lived at home with her mum. They hadn't lived in a pretty house or with a sea-view and her mum had never driven, let alone owned a car, so their lives had been ruled by bus timetables whenever they wanted to go anywhere. Their estate could have benefitted hugely from banks of grass and flowers.

'You're very lucky growing up on such a pretty island, Gabe.'

'I know and I do appreciate it. In fact, leaving for work can be quite a wrench at times, but I know I'll always come back.' He reached out and took one of her hands in his. 'Do you envisage staying here for long, Daisy?'

She hadn't decided, but being with him right now and having her hand in his made the thought of never leaving this place very tempting. 'I would like to,' she admitted. 'Now Mum has gone and what's left of her belongings are in storage, I don't have anywhere else I need to be.'

'That's sad,' he said honestly. She was grateful to him for not holding back with his thoughts; it was refreshing having someone talk about her feelings.

'It is, I guess, but I can't change how things are.'

'Don't you have any brothers or sisters?' he asked, letting go of her hand to manoeuvre the car through a particularly tight bend in the road.

'No, you?'

'I'm an only child too,' he said. 'I always wanted a brother or sister, but I think my parents were so stunned by my unexpected appearance into their fun-filled world and having to make time in their workload to bring me up that they didn't dare have a second child.'

Daisy couldn't imagine making a child of hers feel like an inconvenient intruder. 'I'm sure they were thrilled to have you once they got over the shock of being parents?'

'I'm not so sure it was that easy for them,' he laughed. 'I was very inquisitive and always running off and climbing cliffs when we went to the beach, or jumping off rocks. I was the first one to tombstone off the harbour wall at Bouley Bay with my friends and my mother nearly went mad with fright each time I was carted off in an ambulance, or the police had to inform her that I'd had yet another accident. I don't think they were at all surprised when I told them I wanted to be a marine explorer.'

'Poor people.' She couldn't help feeling sorry for them now, though picturing someone as dramatic as Francesca trying to cope with such an adventurous child was also amusing. 'No wonder they kept going away to work; they probably needed the break.'

'Hey!' he reached over and tickled her side with his free hand. 'You're probably right though.'

They slowed down as the car reached a small village and Gabe turned left down a long road. 'The locals call this Hydrangea Avenue,' he said.

Daisy opened her mouth to speak but was silenced by the avenue of pink and blue hydrangea bushes in full bloom on either side of the long road, a row of equally magnificent chestnut trees standing proudly behind them. 'It's beautiful,' she gasped, making a note to come here and paint the route towards the bay.

He slowed down halfway along the road and turned into a smaller road which meandered for a few minutes until they came to a packed car park where Gabriel finally managed to find a small space.

'We have to walk from here,' he said, getting out of the car and walking around to the passenger side to open Daisy's door for her.

She stepped out and watched as he went to the back of the car and retrieved a hamper and rolled-up blanket from the boot. 'We're going on a picnic?'

'Of sorts,' he said, locking the car. 'Come on, it's this way.'

She walked with him across a couple of fields. 'What's that?'

she asked, looking at a strange arrangement of large granite stones.

'That's a dolmen,' he said. 'It was used as a burial chamber.'

Daisy hadn't expected that answer. 'Are there bodies buried in there?'

He shrugged. 'I'm not sure. I seem to recall my dad talking about it once when he brought me here for a walk when we first came back to live here. I think it's about four thousand years old and they used to believe that it had been built by fairies, or that's what he said anyway. It's owned by the Société Jersiaise now. They look after a lot of interesting places on the island, as do Jersey Heritage. I'll have to take you to some of the other sites.'

'I'd love that,' she said, peering at the ancient monument. She stared at it for a moment then, hearing the chords of a beautiful tune coming from behind a high row of pine trees, hurried to catch up with him.

In her rush, she tripped over a stone in the soil and Gabriel grabbed hold of her arm before she fell. Regaining her balance she groaned. 'Mum always used to moan about how clumsy I am.'

He took her hand in his. 'Come on, we'd better get moving otherwise there won't be anywhere to sit.'

Intrigued by the sounds of voices and beautiful music emanating from behind the trees, she walked a little faster to keep up with him. Daisy watched where she was placing her feet so that she didn't trip again. Excitement bubbled inside her; something was going on and she couldn't wait to discover what exactly it could be. A sparrowhawk hovered in the field nearby and the music got louder.

They strode through the trees and Daisy gasped. In front of them sat groups of people on rugs and coats, watching a band serenading them as the sun, turning the surrounding sky golden orange, was getting ready to set in the channel ahead of them.

'Oh Gabe,' she murmured. 'This is enchanting.'

He looked down at her and smiled. 'I'm glad you like it,' he said. 'It wasn't until we were on our way here that it dawned on me that you might think we were going to watch bands playing contemporary music. I wasn't sure if you'd want to stay.'

She couldn't imagine anything more romantic as sitting on the grass listening to the harmonic sounds being played by the instruments with the spectacular setting of the beach and sea behind them.

'It's glorious,' she said.

'Now we just need to find a space where we can sit down,' he said.

She looked around the couple of hundred people who'd had the sense to arrive earlier than them. Small children played with toys next to their parents and dogs, some sitting, guarding their owners, others snoozing on the rugs while their owners relaxed with glasses of wine as they enjoyed the atmosphere.

Daisy spotted someone waving at them and tugged gently on Gabe's hand. 'That guy over there is trying to get your attention,' she said quietly, not wishing to disturb the audience.

Gabriel looked over. 'It's Ed,' he said. 'He works at a manor house not too far from here, in the gardens. Shall we go and see if they've got space near them?'

Desperate to sit down and take in the atmosphere of the evening, Daisy nodded. 'Yes. I think we're starting to annoy the people behind us.'

They stepped carefully over feet and glasses that were in their way, reaching Ed and his friends a short while later.

'Good to see you,' Ed said, taking the hamper from Gabe and indicating a space next to him. 'Make yourself at home.'

Gabriel unrolled the blanket and placed it down on the grass, giving Daisy room to get comfortable next to Ed before sitting down on her other side.

'Hi, I'm Ed,' said the man who looked rugged and outdoorsy, yet somehow still refined. 'This is Izzy, my girlfriend, and her friend, Jess, and Alex, Izzy's brother.'

'Hi,' they all said in unison.

'Good to meet you all,' Daisy said shrugging off her jacket in the warmth of the setting sun. 'This is incredible,' she said. 'I've never experienced anything like it.'

'Good, isn't it?' Izzy said. 'They say this place has a natural amphitheatre which is why the sound is so good.'

'The backdrop of the bay is pure luck,' Ed said, putting their hamper down in front of Daisy. 'If you haven't got enough of anything let us know. Izzy packed a hamper for us and I think she was expecting to stay here for a couple of days.'

Izzy elbowed him and giggled. 'Ignore him, I just wanted to be sure we had everything we needed.'

'Including cake forks and piccalilli,' Ed said, shrugging. 'Whatever that is. It looks like it could be radioactive.'

Daisy couldn't help laughing at his teasing. She'd always hated the taste of piccalilli, despite her mother's insistence that it was delicious. Gabriel handed Daisy two glass flutes, took out a bottle of champagne and opened it.

'What are we celebrating?' she asked.

'Being here,' he said simply, as he poured the golden bubbly liquid. He placed the bottle against one of the sides in the hamper and took a glass from her. 'To you being here in Jersey,' he said, clinking his glass gently against hers. 'To a wonderful summer.'

'I'll drink to that,' she said, taking a sip.

Gabriel sat cross-legged next to her as they listened to the beautiful tunes filling the air around them. As one tune ended, he leant down and pointed through the trees. 'There's another Napoleonic tower lording it on the rock in the middle of the bay, and down there is a small white house that can be rented out for the odd night.'

She had to move slightly to get a glimpse of each of the properties. 'Is that white stone lighthouse over there on the left Corbière?'

'It is,' he whispered.

'Wow, it's breathtaking,' she said. 'It's so wild and unspoilt down here and that gorgeous sand makes me want to go down there and run into the water.'

'Nothing's stopping you from doing that, if you'd like to,' he said.

'Maybe after this concert has finished,' she teased.

'I'm glad you like Jersey,' he said, his voice quieter and more serious, his cool breath on her neck sending sensations through her body.

'How can I not like it; each bay is different to the last and everything is so pretty. I love it here.'

As the music played, the sun slowly lowered and Daisy realised she was leaning against Gabriel. She wasn't sure whether to move slightly away and sit up straighter. As if he'd heard her thoughts, he put his arm around her shoulders and rested his head against the top of hers. It was a perfect moment. She closed her eyes and lost herself in the music.

'Move over, Gabe.'

Gabriel tensed and sat up. 'Bella, I didn't realise you'd be here this evening.'

'Why shouldn't I be?'

Daisy opened her eyes at the sound of the clipped female tone. The beautiful woman with the dark shiny bob and large brown eyes was gazing down at Daisy. She looked at Gabriel and raised a perfectly threaded eyebrow. 'And this is...?'

Daisy forced her best receptionist smile and offered her hand to the woman. 'Hi, I'm Daisy,' she said. 'I work at the Encore.'

'Nice to meet you, Daisy,' Bella said. She gave Daisy a knowing smile. 'I couldn't help noticing you were looking very cosy with my husband.'

'Your...' Her breath seemed to be sucked out of her. She willed the woman to laugh and tell her that she was joking. When she didn't, Daisy took a deep breath. Gabriel's arm dropped away from her. No one was laughing. She turned to stare at him.

Gabriel groaned. 'Daisy, I should have mentioned this before now,' he said, glaring at Bella. 'This is Bella, and yes, technically, she's my wife.'

Daisy couldn't speak. She could have cried, but wasn't going to let herself down by making a humiliating situation even worse. Refusing to look at Gabriel, she forced a smile onto her face and said. 'It's good to meet you, Bella. Do you want me to move over a bit so you can sit down?'

Bella shook her head. Daisy noticed that she'd suddenly turned rather flushed. 'Oh dear – I was just being silly. Don't worry about me, I'm old news. I won't stay; I'm meeting friends. I just thought I'd pop by and say hello.'

Daisy watched the long, tanned legs step carefully over people as Bella made her way to a larger group of people sitting close to the band.

She got the distinct feeling that the others didn't know what to do or say, and when they began busily delving into their picnic hamper and handing out food, Daisy turned to Gabe and in a low voice said, 'You didn't think to mention that you were married?'

His stricken look only served to show how guilty he felt, but she had no sympathy. The pain in her chest made her wince.

'Why didn't you tell me, Gabe? How could you take me out and spend time with me knowing you had a wife waiting for you at home?'

'It's not how it seems,' he said, taking hold of her hand. 'Please, let me explain—'

She snatched it away from him. 'Don't touch me,' she whispered between clenched teeth. 'I don't date married men, under any circumstances. Do you understand?'

'Daisy, it's not like that, honestly.'

She narrowed her eyes at him as white rage pumped through her system so strongly that she thought she might scream. How could she have been so stupid? She shouldn't be surprised that Gabe wasn't single, but a wife?

'We're not together any more, like she said. Our relationship has been over for months. It never really began, if I'm honest.'

'Are you divorced?'

He hesitated. 'No, but we will be.'

'When?'

'In two years' time.'

'What?'

Her evening was ruined. She couldn't bear to be near him for another second. She grabbed hold of her jacket and small bag and stood up. Gabriel went to stand. 'No, you stay here,' she said quietly, not wishing to alert those nearby to her trauma.

'But Daisy, how will you get home?' He stood up ignoring her pleas.

'I travelled around Asia by myself,' she said. 'I think I can find my way back to the hotel.'

'I'm taking you,' Gabe said, bending down and grabbing hold of the hamper. He handed the half-empty bottle of champagne over to Izzy and scooped up the rug.

'I can give Daisy a lift home,' Ed said.

'No, it's fine,' Gabe said. 'Thanks though.'

'Will you sit down?' an angry voice hissed at them. 'Some of us are trying to enjoy our evening.'

Daisy marched off towards the pine trees and the peace of the field beyond. She could hear Gabriel apologising to the man for interrupting the performance followed by his footsteps as he ran to catch up with her.

'Daisy, please,' he said, stopping in front of her so that she couldn't keep walking away. 'I'm not lying when I say that Bella and I are no longer a couple. I wouldn't cheat on someone, I promise you that.'

Daisy took a deep breath to try to calm down. 'I'm probably overreacting but I feel such an idiot.'

'Why?' he asked, trying and failing to take hold of her hand. 'How were you to know?'

She closed her eyes briefly and stared at the ground. 'I've been acting as if I know you well, when all the time I'm the only one who obviously didn't know about you and Bella.' She looked up at him. 'I wish you'd told me, Gabe, that's all.'

'I know,' he said. 'I couldn't really find the right moment and I didn't want to spoil the evening. I think Bella's actually really embarrassed about it – she's always been a bit of a joker and comes out with things she regrets afterwards.'

Daisy sighed. 'Look, I think I just need to go back to the hotel and think for a bit.'

'I understand,' he said. 'Let me drive you.'

They drove back in silence. Daisy pushed away the image of Bella's face as she told her about her and Gabe and cringed.

'Are you OK?' Gabe asked, glancing at her.

'Fine,' she said, relieved to note that the road he'd just turned down was the one directly before the hotel. Only a few more minutes and she'd be alone to mull over what had happened.

He stopped the car and went to get out. 'No, it's fine,' Daisy said. 'You go back to the picnic.' When he opened the door, she added, 'I'm going to go and paint for a couple of hours.'

She got out of the car and watched him drive away. He didn't seem very happy but right now she just wanted to be left alone.

* * *

The following morning Daisy got up early after a sleepless night and, choosing a quiet place down in the hotel valley, set up her small easel. Two hours later, with very little paint having been placed onto the canvas, she came to the conclusion that what had happened the previous night with Gabe was exactly the reason why she wasn't ready for another relationship. She was better single. At least that way she knew where she stood and there'd be no nasty shocks sideswiping her when she least expected it.

5

GABRIEL

Gabriel rubbed his face with his palms. 'Idiot,' he groaned. He'd been too busy enjoying this chance of spending time with Daisy again to risk ruining it by mentioning his wife's existence when they'd first met up again. He leant against the orangery door and checked his mobile for the tenth time that hour. She didn't want to speak to him.

'I'm going out for a bit,' he shouted.

Luke looked up from the window frame he was finishing and scowled. 'Try not to be too long, I'm going to need all the help I can get if this work is to be finished on time.'

Gabriel knew he was right, but he couldn't leave Daisy to stew any longer than he already had done. 'I'll be back as soon as I can; there's something I need to do first.'

He didn't blame Luke for looking unimpressed; after all, he was the one helping Gabe out, not the other way around.

He'd managed to upset too many people recently, he thought, as he got into his car and drove off to find Daisy. When he'd phoned the hotel earlier Fi told him that Daisy had gone out. She hadn't mentioned going shopping – probably because that wasn't really Daisy's thing – so he assumed she must have gone some-where to paint. He turned at the next lane and headed for his grandmother's house. Daisy was aware that he and Luke were spending the day working on the orangery, so she would have expected him to be hard at work at the hotel, and he suspected she'd be making the most of him being away from his grand-mother's house to paint in the garden.

'What are you doing here?' Lydia asked a short while later, as she strode around the side of the house. 'I thought you couldn't leave the hotel until the orangery was finished.'

He turned off the engine and stepped out of the car, kissing his grandmother on both cheeks. 'I needed to speak to Daisy. I left messages for her at reception and in her room, but she's not called me back.'

'Did you try her mobile?'

'She doesn't have one for some reason,' he scowled. 'It makes getting in touch with her rather difficult.'

Lydia tilted her head to one side. 'You haven't upset her, have you, Gabriel?'

He exhaled sharply. 'She met Bella.'

His grandmother's face fell. 'Oh no.'

'Yes. She came to the sunset concert at Grantez last night and told Daisy exactly who she was.'

Lydia frowned at him. 'Oh Bella. Still the same. Have you explained things to Daisy?'

'I've tried, but she seems to be avoiding me. Is she here? I thought she might have come to do some painting.'

She shook her head. 'She was, but she offered to take Jack for a walk down on the beach. She said she wanted to do a bit of beachcombing and see if she could find a few bits to collect for her room.'

'I told her yesterday how much people find after storms,' he said, half to himself, relieved to have discovered where she was. 'I'd better go and find her. Try to speak to her, if she'll let me.'

He ran across the lawn to the end of the garden, opened the small driftwood gate that Lydia had had installed to keep Jack from escaping down to the beach, and hurried down the stone steps to the beach below. He stopped halfway to raise his hand to shade his eyes from the piercing sunlight to scour the sandy beach for Daisy. He spotted her about two hundred metres away, following Jack who was sniffing around something dark in the sand by the water's edge. He smiled. She was so lovely, and he might have blown it with her. He ran down the rest of the steps towards her on the fine white sand, but as the object Jack was sniffing came into view, he staggered and nearly fell.

It was a rusted, cone-shaped object, with tail fins just discernible. A World War Two unexploded bomb. Occasionally these were washed up on the shore after intense storms and most of the locals knew not to go near them but to report them to the police. But Daisy would have no idea.

He ran faster, calling Daisy's name. She needed to get away from it, and fast. Who knew when this thing could explode? She seemed to be calling the dog away, but Jack was refusing to take any notice. Gabriel's heart contracted painfully when he saw Daisy running towards the object to fetch him.

'Daisy!' he shouted. 'Come away from there!'

She didn't even react. It dawned on him that she couldn't hear him against the waves that were crashing near her feet. He was horrified to see her standing, arms folded as she spoke to the dog. Jack turned and ran closer and Gabriel screamed her name to distract her. But she still couldn't hear him. He sprinted towards her.

Daisy and Jack reached the bomb as he called her name

again. She looked up in his direction, shocked to see him racing towards her. 'I don't really want to talk now, Gabriel,' she said.

'Get back!' he shouted, wanting her to listen, but not wishing to alarm her.

She scowled at him. 'What's the panic?' she asked as he reached her, grabbed her arm and pulled her away. 'Hey, let go of me, you're hurting my arm.'

She looked stunned by his actions, but he didn't care. He scooped Jack up in one arm and dragged Daisy off as fast as he could.

As soon as they were about a hundred feet away, he stopped. Daisy snatched her arm from his grasp. 'How dare you manhandle me like that?'

'Sorry,' he said, hating the accusatory glare she was giving him. 'I needed you to get away from that.'

'What?'

She looked a little frightened and it dawned on him that it might not have anything to do with the bomb. Her expression changed and he thought for a moment that she wanted to punch him. Placing a hand on her shoulder, he turned her to him. 'I didn't mean to be rough, but that thing Jack was sniffing at is a bomb.'

Her eyes widened for a second and then she smiled. 'Are you on something?'

He shook his head. 'I'm deadly serious,' he said. 'Can you hold him for a minute?' he asked, handing Jack into her arms. 'I don't want him to go back and sniff around that thing.'

He took his mobile from his pocket and called the police, reporting what he'd found, and then called another number, giving them the same story. By the time he'd ended the call she was walking further away.

'How the hell do you know that's a bomb?' she asked, obviously not sure she believed him. 'Is this some sort of game? Because after last night I'm really not in the mood.'

Gabriel could see she wasn't going to let him off easily. 'It isn't a game,' he said. 'We need to move further away from it. We also need to make sure no one else gets near.' He checked his watch. 'They should be here soon.'

'You're serious, aren't you?'

'I wouldn't joke about something like this,' he said, a little annoyed.

'OK, so where will this bomb have come from then?'

'It's probably a German shell from the occupation and was probably fired from one of the gun emplacements along the coast.' He heard the sirens seconds later.

'They can't have got here so quickly,' she said, looking doubtful as two of the parish honorary police arrived. They drew up in their car and came over to speak to Gabe.

'Is that it there?' one of them asked. Gabe nodded. 'Blimey, that looks like a fifty pounder to me,' he said, taking his phone from a pocket in his neon yellow jacket. 'I'll call the bomb disposal guys.'

'We need to make a cordon, at least one hundred metres away,' the older one said.

'Ahh, it's young Gabriel Wilson,' the other man said, after he'd finished his call. He held his hand out to Gabriel.

'Good to see you again,' Gabriel said. 'Do you want me to wait here until more men arrive?'

'That would be good. If you could stand further back and ask the lady to take your grandmother's dog back home?'

Gabe nodded and did as he was told. As he and Daisy walked the short distance away, he explained the situation to her. 'These two guys are honorary police – volunteer police officers who take an oath in the Royal Court and assist the centenier to keep order in the parish. We have them for all twelve parishes in the island and they do a brilliant job.'

Daisy looked intrigued. 'I thought they *were* police by their uniforms and markings on their cars. They seem well organised.'

'They are. They live nearby which is why they got here so quickly.'

She stared over at the men who were waving other beach-combers away. 'It's so different here to back home, despite the scenery looking similar in places.' She looked towards the bomb. 'I never expected something like this to happen in Jersey,' she said. 'Do many bombs get brought up on to the beaches after all this time?'

He was relieved she seemed to have forgotten about their disagreement. 'No, not really. It can happen after a particularly violent storm and we had one of those the other night. I've seen one before down at St Ouen's beach. The German army used to test fire various weapons during World War Two down there, so you do get the occasional bomb being brought in on a particu-larly rough tide.'

'I've seen the large bunker from the ferry when I first arrived in Jersey,' she said. 'Someone on the boat told me that it was one of many bunkers built by the Nazis during their occupation of the island.'

'That's right,' he said, enjoying being able to share some of his island's heritage with her. 'They're being excavated all the time. Some people think they're ugly but most of the locals are so used to them I don't think we notice them half the time. There are anti-tank gun casements, old machine gun turrets, and restored underground bunkers. There's one in St Ouen where you can see a vast range of artefacts, including an Enigma machine.'

Daisy's eyes widened. 'And you can visit these places?'

'Yes. They're well worth a look, even if you're not that interested in World War Two or the occupation. It's fascinating to think that this island and the other Channel Islands were completely taken over by the Nazis for five years.'

'It's frightening when you think about it.'

He nodded. 'It is. There's so much I could tell you,' he said, as he led her further away from the unexploded bomb. 'For example, did you know that Alderney was a concentration camp, and that Hitler's Organisation Todt used slave labourers and others pressurised into working on his Atlantic Wall?'

'No, I didn't. How horrible. What's the Atlantic Wall?'

'When you go to St Ouen's beach you'll see the enormous concrete wall stretching along most of the beach; that's part of Hitler's Atlantic Wall. It's a fortification system that stretched from Norway, across northern France to Spain, and here in Jersey and was meant to stop the allies invading.'

'And to think how recently this all happened.'

He didn't want her to only think of the island in terms of the occupation and added, 'The Gunsite Café in St Aubin's bay is an interesting place to have lunch.'

'Lunch in a bunker?' she said smiling. 'How odd is that?'

Relieved to see her become a little more jovial, he remembered that he still had to tell her about Bella. He took a deep breath and gave her what he hoped was an apologetic look. 'Daisy, I really am sorry I didn't tell you about Bella. I just couldn't think how to.'

Daisy frowned. 'You have a wife, Gabe. How can you not think I'd be interested in something like that?'

'I know, and I was planning to tell you. But we're over; we hardly even see each other any more. Except at work, of course.'

'She's a marine explorer too?' Gabriel nodded and Daisy sighed. 'Look, Gabriel,' she said, hoisting the podgy little dog higher in her arms. 'I've got enough issues of my own to deal with. I don't need to become involved with a married man, too. I know you think I'm making more of this situation than is necessary, but, well, I suppose it's because of my parents and my father not being there for my mother. He turned his back on her when she needed him most and married someone else. I don't want to go through life being embittered like Mum was and ending up resenting you. I'd rather remember what we shared in Vietnam and enjoy those memories.' She hesitated. 'Also, don't forget you're the son of my employers and my job and where I live is through them. If I fall out with you I'll only feel I have to leave and will then need to find somewhere to live and work all over again. I'd rather not do that if I can help it.'

In the time they'd been talking Gabe hadn't noticed that the bomb disposal unit had arrived and already prepared the device for detonation. He became aware of someone calling for everyone to stand back just as Daisy turned to walk back to the house when a blast echoed around the beach. Daisy stumbled and he rushed to her, grabbing Jack from her hands.

He turned to look as the sand and oily mass of metal and rotten debris exploded into the air.

'Bloody hell,' she exclaimed, holding on to his arm. 'I was standing next to that thing a short while ago.'

'You were.'

She looked up at him wide-eyed and obviously a little shocked. 'Thank you for, well, saving me from that.' She pointed towards the spot where the sand was now settled in a heap and the smoke was slowly dispersing, her finger trembling.

He hugged her to him with his free arm, while holding tightly to Jack with the other. The poor little dog was now trembling against his chest. 'It's OK boy, nothing to worry about.'

He waved at the police and they nodded for him to leave.

Gabe took Daisy by the hand and walked over to the stairs to his grandmother's garden.

At the top of the stairs he closed the gate behind them and placed Jack onto the grass, who promptly raced off into the safety of Lydia's house.

Daisy tucked a stray strand of blonde hair behind her left ear. 'Your quick thinking probably saved my life and Jack's.'

He could see she was shell-shocked by the incident and went to step closer to her. She raised her hand to stop him. 'I'm not ready to talk to you about anything else though,' she said. 'I'm still upset about yesterday. When I calm down, I want you to tell me everything. I need to know exactly when you and Bella married and your situation with her because I won't let anyone make a fool out of me.'

'I have no intention of doing that to you, Daisy,' he said. 'Can't we talk about this now?'

She walked away. 'I said I'll discuss this with you when I'm ready, Gabriel.'

He watched her go. Ordinarily he'd have offered her a lift back to the hotel, but he could tell she was in no mood to accept anything from him right now. He walked slowly towards the house.

Just before he reached the terrace his grandmother came from behind one of the flower borders. He remembered telling Luke he wouldn't be long. 'I'd better get back to help with the work at the hotel. I'll see you later.' He leant forward and kissed her on the cheek. 'I'll put it right somehow.'

'I hope so,' his grandmother said. 'Daisy is a lovely girl and I think she's hiding a lot of pain inside her. I'd hate for her to get hurt.'

He didn't argue.

She stroked his arm. 'Don't look too forlorn,' his grandmother said, accidentally smearing his elbow with earth from her trowel. 'I'm sure she'll give you time to try and explain what's going on between you and Bella.'

'Nothing is going on, Nan.'

'I'm not the one you need to persuade of that. Daisy is.'

He walked towards his car and, on the drive back, thought about the beautiful woman who had been his childhood sweetheart and who he'd split up from a year before meeting and falling in love with Daisy. Bella was kind and beautiful, if impulsive, and she'd always hold a special place in his heart, but he'd never love her like he loved Daisy.

Arriving at the hotel, he smiled at Fi across the reception desk. She didn't smile back. Word didn't take long to get around this place, he mused. He hurried through to the back of the hotel to his father's wood-panelled office and sat down.

'Bloody fool,' he murmured, resting his elbows on the mahogany desk and lowering his face into his hands.

'Am I disturbing you?' Bella asked from the doorway.

He jumped, glanced up and shook his head. 'No, it's OK,' he said. 'Come in.'

She walked in, her long tanned legs disappearing into a pair of khaki shorts. 'Has this got anything to do with me speaking to Daisy yesterday?'

Bella sat down. She knew him far too well for him to get away with any denials.

He sighed. 'I'm afraid so.'

She crossed one leg over the other and rested her hands on her knee. 'Have I made things difficult for you?'

He stared down at the blotter on the desk. 'Maybe. I was going to tell Daisy, but hadn't quite got round to it.'

She rested her hand on his forearm. 'Sorry, I shouldn't have said anything. Maybe I had a spark of jealousy for a second, seeing you so relaxed and happy with her. Do you want me to speak to her?' She smiled. 'I'm sure she'll be OK once she understands the full picture.'

'No, I think I'd better do it.'

She stood up and sat on the edge of the desk next to him before reaching out her arm and stroking the side of his face with her right hand. 'Poor baby,' she murmured, just as the door opened and Daisy looked in.

Gabriel heard her gasp and looked up. Bella turned and pulled her hand away from his face as he stood up and called after Daisy. 'Wait, Daisy,' he shouted, as the door was slammed in his face.

'Damn, that was crappy timing,' Bella said, looking concerned.

'Sorry, I'm going to have to go after her,' he said. He reached the door, but before leaving he remembered that Bella had asked to come in and see him. 'Is there something you want to speak to me about?'

She shook her head. 'Nothing that can't wait,' she said, waving for him to go.

He couldn't tell which way Daisy had gone, so ran through to reception first and asked Fi, 'Did Daisy come this way?'

Fi shook her head. 'No, why?'

'Nothing,' he said. 'But if she does please tell her that I need to speak to her, urgently.'

'Will do,' she said.

He turned and ran through to the back of the hotel, heading for her room. He knocked, calling for her to open up. One of the waitresses popped her head out of her door. 'She's not there,' she said, smiling when she saw it was Gabriel. 'I can come and help you look for her, if you'd like.'

'Thanks, but that won't be necessary,' he said, heading out of the hallway, down the stairs and out to the gardens.

He stopped at the top of the pathway leading down to the valley behind the hotel. Staring out from one end to the other, he tried to see where she might be, but couldn't find her. He groaned, running down the stone steps to get a better view along the pathways. 'Daisy!' he shouted.

Realising that holidaymakers would be trying to relax in the peace of the beautifully landscaped valley, he decided he daren't call again. When she didn't answer, he turned to go in the opposite direction, nodding a hello to guests as he passed.

Where had she got to? he wondered, trying not to look harassed. He didn't need any of the guests noticing his panic. After all, they might assume that there was a problem with the hotel and after the recent fire, that was the last thing his parents needed.

He hurried down the pathways, looking across to the other side of the narrow valley and down along the row of geometric ponds. Nearing the end, he was about to give up and return to the hotel to look for her there when he spotted a foot sticking out from behind one of the palm trees. Recognising the toe ring Daisy wore on her right foot, he hurried over to her. She was sitting on the grassy verge next to the end pool, resting back against the trunk of the tree, her eyes closed as she listened to something on her iPod.

Gabriel watched her for a few seconds, marvelling at how pretty she was and desperately trying to form a coherent sentence to persuade her to listen to him.

Daisy must have sensed him standing by her and opened her eyes. She glared at him and went to stand up, but Gabriel sat down next to her and as soon as she'd removed her earphones he said, 'Please, Daisy, let me at least try to explain what happened between me and Bella.'

She glanced around them. He watched her smile at a couple of the guests before turning her attention back to him. 'I think this is probably not the wisest place to start opening up about your private life, don't you?'

She was right of course. 'Yes. Where do you want to talk, then? We could go for a drive somewhere, have something to eat, or a walk maybe?'

'I've got a few hours off and Fi said Luke had been looking for you, so you should be over at the orangery with him, not here. I need to make the most of some peace in the sun.'

'You've got one hour,' he said, aware that he was pushing his luck with Luke. 'I'll be back here to get you and then maybe you'll let me explain.'

'Fine,' she said after some thought. 'As long as we can walk. I don't want to be inside a car on an afternoon like this.'

Before she had a chance to change her mind, Gabriel left her and ran back to the orangery to make amends with Luke for his tardiness.

'Good to see you've remembered to come back,' Luke scowled. 'I do have other things I could be getting on with, you know.'

'Yes, I'm sorry.' Gabriel appreciated that Luke was taking time out from his busy life and work schedule to help them out, and said so.

Luke grumbled something Gabriel couldn't hear, then added, 'You're here now, so pick up that brush and help me finish varnishing these frames. They're going to need several coats, and if you don't want them to be sticky when your guests arrive, we'll have to finish working on them sooner rather than later.'

Gabriel did as he was told, relieved Luke was still here working on the repairs at all.

'Fi brought me a coffee a little while ago and we got chatting. She let it slip about your wife introducing herself to your girl-friend. She didn't mean to, so please don't be angry with her.' He frowned disapprovingly at Gabriel. 'That must have been awkward though?'

'I must remember to thank Fi for that,' he said, irritated that she'd been gossiping about him and making a mental note to speak to her. She probably didn't mean anything by it, but it wasn't very professional. 'It isn't quite as it seems, though. Firstly, Bella and I aren't together any more and the divorce is just a tech-nicality. Secondly, Daisy isn't my girlfriend, more's the pity.'

'Keep varnishing,' Luke said, indicating the brush Gabriel was holding down by his side.

'Sorry.' He did as he was told. 'Bella really is just a friend now, apart from the marriage certificate connecting us. As soon as we can get divorced we will. Both of us look forward to being free from the other.'

'Good, I'm glad,' Luke said. 'I don't know Daisy, but from what Fi tells me she's a pleasant girl.'

'She is,' Gabe agreed.

Finally, having completed the tasks Luke had given him, Gabriel helped him pack up his pick-up truck and thanked him again. He noticed the time and went to find Daisy, relieved to find her exactly where he'd last seen her.

'I'm sorry for taking twice as long as I'd promised,' he said, wondering how many times he'd end up having to apologise to people today.

'I did pack up when you didn't come back,' she said. 'But when I passed the orangery and saw you hard at work with Luke, I thought I couldn't blame you.'

He gave a sigh of relief. 'Thank you.'

She shrugged. 'I want the party to be a success. Your parents need the takings, especially after having to cancel that wedding. If that means me having to wait to go for a walk, then it's the least I can do for them,' she said.

Delighted she was still happy to go for a walk with him and determined not to give her the chance to change her mind, he reached out his hand.

'Here, let me,' he said, taking her hand and helping her to her feet. He didn't miss her hesitation. 'We can go through there,' he said, pointing through a gap in the hedge. He wanted to get on with it without having to go via the rest of the hotel grounds and chancing bumping into Bella or Fi. The last thing he needed was Daisy to have any reason to decide not to go with him. 'We can reach the Railway Walk from there.'

Distracted by this suggestion, he saw her confusion. 'I didn't think there was a railway here,' she said, brushing a few stray blades of grass from her skirt.

'I'll tell you about it while we go.' Recalling that he was supposed to be on duty, he added, 'I'd just better send Fi a text letting her know that I'll be gone for about an hour if she needs me for anything.'

Daisy took a pair of sunglasses from her red-and-blue striped basket and put them on while he sent his text.

He led her to the gap in the hedge and held back a couple of small branches as she stepped through to the field on the other side.

'Is this private property?' she asked.

'Yes, but I know the owners. They've always been happy for me to come through here.'

They walked along the edge of the ploughed field as it sloped downwards. Reaching the end of the field, they climbed over the five-bar gate and onto the road.

'The Railway Walk is this way,' he said, pointing to their right.

'You were going to tell me about the railway,' she said, stopping to take off one of her espadrilles to shake the dust out of it.

He waited for her to put her shoe back on. 'I don't know too much about it,' he said honestly, 'but I believe a railway linking St Helier to St Aubin first ran in the nineteenth century. It was added to by the owner of a quarry in La Moye, just along there,' he said, indicating in front of them. 'Other sections were added until it reached Corbière, which is where we're heading now.'

'I should imagine it was a beautiful journey.'

'I don't think carriages were added for passengers until the mid-twenties. I think it was mainly for business use before then.' He was enjoying her interest and the distraction from his own story. 'It did build up to about a million passengers a year, I think.' He tried to recall what his father told the guests when they ever asked about the railway. 'I suppose people began owning their own cars and travelling by buses after that, so it declined in popularity. I think it was scrapped in the mid-thirties.'

'That's such a shame,' she said, as they walked along the hardstanding making up the pathway.

Gabriel enjoyed the shade the overhanging branches were giving them in the extra-warm August afternoon. 'I think this stretch was used by the Nazis during the occupation to help them carry guns and equipment for battery placements they were building as part of their Atlantic Wall.' She looked a little confused, so he added, 'To build the bunkers you've probably seen along the coastline that I was telling you about. It was scrapped again soon after the end of the war. It's sad really.'

'It is,' she said. Pulling a camera from her basket, she stopped to take a picture of the curved pathway in front of them, edged on both sides by trees, shrubs, and colourful flowers. She pointed through the opening in the trees to their right. 'What's that over there? Is it a playing field?'

He nodded. 'Yes, there are pitches for things like football and hockey. There's also a gym and an indoor pool if ever you want to join. I could show you around if you like?'

'No, it's fine, thanks.'

Not to be deterred, he added. 'Over there is the airport and if you go in that direction,' he said, pointing somewhere in between the two, 'you'll go over the sand dunes and down to St Ouen's Bay.'

'Where I'll find the Five Mile Road and quite a few of the bunkers you were talking about?'

He smiled at her. 'That's right. Great surfing too.'

They continued walking in silence. It was almost deafening and as hard as he tried, Gabriel couldn't ignore what he had to do next. He waited until they'd crossed over the road to the final strip of the walk taking them closer towards the Corbière lighthouse.

'We were childhood sweethearts,' he said finally.

She stopped walking and stared at him for a few seconds. 'I presume you weren't a couple when we hooked up in Vietnam?' It was part accusation, part question.

He took hold of her hand. 'No, we weren't,' he said. 'Bella and I split up soon after we left university. She wanted us to move into a flat together but I wasn't ready.' He recalled the tearful threats she'd given him, shocked when she'd gone through with them and left him to move to France to work for a few years. He gave a precis version to Daisy.

She frowned, snatching away her hand from his grasp. 'If you weren't together when you came to Vietnam,' she asked, raising her sunglasses up on top of her head so he could see her piercing blue eyes staring at him, 'then how come you got together and married such a short time after I'd left?'

'It wasn't that short a time,' he said, trying not to become angry at the memory of her promising to contact him and then not doing so. 'If you recall, you were going to let me know when we could see each other again.'

She looked a little sheepish and shrugged. 'I had a lot going on.'

He took hold of her gently by the shoulders. 'Daisy, you're acting as if I jilted you.' He studied her face, unable to miss the hurt but not wishing to take all the blame for what had happened since they'd last been together as a couple. 'I emailed you for months, your number wasn't recognised and I had no other way of contacting you. You weren't on any social media sites that I looked at, so how do you expect me to know that you're still waiting for me?' He could hear his voice getting colder and quieter the more he tried to reason with her. 'I loved you. I was hurt to think you'd forgotten me so easily, after all we'd shared together.'

'I understand that, but it hurts that you not only got back together with your ex but that you rushed off and married her.' Daisy marched away from him, head down.

Stung by her outburst, Gabriel followed, soon catching up with her. 'Hey, that's really unfair,' he said. 'It wasn't like that.'

Daisy stopped. 'Then why did you get back with her?'

'Because she was pregnant with my baby,' he said, the pain of his words and recalling the misery that lay behind them making him wince.

6

DAISY

Daisy flinched. 'She had your baby?'

He cleared his throat. 'No, she miscarried at five months,' he murmured.

Daisy's heart pounded at the shock of this news. She couldn't think what to say.

'After not hearing from you for over a year,' he said, 'Bella and I met up with each other when we were each out with friends in town. One thing led to another...' He looked down at his feet and exhaled sharply. 'I'm not proud of what I did. I still loved you, so it was unfair to Bella, which was why I felt doubly certain that I had to marry her when she told me she was pregnant.' He sighed heavily. 'I'm sorry, Daisy. It was a mistake and we both know that now.'

Daisy didn't know what to say. 'How heartbreaking for you both,' she whispered, tearing her eyes away from the sadness in his. She turned and began walking. 'I'm sorry for you and Bella, really I am,' she said. 'But I'm going to have to think about this.' She was heartbroken to think of him preparing to be a father to another woman's baby. How different to her own father who'd made promises to her mother he hadn't kept. At least Gabe had stood by Bella and not let her down. It occurred to her that maybe she wouldn't be so distrustful of others if her father had been around more. She had no right to feel badly towards Gabe when she had no claim on him, but she'd dreamt so many times of their future together and it always involved a brood of tousle-haired boys and girls playing on a sandy beach somewhere.

'I really am sorry,' he said, walking next to her.

She could tell he meant what he said. 'It must have been a difficult time for you both.' She struggled to resist from adding anything further, but her resentment of what he'd done overtook her best intentions. 'You must have married pretty soon after sleeping together though.'

'Three months,' he said quietly. 'We weren't together long because as soon as she lost the baby, she told me she was returning to France and wanted to put the whole mess behind her.'

'So, it was her choice to leave you?'

'It was mutual,' he said quietly. 'I couldn't help missing you and she wasn't ready to settle down.'

'Will your divorce be final soon?' she asked, desperate to find something positive to cling to.

'Not for a while, like I said.' He moved to avoid collision with a small child on his bike.

'Why not?'

'Because in Jersey you have to be married for three years before you can start divorce proceedings.'

'So, you can't begin divorce proceedings for another two and a half years?' He nodded. 'How can I think about getting back together with you while you're still married? I grew up with occasional visits from my father because he married someone else soon after my mother became pregnant with me. I've told you this already,' she said, not enjoying being so open about her issues with her past. 'I'm sorry, but I can't contemplate seeing a married man now; it's too close to home.'

'I'm sorry about what happened between your parents, Daisy, and I can't imagine how you feel, but this is different. My marriage to Bella is over in all but name. It's a legality, nothing more,' he said. 'Seeing you again has brought back all the feelings I had for you when we were away. I want to try and make things work between us.'

'How?' she asked, sensing a laugh rising up through her body, or maybe she was about to cry.

'I don't know,' he said, taking her hands in his. 'But I'll work something out. I promise.'

She swallowed and looked down from his face. She wanted him so much, but this was so complicated. Daisy pushed her resentment away, instantly feeling guilty for being so selfish. Maybe she was just jealous. After all it wasn't really Gabe's fault that things between them had turned out to be more complicated than she'd expected. She hadn't exactly been open with him about Aaron and her issues, and her resentment of her father wasn't his fault.

'I think we should go back to the hotel now,' she said, unable to bear feeling so envious of some other woman. She wasn't a jealous person usually and this alien emotion nauseated her.

'But I haven't shown you the lighthouse yet,' he said.

'I think we've done all we needed to do this afternoon, don't you?' She looked up at him and waited for him to answer.

He nodded. 'Fine... You're right. It's time to go back.'

They walked back in silence. She stole a glance up at him and saw such sadness in his face that for a second she felt cruel. She'd been the one who promised to contact him and hadn't. It's my own fault, she realised. If I had answered his emails like I wanted to then none of this would have happened. She'd had her reasons though, despite how much she wanted to turn back the clock, and nothing could change what she'd had to cope with then. She pushed the image of Aaron to the back of her mind. She couldn't cope with thinking about him right now. 'Life's a real pain sometimes,' she said, not meaning to voice her thoughts.

'You're not kidding.'

They arrived back at the hotel valley and Daisy stopped and turned to him. 'Let's go our separate ways from here,' she said, unable to bear being with him and her thoughts a moment longer. 'I'm going to go to my room for a bit and I think you need to go and see if Fi needs anything.' She checked her watch. 'I've got to be back on reception in just over an hour and need to shower and chill for a bit first.'

'Why don't you have a swim?' he suggested. 'The pool is lovely and cool enough to be refreshing.'

'I thought the staff weren't supposed to swim in the pool.'

He shrugged. 'They can as long as they're discreet and it's not in the middle of the day. It's usually quiet round about now, so why not make the most of it?'

'Thanks,' she said, grateful to him for the suggestion. 'I will.' Without waiting for him to say anything else, she walked up the stairs closest to the staff quarters to go and change into her swimming costume. Stepping inside, she pushed her window as wide as it would go to let in some much-needed fresh air – not that the humid evening was allowing much relief inside the room. She pulled off her skirt and top and changed out of her underwear and into the red halter-neck bikini she'd bought when she'd been given the job in Jersey. There wasn't any point coming to work on a holiday island and not make the most of the glorious weather, she'd thought.

A lifetime living on the outskirts of Devon hadn't really

prepared her for island life, though one thing she hadn't had any trouble getting used to was the glorious weather. We might only be a couple of hundred miles south of the coast of England, she thought, but this place seems almost tropical at times. She loved this island and whether Gabriel was staying or not, she hoped to be able to stay here for the foreseeable future.

She put on a loose-fitting cotton dress and flip-flops and walked outside to the pool area. She looked around, relieved to see that only the pool attendant was out there, tidying up the seat covers and straightening tables. The guests must be out seeing the island, she decided. Slipping the dress over her head, she placed it down with her towel on one of the chairs in a far corner to the entrance of the area. She walked over to the edge of the pool, dipped the toes of her right foot into the water and then without giving herself time to think, dived in.

Her warm skin stung briefly when it touched the cool water. The otherworldly feeling of gliding through the water, unable to hear or feel anything or anyone around her, was bliss. She opened her eyes and swam to the shallow end, coming up for air with a smile on her face. Wiping the water from her face, she smoothed her wet hair back from her forehead, looking towards the arched front double doors of the hotel just as Gabriel emerged accompanying a couple of guests to their taxi. He stopped and gave her a smouldering look. She felt a pang so strong that all her good intentions of not falling for him were lost in an instant.

Unable to tear her gaze away from his, the message of his regret came across perfectly and for a second she wondered if maybe she'd been too quick to dismiss the prospect of the two of them ever being able to move on from this. The man standing next to Gabriel realised he wasn't paying attention to what they were saying and Daisy saw him look over in her direction, giving her an approving look. She bent her knees so her shoulders were in the water when the woman also looked in her direction, no doubt to see what they were staring at. She smiled at Daisy and said something to Gabriel, who reddened slightly, shook his head, and opened the taxi door for them.

Daisy swam to the other side of the pool. Not wishing to be the centre of so much attention, she hurriedly got out, and grabbed her towel and wrapped it around her chest. She picked up her bag, slipped on her flip-flops and went around the side of the hotel to return to her room. She heard the taxi purring down the curved driveway and slowed her step. How could she really expect this situation to continue? she wondered miserably. Gabriel had his issues, as well as a divorce to deal with, and was certainly going to be around for the next month while Francesca and Rick were working, and as difficult as it was going to be, she couldn't let Lydia down by leaving.

It wasn't only that she had nowhere else to go, but also that she didn't back out of her contract – she'd agreed to work the entire season at the Encore. She would just have to keep her head down and work hard, saving as much as possible so that she could maybe share a flat with someone who had residential qualifications here on the island. Gabriel wouldn't be here too long, she decided; he had too many interests elsewhere with his marine exploration.

* * *

After a few days of trying to do just that, Daisy was working on a group booking at reception when Lydia walked up to the desk. 'Hello,' she said, her short white hair as immaculate as ever.

'Hi,' Daisy replied. 'Isn't this weather glorious?'

Lydia nodded. 'It is, thankfully. The guests are always so

much happier when they can plan their days to the beach or simply relax by the pool.' She nodded a greeting to a passing gentleman who raised his Panama hat slightly in acknowledgement. When he'd stepped outside, Lydia added, 'I haven't seen you in my garden recently. Is everything all right?'

Embarrassed to have appeared rude and to have caused Lydia concern, Daisy blushed. 'Fine, really. I've just been, um, busy with this and that.'

Lydia looked either side of her to check no one was around, and bending in slightly said, 'So your absence has nothing to do with my grandson's little bombshell the other day?'

Daisy frowned. 'I'm sorry?' She hadn't expected him to share their argument with his grandmother and was mortified to think they'd been discussing her behind her back.

Lydia shook her head. 'I think that came out a little oddly. I have a confession to make to you.'

Not another confession, Daisy groaned inwardly. 'What is it?' she asked politely, not really wishing to know.

'I overheard your conversation with Gabriel in my garden.'

Daisy racked her brains to think what they'd actually said. She didn't want to offer any information if it was incorrect, so shrugged. 'Sorry, I can't recall what we were talking about.'

'His marriage to Bella,' Lydia said gently. 'I'm sorry, I hadn't meant to eavesdrop, but I was working on a small shrubbery and you two stopped in front of a couple of the bushes and there didn't seem to be the right time to make my presence known to you. Are you all right?'

Daisy was unable to hide the look of hurt on her face. 'It was a shock,' she said quietly.

Lydia nodded. 'I'm sure it must have come as a terrible blow.' She put one hand on her chest.

It occurred to Daisy that Gabriel's secret had brought back

unexpected memories for Lydia too. Daisy could see she was troubled by them and hurriedly forced a smile. 'I'm fine now though, honestly,' she fibbed.

Lydia studied her face and Daisy couldn't help looking away, aware that she could see right through her attempts at bravado. 'I think we should sit down and have a chat, woman-to-woman. Pop round after your shift, if you want.'

'I'd like that,' Daisy admitted. It would be good to speak with someone she trusted, even if that person adored Gabriel above anyone else.

After her shift was over, Daisy caught a bus to Lydia's house and the two of them went for a walk down to the end of her garden and onto the beach below.

'I'm glad you invited me to do this,' Daisy said, stepping out of her flip-flops and holding them in one hand. 'I think one of my all-time favourite things has to be walking barefoot on a sandy beach.'

'I agree,' Lydia said, pushing the front of her straw hat down a little further onto her forehead. 'Please don't think too badly of Gabriel,' she said. 'He means well even if he's made some choices I find difficult to accept.'

'Don't you like Bella?' Daisy asked, hoping she wasn't over-stepping the mark where her employer was concerned.

Lydia stopped walking and looked at Daisy, the intensity of her icy blue gaze reaching deep into her soul. 'I do like her.' She rested a hand on Daisy's shoulder. 'She's a lovely girl, although I'm sure that's not what you'd prefer me to tell you.'

Her honesty stung, but Daisy was grateful to Lydia for being so open. At least this way she could be sure she was telling her the truth.

'A few years ago,' Lydia continued, 'I would have been delighted to welcome her to the family.'

'Oh? What's changed?' Daisy asked, confused.

'I think I should be honest with you about my feelings for Bella. Her family were good friends with Francesca and Rick, so when Gabriel and she were teenagers it was probably not too unexpected that they began dating each other. No one foresaw them continuing that relationship though, and I think you should know that Francesca is more than a little disappointed that Bella and Gabriel are getting a divorce. She'd been looking forward to, well...'

'Becoming a grandmother?' Daisy offered, when Lydia struggled to find the right words.

Lydia threw back her head in laughter. 'Oh my word, no, never that.' She shook her head. 'Francesca isn't nearly ready to be a grandmother, but she did like the idea of her best friend's daughter marrying her son.'

Lydia began walking again and Daisy kept in step with her. 'So what you're trying to tell me is that my boss isn't going to be too pleased to discover that Gabriel and I have a history, however small.'

'Exactly.'

It gets better and better, Daisy thought, bending down to pick up a piece of green glass made opaque by years of being tossed about by the sea. She quickened her step to catch up. Wanting to change the subject she said, 'Gabriel is as dark as you're fair.'

Lydia smiled. 'You think it's strange because Francesca and Rick are pretty fair too. His grandfather was dark, though.'

Daisy nodded.

They walked in silence for a moment and Daisy began to think that Lydia had forgotten she was next to her. Not wishing to disturb the woman's thoughts, she concentrated on listening to the waves as they broke against the shoreline near to them.

'His grandfather was very handsome,' she said wistfully. 'His name was Lorenzo and he was Italian. He was the reason I gave up acting and disappeared from the public eye.'

Daisy was intrigued to hear Lydia's story. 'That's so romantic,' she said, longing to have that sort of thing in her life. 'You must have loved him very much.'

Lydia nodded. 'It was a magical time. We met when I was filming on location in Naples. He was one of the supporting actors and we only had a couple of short scenes together. I was out walking in the city one day. I'd gone off wandering and got lost, and he happened to discover me trying not to panic as the sun set. He offered me a lift on the back of his Lambretta.' She laughed. 'I was shy back then and tried to argue with him but he told me the streets were dangerous and that he would walk next to me if he had to, but he wasn't leaving me alone. So, in the end, I gave in and went back to the hotel with him.'

Daisy sighed. She could picture a younger version of Gabriel insisting that Lydia Grey accept his offer of a ride home. 'How lovely. What happened next?'

Lydia smiled. 'I used to see him around the set most days, and then he disappeared for a few weeks. I was devastated and it was then that I realised I'd fallen in love with him. When he returned, I was ecstatic and so when he secretly asked me out to visit a new galleria that had opened up I agreed and went with him. We saw each other every day after that until shooting ended.'

'Is that when you came back to Jersey?'

Lydia nodded. 'My mother insisted I return. I'd tried to confide in her about Lorenzo, but she didn't want to know. She was determined that I would marry an Englishman with money, who could give me the life she'd never had. She was very ambitious for me.'

'But you obviously saw him again because you had Francesca together.'

Lydia took her hat from her head, smoothed down her hair, and replaced it to shield her pale face from the sun. 'He came here, to Jersey, to try and see me, but my mother lied and told him I was away filming. But I was lucky – I'd broken my stiletto heel when I was in town so I came home early and saw him walking down our front path.'

'How lucky,' Daisy murmured, entranced by the romance of Lydia's story.

'I didn't realise what my mother had done until I got back home again later that evening, but by then Lorenzo had given me the name of the small hotel where he was staying as well as his address in Italy. We secretly spent every day together for the rest of his brief trip and it was then that I became pregnant with Francesca.'

'It's like something you'd see in a movie,' Daisy said dreamily.

Lydia pulled a face. 'No, it was terrible. My mother was horrified when I told her. I stupidly thought she'd insist Lorenzo and I marry, but instead she planned to take me to her sister's in Scotland to have the baby and then for it to be adopted.'

Daisy gasped, shocked to hear how Lydia had been treated by her own mother. 'How did you manage to keep your baby?'

Lydia picked up a seagull feather. She held one end and pulled the soft white strands slowly through her fingers. 'I managed to send a letter to Lorenzo telling him where we were going. He arrived in Jersey the morning we were due to leave for Scotland and we ran away together.'

'How?'

'On a friend's boat. He sailed us to St Malo and from there we travelled by train down to Lorenzo's flat in a small village outside Rome.' Lydia smiled at Daisy and she realised she must have a gormless expression on her face. 'Let's sit here,' Lydia suggested, leading her to a bank where some grass clung on in the sand. 'It's so hot I could do with a rest.'

'Of course.' Daisy sat next to her and pushed her feet deep into the soft tiny grains of sand.

'Where was I?' Lydia frowned, then before Daisy could remind her, stared out to sea. Daisy could almost see the older woman's past catching up with her. Her face took on a haunted look and she wondered if maybe asking her to divulge her history to her might not be the best thing she could have done.

'If it's painful for you to recall all this and you don't want to tell me, I'll understand,' she said.

'No, its fine. I need to remember. I forget sometimes and reminisce about Lorenzo, making him out to be the perfect gentleman, which he was not. He was my first and only love though.'

How sad, thought Daisy, for such a beautiful woman to have only loved one man and lost him. 'When did you part?' she asked, intrigued, but concerned at her direct question.

'Francesca was two when I discovered he had a mistress.' She looked at Daisy. 'She was a beautiful Italian girl he'd fallen in love with. His first love.'

'Like Bella is to Gabriel?' Daisy asked almost to herself.

Lydia nodded. 'Yes, like that.'

She felt a pang in her heart, but couldn't blame Lydia for telling her the truth.

'Sorry, but it is very similar,' Lydia said, patting Daisy's clasped hands. 'Lorenzo loved his daughter, very much, but became more demanding of me. I think he loved me, but I began to believe that he loved the idea of me, more than me as a person. I'd been this untouchable actress, courted and photographed, someone to admire. When I was heavily pregnant and then afterwards he used to come home and I'd catch him watching me – no make-up, creased clothes, and definitely not being coveted by other men. I'd gone from being a goddess in his eyes to his laundry maid and he seemed unable to hide how very let down he felt by me.'

'But that's so unfair,' Daisy said, hurt on Lydia's behalf. 'You were bringing up his baby.'

Lydia nodded. 'I thought so too, but he hadn't wanted a baby with me, he wanted someone to adore. I think his mistress was always glamorous. I've often thought she'd have suited him much better than me.' She wiped her eyes with her fingertips. 'It was all rather a mess in the end.'

Daisy could feel the pain that these memories still stung Lydia. 'I'm sorry.'

'No, it's fine. It was so long ago and if I'd fallen in love with someone else after Lorenzo then maybe this wouldn't still hurt me so much, but I didn't and it does.'

'Did he mind you leaving him?' Daisy asked doubtfully. She'd found it hard enough to break away from her own past and emotional blackmail was always a difficult thing to fight, she'd discovered.

Lydia laughed, and a pained bitter sound came from her mouth. 'It was horrendous. When he discovered I was planning to leave him, he locked me in the flat and wouldn't let me out. Thankfully I'd made friends with a daughter of one of the neighbours. She'd been a fan of mine and so kindly posted a letter for me to my agent. He was furious with me for eloping with Lorenzo, but thankfully still had offers coming in for work for me. He had connections in Italy and sent two brothers round, who were heavies of some sort. They got me and Francesca away from Lorenzo.'

Daisy couldn't help wishing she had backup like that. 'That must have been traumatic.'

Lydia sighed. 'It was terrifying at the time and he was furious and threatened me with all sorts, but I hid at a friend's flat in London and eventually he agreed to let me stay in England with Francesca. He never agreed to divorce me and eventually I gave up fighting him for my freedom. I'd got away from him and that seemed enough. It didn't stop me being hurt when I discovered through the neighbour's daughter that he was still seen with his mistress and eventually moved her into our home.'

'Did you ever see him again?'

She shook her head. 'He wrote to Francesca when he was a bit older and calmer, sending the letters to my parents. They met up once or twice, which I was relieved about.'

'How sad.'

'So, not as romantic as you'd expected, was it?'

Daisy shook her head. 'No, it wasn't.'

'But I comfort myself with the fact that Gabriel inherited his grandfather's good looks.' She looked at Daisy and pulled a face. 'Gabriel might have been in love with Bella and married the girl, but she isn't his mistress and he would never treat a woman like his grandfather did.'

'Good, I'm glad,' Daisy said. Then she had a disturbing thought. 'If anything, I'm the mistress in this scenario.'

'You're not sleeping with him, are you?'

Daisy widened her eyes, embarrassed to have been asked such a question by Gabriel's own grandmother. 'No, I'm not.'

'Sorry, it's none of my business really.' She took one of Daisy's hands in hers and squeezed it gently. 'Give him a chance to sort this mess out with Bella. It would be a terrible shame if the two of you couldn't be together when you obviously have feelings for each other. Give him time.'

Daisy nodded. She didn't like to say that they didn't have much time. She wouldn't stay at the hotel longer than the end of the season and Gabriel was leaving in less than a month to go and return to his project work in South Africa. He might come back, but for how long?

'You look troubled,' Lydia said. 'What's the matter?'

'Nothing,' Daisy fibbed. She wasn't going to put his grandmother in the difficult position of playing referee to them both. The last thing she needed was to have to make a choice between Daisy and Gabriel, because Daisy knew full well that she would always choose her grandson, and that was exactly how it should be. 'Isn't this the most glorious view?' she asked, to divert Lydia's attention.

Lydia watched her briefly but when Daisy looked out across the sea, Lydia followed her gaze. 'It really is wonderful. I love travelling and always enjoyed working abroad, but I'm never happier than when I'm sitting on one of the beaches on this island.'

'I can see why,' Daisy said.

They sat in companionable silence for a while, each lost in their own thoughts. Daisy couldn't help wondering what it must have been like to be in a love affair that encompassed your entire world. Poor Lydia, to have suffered so cruelly at the hands of the one man you loved so much that you still felt the pain keenly sixty years later.

The tide slowly worked its way towards them until Daisy, lost in thought, gasped as the cold, salty froth of the sea licked against her toes.

'Gosh, I was dozing off then,' Lydia said, smiling at her. 'This is almost too relaxing.'

'I enjoyed this evening,' Daisy said.

'So did I,' Lydia said. She didn't speak for a few minutes before continuing. 'I don't want you and Gabriel to fall out over Bella. You seem to click together so beautifully.'

Daisy didn't want to offend Lydia, but felt she had to be honest enough to let her know that sorting out their issues probably wouldn't be as easy as she hoped. 'I've had a lot of emotional stuff to deal with these past two years,' she confided. 'I'm not ready to open myself up for more heartache.'

Lydia nodded. 'I understand. Although, surely being friends with each other won't lead to difficulties? He'll need your support, I'm sure.'

Daisy didn't like to argue, so nodded, even though she didn't agree with what Lydia was proposing.

7

DAISY

Two days later, Lydia sent one of the waitresses through to Daisy's room with a note asking her to meet up in reception in ten minutes. Grumbling to herself, Daisy stood up from her bed where she'd been dozing and cleaned her teeth, brushed her hair, and changed into a pair of shorts and a fresh T-shirt. When she arrived downstairs, she was concerned to see the usually calm lady in a bit of a flux.

'What's the matter?' she whispered, hoping there hadn't been any bad news.

Lydia sighed. 'Gabriel is working with the volunteer group at Noirmont on one of the bunkers and texted me to say he'd heard that an important letter he's been expecting has been sent here for him. I promised to deliver it to him, but forgot I'd planned a meeting with some tourism executives this afternoon. Can you drive?'

Confused by the change in topic, Daisy said, 'Yes, but I don't have a car.'

Lydia held up a set of keys. 'These are for a hotel car, which your contract means you're insured on. Are you OK to drop it off for him?'

She nodded. Lydia motioned for Fi. 'Pass me that large envelope over there will you, dear?'

Fi winked surreptitiously at Daisy as she turned, then picked up the envelope and handed it to Lydia.

'Please take this as soon as you can to Noirmont.' She frowned. 'Do you know where that is?'

'Sorry, no,' Daisy said with relief. Somebody else would have to go. She wasn't in the mood to take anything to Gabriel. They hadn't seen each other to talk to for days and she was quite happy with leaving things as they were.

'Fi, pass me a map please.' Lydia pointed at the pile of maps kept at the back of the desk for tourists.

Damn, thought Daisy; she should have known Lydia wouldn't just accept her answer. She followed Lydia to the reception desk and watched as Fi unfolded a leaflet. Lydia pointed to a place on the west of the island. 'This is where we are, and here—' she manoeuvred her finger around the map, tracing a route along winding roads before ending on a section where small boxes depicting the cluster bunkers where Gabriel was likely working were printed '—is where you'll find Noirmont. Drive to the end where they've parked their cars and you'll soon find him, I'm sure. Just ask anyone there, they'll know him.'

She handed the envelope and keys to Daisy. 'The car is parked at the back of the hotel. If you have any problems, just give Fi a call on the main line.' She smiled at Daisy. 'Thank you for doing this for me, dear.' She glanced at her watch. 'Sorry, I'm going to have to dash.'

Fi giggled and turned her back on Daisy when the phone rang. 'Don't look so bloody miserable; I'd much rather you work my shift and let me go and pay a visit to Mr Gorgeous.'

Left with little choice, Daisy took the keys and envelope and went through the hotel to where the little, battered run-around car was kept.

The drive through the tree-shaded lanes was fun. So much fun in fact, that she took the wrong route twice, the first time going down a long windy hill ending up facing St Aubin's beach, and the second time she went right down a wooded hill to Ouaisne Bay. The third time the road took her to the open headland where massive concrete bunkers lay all around, a network of relics from the Nazi occupation that fascinated Gabriel so much.

She parked and got out, locking the car as she surveyed the open area and tried to work out where he could be. She tucked the envelope under her arm and putting her hand up to shield her eyes from the sun, tried to find him.

So many people walking around, she noted. Families stopped to pose for photographs, locals were walking their dogs, and children ran around screaming with excitement. It was difficult to imagine that only seventy years before this had been a place of strict regime instilling fear into the locals still living on the island.

She heard his laugh first. The sound made her stomach contract and her heart pound. She hadn't heard him laugh like that since they were in Vietnam. Hearing this sound made her spin round to face his direction, dropping the envelope and cursing when she went to pick it up and the wind blew it away from her. 'Crap!' she cried, running after it, trying to stamp on it only for it to fly off out of her reach.

'Oh no.' She tried not to panic, but the thought of it slipping over the edge of the cliff face was too much for her, remembering how important Lydia had made it sound. 'Help!' she cried, to anyone within distance.

A few people looked up, and two teenage boys giggled and nudged each other as she ran past them. Needing to go faster, she kicked off her flip-flops and followed the envelope, but had barely gone a few feet when she tripped on a large stone. Daisy stared after the document as it flew over one of the bunkers and landed on the other side. Had it gone over the edge of the headland? she wondered in a panic. It was too late to worry about it now, she thought, trying her best not to cry as her toe pounded in pain.

'Is this what you were trying to catch?' said a familiar voice.

She didn't have to look up to see Gabriel standing next to her, but did anyway. 'Yes.' She winced as her toe smarted.

He crouched down next to her, inhaling sharply between his teeth. 'That looks painful, and it's already bruising. Here, let me help you up.' She nodded. 'We have a first-aid kit down in the bunker, if you'll let me take you there.'

'Thank you,' she said, squeezing her eyes together as she placed her foot down on the ground. She'd never been inside a bunker before. In fact, this was the closest she'd been to any, but she hoped that access wasn't going to be difficult. From what she'd seen there weren't any obvious doors leading into the concrete building. She hopped next to Gabriel with one arm around his waist as he took most of her weight.

'What brings you here? Is Nan with you?'

She shook her head. 'No, she's in a meeting, but she asked me to bring that to you.' She indicated the envelope he was holding in his free hand.

'Did she read it?'

'I'm not sure,' she answered through clenched teeth. 'She said it was important and that you'd want to see it as soon as possible.'

'Oh, OK. Thanks for bringing it.'

'No problem,' she said, wincing when her good foot landed on a sharp stone and her ankle almost gave way.

He held her more tightly, stopping her from falling over. 'Let's take a breather on that bench,' he said. 'I'll have a look and see what you've brought me.'

She had to stop herself from groaning in relief as he helped lower her onto the wooden bench, dedicated to someone who obviously loved this place during their lifetime. Gabe sat down next to her, the heat from his bare leg against her own sending electric currents shooting through her thigh. He didn't seem to notice as he ripped open the top of the self-seal envelope.

Pulling out the document from inside, Gabe narrowed his eyes. She could tell this wasn't something that made him happy.

'Is everything all right?' she asked hesitantly.

He shook his head.

'Bad news?' She hoped it wasn't, but by the troubled expression on his face this document contained information that displeased him greatly.

'Afraid so,' he said. He tapped the cover letter with his index finger. 'Our funding's been pulled.'

'No, that's awful.' Surely there weren't many projects for marine explorers to cover. She recalled him telling her stories about his exploits and conservation plans when they were in Vietnam together, so understood how keenly he'd feel this unexpected halt to his plans. 'Didn't you have an inkling they would do this?'

He shook his head. 'Not exactly,' he said quietly. He stared out across the rolling waves in the channel at the end of the headland. She rested her hand on his knee, only vaguely sensing that it might be construed as being a little forward in the circumstances. She didn't care. Regardless of their differences, he was someone she cared about and his beliefs were important to him and therefore to her. 'I'm so sorry,' she said. 'Isn't there anything you can do?'

'If you can wait here a moment, I'll go and tell the guys that I need to get back to the Encore. I'll take you back in the hotel car and make a few calls, see if there's anything I can do to change their minds.'

He disappeared down a ladder into a hole that must have been the entrance to the bunker he'd been working on and she was relieved not to have had to follow him inside. He soon came back out of the bunker closely followed by another tall, dark man who had an air of authority about him that was hard to miss. He was very handsome and looked similar to the actor Henry Cavill, who she'd only recently discovered came from Jersey. Surely it couldn't be him, she thought. Daisy stood up, flinching in pain as the pressure on her foot increased as it touched the grassy soil beneath her.

'Daisy, this is Sebastian Fielding,' he said, indicating the man next to him who, she noticed, also had a beautiful smile. She decided that his photos in the *Gazette* hadn't done him justice. In fact, she thought, he would have been almost too good looking if it hadn't been for his slightly crooked nose, brought on by someone breaking it at some point in his life, she guessed.

It dawned on her that Gabriel had said his last name was Fielding. She smiled at him. 'You must be Fi's older brother. She talks about you a lot,' she said, smiling and holding out her hand for him to shake.

He took her hand in his and nodded. 'I am, though I can imagine that more often than not she's telling you how mean I can be,' he joked.

'Not at all,' she lied. 'Although I gather you don't like the thought of her going to Glastonbury by herself, which seems pretty mean to me.' She laughed, relieved he could tell she wasn't being serious.

Sebastian shrugged. 'My sister is very independent and even I wouldn't have a problem with her going to the festival with a group of friends, but she intended going by herself for a "laugh" and seeing who she met along the way. If I know Fi, that's a ticket for disaster.'

Gabriel laughed. 'True, but then again, I know from experience that women are usually more capable of looking after themselves than us blokes when it comes to travelling.'

'Probably because they've got the sense to stay away from anything that seems a little dangerous,' she said. 'I understand your concerns, but Fi's pretty tough.'

He laughed. 'I'm sure you're right there. But not paying for her ticket made her so furious she went and found a job and that's why she's now working for Francesca and Rick at the Encore. And she loves it there.'

'That's good to hear,' Gabriel said.

Sebastian nodded. 'She talks about you a lot,' he said to Daisy. 'You've been very kind to her since you've been here, showing her how everything's done and never getting cross with her when she makes mistakes.'

Daisy shook her head. 'She's very clever and the guests love her. She's the most cheerful person I've ever worked with.'

'That's good to know. She's a great kid, even though I say so as her brother.'

Daisy went to step forward and winced.

'We'd better get going,' Gabriel said. 'I'll give you a call later and maybe you could join us for a drink sometime with Paige.' He turned to Daisy. 'You've not met Sebastian's fiancée Paige yet, have you?'

She shook her head.

'Daisy's only been in Jersey a couple of months, so hasn't had a chance to make new friends yet.' He turned his attention back to her. 'You'll get along with Paige, she's very friendly. She's a shoe designer.'

'Wow,' Daisy said, impressed. 'I've never met a designer before.'

'We'll arrange something,' Gabe said, putting an arm around her waist. 'Speak soon, Sebastian.'

Daisy waved goodbye to the man and hobbled off towards Lydia's car with Gabriel. 'A shoe designer,' she repeated. 'How exciting.'

'She's lovely,' Gabriel said. 'In fact, I've got a group of friends I'd love to introduce you to if you wouldn't mind.' They reached the car and he pressed the fob to unlock the doors, helping Daisy settle into her seat.

'I'd love to meet your friends,' she said honestly. 'One day.'

He looked disappointed but nodded. 'I understand,' he said.

She knew he couldn't possibly have an inkling about how she felt. He knew so little of her past. And after all, didn't he have both his parents still married to each other and despite their occasionally noisy exchanges, seemingly very happily, too? No, he couldn't know how she felt and she was far too embarrassed by her past to ever share it with him. She liked this new life where everyone just knew her as Daisy the receptionist.

They arrived back at the hotel and Daisy insisted that Gabriel go and make the phone calls and emails that he needed to make to try and save his project.

'I'll be fine,' she said, making her way to the housekeeper's back office and knocking on the door.

The door was opened by Mrs Vines, the housekeeper, and she showed her in. 'Sit over there, Daisy.' She squinted and bent down to inspect Daisy's foot. 'What have I said about those dreadful slipper things you insist on wearing? They give your feet no protection. It's a good thing you're not one of the chamber-maids or waitresses,' she said. 'At least you can sit behind your desk and carry out your work with a damaged foot.'

She left the room and returned with a tub of warm soapy water and some cloths. 'Here, put your foot up on my knee and let me see to this.' Daisy did as she was instructed and Mrs Vines cleaned her foot, tutting noisily several times. Drying the foot carefully, she applied some ointment and bandaged it carefully.

'Right, my girl, you take care of that foot. It should heal very quickly. You're lucky it wasn't worse.'

There was a knock at the door. 'Come,' the woman barked.

Gabriel opened the door and put his head around, giving a sheepish smile at the older woman who beamed back at him. 'How's the patient?' he asked.

She tutted once again. 'I presume she was with you when it happened?'

He nodded. 'Yes. Nan sent her on an errand to find me at Noirmont.'

That must have been an acceptable answer, because she patted Daisy's ankle and stood up. 'She's fine, but I think she should wear more sensible sandals if she's going to be running around over bunkers.'

Daisy bit her lip to stop from giggling at the image the woman's words conjured up. She cleared her throat. 'Thank you,' she said. 'I'll try and buy something a little less dangerous next time I have an afternoon off.'

8

GABRIEL

Gabriel went to accompany Daisy out of the housekeeper's office, but she called him back.

'One minute, Gabriel,' Mrs Vines said, as he held the door open for Daisy to leave. Daisy gave him a surreptitious grin and raised an eyebrow. He wasn't certain but he could have sworn he heard her giggling to herself as she limped down the corridor towards the staff quarters. He closed the door and turned to face the woman who had been his parents' housekeeper at the Encore since the hotel opened when he was in his early teens.

'Take a seat for a moment, will you?'

He did as she requested, wondering what she could wish to speak to him about.

'Gabriel,' she said, sitting opposite him at her desk. 'You may not think it my place to speak to you about this, but as housekeeper here at the hotel, I take great interest in the well-being of all the staff, especially the young ladies.'

Ah, he mused, so this was about Daisy. 'It's not—' he began, but immediately stopped talking when she held up her hand.

She smiled at him. 'Gabriel, we both know you are a lovely

young man, but I don't think you realise quite how you come across to the girls we have working here, not to mention the guests.'

He didn't like the way this conversation was going, but waited for her to finish.

'You're very good looking and your job, by the very nature of it, might be perceived as, shall we say, rather intriguing. So, I think you need to be aware that where you might think you're being kind to someone like young Daisy, she might take it that you're more interested her in a—' she hesitated '—romantic way. Do you see what I'm trying to say?'

He nodded sagely. 'I understand what you're saying, Mrs Vines.' Although he thought she was wrong. In his experience, women were more interested in the likes of Sebastian or Luke, men with solid jobs, with homes and a solid lifestyle. Not like him with his nomadic way of life. 'But I can't see that anyone would think my job heroic in any way.'

'Daisy certainly seemed to perk up when you entered the room,' she said, looking unimpressed at his disagreement.

'Daisy and I know each other from our travels in Vietnam, so she's an old friend.'

She studied him, her pale blue eyes boring into him. Could Mrs Vines see how he felt about Daisy? She had known him a long time, but he hoped he was able to hide his true feelings for Daisy well enough to stop her from worrying. Daisy had made it perfectly clear that she wasn't going to consider being with him until he was divorced from Bella. If only there was a way round this divorce nonsense of having to wait for another two years. 'Seriously,' he said, hoping he was giving the housekeeper his most sincere look. 'I have no intention of hurting Daisy in any way.'

'Good, you keep it that way. Because, as much as I like you,

Gabriel, I won't hesitate to bring this to your mother's attention, or even your father's if I have to.'

He doubted his father would have much to say and all his mother would be worried about was losing Daisy as a member of staff. No, he mused, the one person she should speak to if she was so worried about his behaviour towards Daisy was his grandmother. He could see how fond of Daisy she was. The mere fact that she'd invited Daisy to the house to dinner and then gave her an open invitation to use her garden in which to paint spoke volumes to him. He supposed Daisy assumed that his grandmother was this welcoming at her home to everyone. He wondered how Daisy would feel if she discovered that she was the first member of staff to have been invited to his grandmother's home, as far as he was aware.

'I promise you have nothing to worry about,' he said, standing up and giving her a smile.

She relaxed, her severe expression softening now that the awkward business of his private life was over with. 'Good. Off you go then,' she said, as if he was still a teenager.

Gabriel walked to the door and pulled it open.

'Oh, and Gabriel?' she said.

'Yes?'

'You're a good boy really, I do know that.'

He smiled; no one had called him a boy for about fifteen years. 'Thanks.' He turned and left, closing the door gently.

There was a gasp behind him. Gabriel looked over his shoulder to see Fi, her mouth open in horror.

'What's the matter, Fi?' he asked.

'Someone's been a naughty boy?'

'She doesn't just call people into her office to tell them off you know,' he teased.

Fi glanced at the closed door and then walked up to him and

lowered her voice. 'No, but...' She hesitated. 'I know you said I shouldn't gossip but it's not gossiping if I'm talking to you about you, is it?'

'No,' he agreed, eager to see what she had to say.

'I think she must have been telling you off about Daisy. Wasn't she?'

He turned to face her. 'Why? What's being said?' He knew how the other staff loved to talk. They were like a large, sometimes dysfunctional family, some bickering, but all working towards the same goal to make the hotel run as smoothly as possible. He loved being a part of this place, but sometimes, when you tried to keep your private life to yourself, it could be a little irritating to know there were others trying to second-guess everything you were doing.

She raised a shoulder in a cocky shrug. 'Nothing much, but we all know Bella's been here and that you and Daisy were at your grandmother's the other night for dinner, so there's a tote running on who you'll end up with.' She giggled.

Gabriel was sure she'd expected him to find this amusing, but he couldn't imagine why. His heart pounded and he realised he'd clenched his teeth together in fury. He took a deep breath to calm down, not wishing to add fuel to their furnace and said. 'Fi, firstly, I think you need to remember that you work here, for my family and I'd therefore like to suggest that you stop and think before commenting to any of us about the things you might overhear.' Fi had the grace to blush. 'Secondly, if Daisy gets to hear of this she's going to be upset. I want you to tell me who's set up this bet so I can go and put a stop to it.'

Her eyes widened and she shook her head. 'Hell no, I'm not a grass.'

He thought she'd say that. 'Fine, then you go and speak to whoever is behind this and stop it, right now. Tell them I've discovered what's going on and I'm bloody furious.' He calmed down a little realising she was beginning to look upset. 'Look, I'm not having a go at you. You're young and still learning how things work here.' He sighed, feeling tired of the whole situation. 'You're also only the messenger, but Daisy's your friend too. Surely you don't want her to be hurt?'

'Of course I don't,' she said, tears welling in her eyes.

'Then you need to help me stop this. OK?'

'Yes.'

'Thank you.'

He walked away from her, seething with irritation. Sometimes working closely with others could be a hindrance on your life. He hoped Daisy didn't think he'd been discussing their business with others. He knew she'd hate something like that. The divorce might take two years but he needed to make an appointment to see a lawyer and set the divorce in progress. He was sure Bella would agree to sign the paperwork.

The following morning he was sitting in his father's office ready to call his lawyer as soon as nine o'clock rolled around. He dialled the number of his father's close friend and legal advisor but could only get hold of his secretary. Gabriel explained the situation to her about Bella and their failed marriage. The secretary claimed it should only be a matter of weeks to draw up the papers, and an elated Gabriel hung up, happier than he had been in weeks.

Later, he walked passed Daisy and Fi at reception and opened his mouth to wish them a good morning when a piercing scream made them all turn sharply towards the swimming pool.

'Damn,' Gabriel said, recognising the panic in the voice calling for help. He ran out of the entrance, across the driveway and down to the nearby pool area where he saw a small boy floundering and the mother shouting at him to swim.

The panic on the child's face as he disappeared down under the water shot through Gabriel. He kicked off his trainers and dived into the pool, surfacing under the child, grabbing him under his arms and lifting him up out of the water. Then swimming to the side of the pool where Daisy bent down to reach the child, he held him up to her, helping her pull the spluttering boy onto the side to his crying mother.

The child coughed, crying noisily, reassuring Gabriel that he was perfectly fine, if a little shocked by his accident. He checked that the little boy wasn't cut anywhere and looked up at the mother. 'He's fine,' he soothed. 'I'll get him a towel and maybe he should sit quietly with you for a few minutes until the shock has worn off.'

There was a commotion behind him.

'You stupid bloody woman,' Gabriel heard a man say. He was about to look and see what was going on when he noticed Daisy gasp. The colour faded instantly from her face and Gabriel stood up and walked over to check if she was all right.

'What's wrong?' he asked quietly.

She shivered despite the heat of the day, but didn't say anything. Staring in the same direction her large eyes widened. Gabriel turned to see what was upsetting her so much. There was an older man, his face puce with rage, arguing with the mother of the boy he'd just rescued.

'He'll calm down,' he said, assuming the man's reaction must be what was bothering her so much. 'He's just had a fright, that's all.'

Daisy didn't speak. She stared past Gabriel towards the pool, silently focusing her attention on the man and woman, who was blowing her nose on a tissue while her son settled down on the sun lounger next to her.

'Daisy?' Gabriel asked, trying to take her attention from the scene that was disturbing her so much. 'What's the matter?'

She shook her head. 'I don't believe it,' she murmured. 'I never saw them arrive. Fi must have checked them in.'

He had no idea what she was going on about. He stood in front of her to block her view. 'Daisy,' he whispered.

She sighed heavily. 'Sorry, Gabe.'

'Tell me, maybe I can help.'

She shook her head slowly. 'No one can help me with this,' she said quietly, almost under her breath.

He looked over his shoulder at the arguing couple. 'Why are they bothering you so much?' He wanted to put an arm around her to comfort her but didn't dare overstep the boundary she'd put up between them. 'Do you know them?'

She nodded slowly. 'Yes,' she said, after a moment's hesitation.

'Who are they?' They looked perfectly ordinary to him. The man was a few years older than the woman. In fact, she looked a bit like the classic trophy wife, very blonde, and sexy in an obvious way. Their rowing wasn't noisy enough to bother other guests and the boy didn't seem at all fazed by their exchange, so he didn't feel like he should be asking them to quieten down. 'Do you want to come to my dad's office and talk about this?' he offered, wanting to help her.

'No, that's not necessary,' she said, staring blatantly at them.

Gabe moved so that his back was towards the couple and they couldn't see Daisy staring at them. 'Daisy, come along. You can't keep watching them so openly, it looks odd.'

'He's my father,' she murmured.

Had he heard right? 'Sorry?'

She looked him straight in the eyes and said loud enough for the couple to hear her. 'He's my father.'

'That's what I thought you'd said,' he replied, turning slowly as he became aware that the arguing had ceased. The man was now peering around Gabriel trying to see who'd just spoken. Aware that Daisy didn't care if they'd heard her, Gabriel stepped back to let her face the older man. He was surprised when neither of them spoke, but simply studied each other. She'd never mentioned her father before and he'd assumed he must be dead.

'Daisy?' The man eventually said. 'What are you doing here?'

Gabriel looked at Daisy to see how she'd react, but her cold expression didn't change. He couldn't help wondering what sort of relationship she had with this man. It wasn't good, that much was obvious. He was distracted by a whimper and turned to the couple. The man's wife looked as if she was about to pass out.

Gabriel said, 'Maybe you'd like to come into the office, sit down and have a chat?'

He wasn't sure what they wanted to do but standing outside around the pool area with other guests arriving wasn't the best audience for them to have this reunion. When no one reacted, apart from the boy showing interest in the girl who had helped haul him out of the pool, Gabriel added, 'Grab your things and follow me.'

He didn't wait for them to reply, but started collecting their towels. The man moved first, glaring at the woman and murmured for her to be quiet and that he'd explain everything later. Gabriel presumed by her reaction that he'd never thought to mention anything about Daisy's existence.

He glanced at Daisy, and seeing she was still glaring at the couple, walked over to her and pushed her back gently to get her moving.

She looked up at him in surprise, as if she'd just registered his presence even though they'd spoken only moments before. 'Where are we going?'

'Inside. Somewhere private. You look as if you'd like to talk.'

'About what?' she frowned.

He lowered his head to hers. 'I think you've come as something of a surprise to this man's wife and son.'

'You can say that again.'

Gabriel pushed her gently and she began walking inside, slowly, staring at the man as she passed. He gave his daughter a sheepish look and then focused his attention on collecting his wife and son's belongings together.

'But I want to swim,' the boy whined.

'Later.' His mother snapped. 'Your father has something he wishes to discuss with us.'

Gabriel wasn't sure that the boy needed to be a witness to what was coming next. He glanced at his watch and said, 'The lifeguard should be on duty any second. If you like, your son can wait with Fi at reception until he arrives. She'll make sure the lifeguard keeps an eye on him while you're not there.'

The mother nodded.

They followed Gabriel inside, Daisy occasionally giving looks at the couple who were now whispering furiously. Her father dragged the boy along with them towards the reception area.

Gabriel asked Fi to watch over him until the lifeguard arrived for his shift. 'Please also send in a tray of tea and biscuits to the office,' he said. 'And don't put through any calls until I say.'

Fi nodded. 'You all right?' she asked Daisy.

'Fine,' Daisy said, looking anything but. 'I'll be back as soon as I can.'

'It's fine, I'll ask Jo to come and cover for you if I need to.'

The four adults made their way to the office. He indicated for them to take a seat on one side of the desk and for Daisy to sit in his father's chair. Gabriel then went into the next-door office to collect a fourth chair for him to sit on.

He re-entered the silent room and realised that he needed to take charge if they were going to get anywhere. 'OK, it seems to me that Daisy is surprised to see you here,' he said to her father. 'Mr, erm...'

'Baxter. Peter Baxter,' said the man, trying to take his wife's hand but she snatched it away and glowered at him in supressed rage. He cleared his throat. 'This is my wife,' he said by way of introduction to Daisy. 'Stella.'

'Yes,' said the woman, finally finding her voice. 'And that poor unsuspecting child out there, who—' she directed her venom at Peter '—almost drowned not ten minutes ago, is in shock to discover that he is not after all an only child but has a sister who must be, what? Twenty, twenty-one?'

'Twenty-six,' Daisy replied.

'So,' continued Stella at her red-faced husband. 'I'd like to know who Daisy's mother is and why you hadn't thought to mention either her or her daughter to me or our son before now?'

Peter shrugged. 'I meant to tell you.'

'When? Next week, next year?'

He shook his head. 'I'm sorry, darling, I really was going to—'

'But it was easier to pretend I didn't exist,' Daisy interrupted. 'Isn't that more like it, Dad?' She put the emphasis on the word and the man winced.

'Daisy, I'm sorry, really I am.' He took a deep breath. 'You know it wasn't all my fault.'

She immediately stood up. 'Don't you dare start blaming Mum for this; I won't have it,' she shouted. 'She brought me up single-handedly, while you went about your happy daily life without a care in the world.'

'That's not true,' he said, looking red in the face. Gabriel wasn't certain but he suspected Peter might be close to tears.

'Daisy,' Gabriel said, trying to calm the tension in the room.

She turned on him. 'And you know nothing whatsoever about my life, so don't start trying to pacify me, Gabriel.' Her expression softened. 'I don't mean to snap at you.' She looked back at her father and Gabriel couldn't miss the hurt in her pretty face as she said, 'She died, you know.'

Peter gasped and now Gabriel was sure he was about to cry. 'No,' Peter whispered, his voice cracking with emotion. 'Penny died? When?'

Daisy sat back down. Gabe could see she regretted telling him in such a cruel way. 'A few months ago. I don't want to discuss it in front of others, but I'll tell you more when we're alone.'

'Well, really,' Stella said. 'I think it's a bit much you wishing to discuss someone who, by the sounds of things, was my husband's mistress.' She narrowed her eyes and added, 'Not while we were together, I hope?'

Gabriel saw Daisy clench her fists. 'She was not his mistress, thank you very much. She was his fiancée, became pregnant with me and before they could be married, your husband buggered off to "find himself".'

'I came back though, Daisy, surely she told you that.'

Daisy glowered at him. 'Not until I was born and she'd had her trust for you shattered. Why would she take you back and fret that you could leave again at any time?'

He leant forward. 'But I wouldn't have done; I loved Penny with all my heart.'

Stella cried out. 'Peter, how could you say such a thing?'

Gabriel could see by the look of horror on Peter's face that he'd forgotten for a moment that Stella was in the room with them and regretted his outpouring about Daisy's mother. 'Darling, I didn't mean... Well, that is to say...'

Stella wiped away tears. 'Did you love her more than me?'

He shook his head. 'No, of course not, dear. I loved Clarissa, but then I met you.'

'Clarissa?' Gabriel asked, thinking that maybe he'd made matters worse by insisting they all come to the office to chat.

Stella addressed Gabriel as if the other two people in the room weren't there. 'His first marriage – to Clarissa – was a disaster, but she was so devastated about miscarrying all her pregnancies that he didn't feel he could leave her.' She looked at Daisy. 'She died too.'

'So I gather,' Daisy said, her expression cold. 'So, how long have you two been together then?' she asked. 'I take it that the little boy out there is my half-brother?'

Stella sat up straighter in her chair. 'Alfie is our son. He's six and we've been together for seven years.'

'So, before Clarissa died, then?' Daisy sneered.

Gabriel could see she was struggling with her emotions and guessed it was because Daisy had just discovered that Peter must have still been seeing her mother when he'd begun a relationship with Stella. He wondered what the story was behind this situation and resolved to speak to her later, hoping she'd confide in him.

He stood up. 'I think you've all been dealt a few unexpected blows today, so maybe you'd like to take some time to let everything sink in. If you need to meet up again and use my office, please let me know, or if there's anything else I can do to help the situation in any way.'

'Thank you,' Peter said, offering his hand for Gabriel to shake. He looked at Daisy. 'I really am sorry, sweetheart. I honestly didn't know about your mum.' He hesitated. 'She was a very private lady.'

'She was,' Daisy said, 'But when she was dying she asked after you many times. I left messages at your office for you to call me but you never did.'

He frowned. 'I promise I never received any messages.'

'Well, I did leave them.'

'I'll look into it, see what happened to them.'

Gabriel thought that if he was trying to pacify Daisy he wasn't going the right way about it and wondered just how well this man did know his daughter. They'd obviously spent some time together over the years because she seemed to be fairly familiar with him, if a little distant, but something wasn't right, that was certain.

'I shouldn't bother,' Daisy said. 'It's too late now anyway.' She walked towards the door. 'I think I'd better go in case I say something I might regret.' She looked at Gabriel. 'Thank you for letting us chat in here,' she said. 'And I'm sorry I was rude earlier. None of this is your fault.'

He followed her to the door. 'It's fine. Anything I can do to help.' He instinctively took her by the shoulders and bent down to give her a kiss on her cheek.

Daisy left the room without saying anything further to her father or his wife.

Gabriel turned and held the door open. He looked at the couple, both lost in their own torment. 'I hope you all find a way to overcome what's happened.'

Peter waited for Stella to leave the room. 'So do I,' he said.

Gabriel closed the door after them and walked over to the office window, staring out at the car park at the back. He hadn't seen Daisy going to her room, so assumed she must have returned to reception.

How like Daisy, he thought, to have a shock like this and immediately return to work. His heart contracted. Seeing her so stunned and hurt had upset him. Despite her seeming resilience and constant insistence that she was perfectly fine by herself, he couldn't help thinking that everyone needed someone in their lives, and at the moment it seemed to him that she didn't have anyone at all.

As he stared out of the window and went over what he'd just witnessed, he could see why she'd refused to be with him when he was still married to Bella. She wasn't going to allow anyone to push her back in their affections. He didn't blame her. He needed to sort out this divorce, and as quickly as possible if he wasn't going to lose his chance of being with her.

He sat down at the desk and dialled his lawyer. He was put through immediately. 'Hi, this is Gabriel Wilson,' he said.

'Gabriel, I'll have to be brief,' replied his lawyer, an old family friend. 'I've got a client waiting in reception for a meeting.'

'I was wondering if you've been able to find a way that Bella and I can bring this divorce forward somehow? Your secretary seemed to think it was possible.'

'Unfortunately my secretary is new and doesn't fully understand the divorce laws. Other than in special situations – of which your divorce is not one – your request for a divorce cannot be heard by the court until you've been married for at least three years. I'm afraid there's nothing you can do apart from wait.'

He felt like someone had punched him in the stomach. 'There must be some way we can make it happen,' he said, trying not to sound pleading. 'I've met someone,' he admitted, hoping it would help sway the lawyer, but knowing that if there was any way he could help Gabriel he would have done so by now.

'I thought as much,' he said, sounding sympathetic. 'But there really isn't anything I can do. Sorry, I'm in a bit of a rush, but if I do come up with anything I'll let you know. I can't see it happening though. I'm sorry, but I won't give you false hope.'

Gabriel sighed. 'I'm grateful for your honesty. Thank you.'

He hung up and replaced the phone on the receiver. Lowering his head into his hands he closed his eyes. He was usually so positive about everything, but this time there didn't seem to be an upside to his situation. He needed to stop panicking in order to think more clearly. There had to be a way to sort this out.

* * *

After leaving the hotel for the day, Gabriel headed over to his grandmother's house for a bite to eat.

'What's wrong, darling?' Lydia asked, when he could only manage half of the omelette she'd cooked him. 'You've barely touched your food and you usually have such a good appetite. Is there something wrong at the hotel?'

He shook his head.

'Then is there a problem between you and Daisy?'

He smiled at her. 'You know me so well,' he said, wondering how it must feel to Daisy not to have someone like his grandmother in her life. 'I've discovered that in Jersey a request for a divorce can't be heard by the court during the first three years of a marriage. I've only been married to Bella for nine months, so I can't get divorced for over two years and Daisy won't consider being with me if I'm married to someone else.'

He watched his grandmother mull over this news. 'Three years? That's ridiculous.'

'What am I going to do?'

She thought for a moment. 'Does Daisy know that you and Bella aren't a couple in any way?'

'Yes, I've told her and I'm pretty sure she believes me.'

'It's not as if you and Bella are still together and you're seeing Daisy behind her back,' she said thoughtfully. 'I don't understand why she's got a problem seeing you.'

'I understand her reasons,' he said, thinking about what he'd learned of her mother's situation with her father. When his grandmother shrugged one shoulder and raised her eyebrows wishing for him to enlighten her, he shook his head. 'I can't tell you, it's her story. But I do know why she feels this way. I just don't know how to sort things out between us.'

Lydia placed one of her hands on his forearm. The cool touch of her palm soothed him in the warm evening. 'Gabriel, you never give in to problems,' she said. 'You always see them as a challenge. Why are you being so defeatist this time?'

He sighed heavily. 'I don't know. Maybe because this time I'm more emotionally involved than I usually am, or because I'm still hurting about losing the baby.'

He realised he was being very negative and forced a smile. 'Take no notice of me. It's been a lousy day and I'm being an idiot. I'll try to think of something, but I've tried the legal avenue and there doesn't seem to be anything I can do to hurry up my divorce.'

'That's a shame,' she said.

She stared at him silently and he knew what she was about to say. Gabriel hated sharing anything with his grandmother that could upset her. Although telling her about his legal situation was something she'd insisted upon knowing, he knew she couldn't do much to help him.

'Gabriel, what was in that envelope I asked Daisy to take to you at Noirmont? Was it about your research project?'

He nodded. 'It was, but it's fine. Nothing to worry about,' he lied.

'Rubbish. They've pulled the funding, haven't they?' she said, giving him a sharp look.

'They've rescinded all funding.' He frowned. 'How did you know?'

'I guessed it might be something like that. I'm so sorry, darling. What are you going to do now?'

He had no idea. Working for his parents at the hotel went a little way to fund his expeditions, but he always needed sponsorship. 'I'm not sure yet, but I'll think of something.'

She smiled. 'Now that's the attitude I'm used to. Stop fretting about Daisy. She'll come round if she loves you. You just haven't known each other long enough for her to want to ignore these other things. After all, what's a few years?'

'We both know that's a very long time when you love someone, Nan,' he said. He bent forward and kissed her on her cheek. 'It's fine though, I'll think of something,' He wished he felt as positive as he sounded.

'I know, darling. You just have to believe it.'

He hugged his grandmother tightly, wishing he had half the faith in himself that she had in him. 'You always think the best of me,' he said, smiling at her.

She stared at him. After a moment's thought she said, 'Darling Gabriel, you've achieved so much in your young life already with your conservation activities and those projects. I admire how much you care and how you've put that caring into saving marine life. You've also always been there when your parents or I needed you. I'm sure once Daisy gets to know you better she'll trust you as I do.'

He wasn't so certain. Not now he'd seen Daisy's reaction to her father and realised just how deep her hurt went. He might come second best to his parents' career, and even maybe to their own feelings for each other, but at least he came first where his grandmother was concerned. He supposed Daisy must have had a similar relationship with her mother, but it had sounded as if Daisy's mother had needed her far more than his independent grandmother needed him. He wished Daisy hadn't been so scarred by her past. The haunted look he saw crossing her face sometimes concerned him and he wished she'd open up to him more.

'She's been deeply hurt,' he said quietly. 'I'm not so sure I'll be able to make her understand how important she is to me.'

They sat in silence, the only sound entering their space being birdsong and the lapping of the waves onto the beach at the end of the garden.

'What will you do about the project?' his grandmother asked. He might have known she wasn't going to leave it alone.

'They're having a meeting tomorrow to discuss the funding,' he said. 'I'll send them a report urging them to rethink their decision and assuring them that we've gone too far now to back out of the work.'

She rested her hand on his arm. 'Is there anything I can do to help?'

He shook his head. 'Thanks, but no. I'm sure it'll be fine.' He hated lying to her, but didn't need his grandmother worrying about having to bail out his project. It was his problem and he was going to have to find a way to solve it. His parents would be back in Jersey in a few weeks and he'd have time to return to South Africa and find a way to keep things going. Until then, he needed to keep track of what was happening at the hotel, with his divorce, and maybe think up new ways to fund his failing enterprise.

He checked his watch and drank the last mouthful of his coffee. 'I'd better get back,' he said. 'We're expecting a few late arrivals and they're return visitors who come several times a year and they'll expect us to welcome them properly.'

'Do you need me to come along to the hotel?' she asked.

He shook his head. 'No, you stay here and enjoy the sunshine. I shouldn't be too late. Maybe we can have a drink out here and a stroll on the beach.'

She beamed at him. 'I'd love that,' she said.

He stood up, kissed her on the top of her white hair and walked away. She was always there for him, he thought, as he got into his car and drove off to the hotel. If only Daisy could experience the same sort of love.

He just wished Daisy would trust him enough to let him devote his time to her so that they could enjoy this beautiful place with its peaceful, meticulously designed garden and valley divided by tiny geometric ponds.

He checked with Fi at reception that everything was in order for the Johnsons. They were the hotel's most honoured 'RVs'. Gabriel knew from their records that almost seventy-five per cent of the visitors to the hotel were 'RVs', or return visitors, and the Johnsons had been coming to stay at least three times each summer since his parents had bought the place. Each time they arrived, his parents always ensured that there was a champagne bucket filled with ice and one of their best bottles of champagne waiting for the couple to drink as they settled in their room. An arrangement of fresh flowers sourced from the well-stocked gardens were always displayed for them on a table and Mrs Johnson's favourite local chocolates stored in the small fridge in the room. It was the least they could do for such valued guests.

He was about to speak to the concierge about booking their favourite restaurant on the Sunday, when he heard a hum of excitement behind him. Turning with a smile on his face, Gabriel saw Mr and Mrs Johnson, arms linked, as they greeted the staff they'd come to know so well.

'Wonderful to see you both again,' Gabriel said, his hand outstretched to shake Mr Johnson's before giving his wife a welcoming hug. 'You're both looking very well. I was sorry not to be here for your last visit to the Encore.'

'My lady wife missed seeing you here,' Mr Johnson joked.

She reddened and nudged him. 'He's such a naughty man, Gabriel,' she said. 'You take no notice of him.'

Joseph, the concierge, immediately appeared next to Gabriel, welcoming the guests and waving his assistant porter over to take their bags to their room.

'Can I offer you a drink in the bar?' Gabriel asked. 'Or would you prefer to go to your room and settle in first.'

'I think we'll go to our room and take a shower,' Mr Johnson said. 'It's blistering hot out there.'

'No problem,' Gabriel said. 'I'll see you a little later when you're ready to come down.'

He waited for them to leave, followed by Joseph and his assistant, and then went to reception to see Fi. He was surprised when no one seemed to be there and was about to walk around behind the desk when Daisy popped up.

'Oh, I didn't know you were here,' she said, eyes wide with surprise. 'Did you want something?'

'I was looking for Fi,' he said. 'I just wanted to be sure that everything had been covered for the Johnsons' arrival.'

Daisy nodded. 'All done,' she said. 'We double checked earlier. Our main priority now is the party that's happening on the weekend. The family start to arrive tomorrow and the rest follow on the next day. I've told the host and hostess that you'll go through everything with them. I hope that's OK.'

'It is,' he nodded. He was used to these occasions, although this one promised to be a little different, but no doubt still fun. He preferred it when his mother or grandmother took over, if he was honest. 'I'm more of an outdoor guy, but I enjoy seeing people having fun, even though I don't seem to have the finesse that my mother or grandmother have for these events,' he said. 'I'll do my best though. Do you have the list of everything I need to go through?'

She looked down at the desk and handed him a copy attached to a clipboard. 'I've given you the checklist the hotel uses for weddings, but it should be similar enough, I think.' She leaned over to him slightly and lowered her voice. 'Is the decorating in the orangery complete now? Francesca said the reception will be held in there and she was concerned that Luke might not be able to finish everything in time.'

'I've arranged to meet him there in half an hour,' he said. 'I'll go through everything then.'

Fi came back to reception. 'All OK?' she said, with a glint in her dark blue eyes. She looked at Daisy. 'If you want to go with Gabe and check through everything on the list, you know, for any future weddings you might have to arrange...?'

'This isn't for a wedding reception though, is it?' Daisy asked.

He was glad she'd missed Fi's point. Today wasn't the day to be joking with Daisy about weddings.

Fi laughed. 'No, it's a Never-Going-to-Retire party.'

'Seriously?'

Gabe understood Daisy's confusion. He found it a little odd and he'd grown up with his parents holding parties for made-up occasions. 'The couple have been acting for half a century,' he explained. 'They wanted to celebrate it in some way.'

Daisy smiled. 'Does that mean we'll meet some famous people, then?'

Fi nudged her. 'You work for three of them,' she said. 'Don't let Francesca ever hear you saying you're excited about meeting other well-known people.'

Gabriel pulled a face at Fi. 'Stop teasing her.' He smiled, hoping Daisy would relax a little. 'She's joking, and yes you will meet people you recognise from the big and small screen.'

'OK, then,' Daisy said. 'I'll come with you and see the routine. I suppose I should know how everything is set up for future reference.' She looked up at Gabriel and he felt his stomach contract. Hell, he wanted to kiss her, he thought. 'Is that OK with you, Gabe?' she asked.

'Sorry?' He wasn't sure to what she was referring and then noticed that both women were looking at him strangely.

'Do you want Daisy to come with you to the orangery?' Fi asked, shaking her head.

'Sorry, yes, that's a great idea,' he said, irritated for acting like a teenage boy in front of them. 'I'll meet you outside the orangery in half an hour.'

* * *

Daisy checked her watch. He was late, but she supposed he must still be chatting to the Johnsons and couldn't really get away. She spotted a tall man with untidy blond hair working inside the room, and by the look of his paint-smeared shorts doubted he could be one of the guests. She went inside to meet him.

'Hi,' she said holding out her hand. 'I presume you must be Luke Thornton.'

He turned to her, a gruff expression on his face. She thought he was probably very handsome under all that facial hair; his eyes were certainly piercing enough. She cleared her throat. 'I'm Daisy, from reception. Gabriel said to meet him here to go through a few things.'

The man seemed to know who she was, though she couldn't imagine how.

He smiled, and after wiping his hand on his T-shirt shook her hand. 'Yes, I'm Luke. You've come to check that all the work's been finished in time for the weekend, I suppose.'

She nodded, a bit stunned at how his face lit up when he looked cheerful.

'There's some damp paint over in that corner,' he said, pointing to an area hidden by a plant stand. 'But that's all. The cleaners are coming in here first thing in the morning to clean up and it'll be dry by then.'

'You've done an incredible job,' Daisy said. 'There seemed to be a lot of damage.'

He shook his head, reminding her of a lion when his untidy hair moved around.

'It was bad enough not to be able to use the place for the guests, but not as bad as it could have been.'

'Luke, hi,' Gabriel said coming up behind her. 'You've done a great job in here, thanks.'

'No problem, I was glad to be able to help your folks out.'

'Are you and Bea coming to the party on Saturday night?'

Luke nodded. 'We are, and a couple of her friends. It should be fun.'

Gabriel nodded. 'I think it will be.' He looked down at Daisy. 'I hope you've had your invitation to come along?'

She shook her head. 'I thought it was for the guests?'

'Not this party. Everyone here is invited. The kitchen staff will be preparing the food, but extra help is being laid on by a small events business, Lapins de Lune. They'll be keeping an eye on the evening.'

Daisy couldn't help being excited. She'd never been invited to such a splendid occasion before and was sure she wouldn't have anything to wear.

'It's going to be fun, you really should come along,' Luke said, glancing at Gabriel. 'You can meet my wife, Bea – she'll introduce you to anyone you don't know.'

Daisy laughed. 'Well, that will be pretty much everyone, then.'

'Then you'll come?' Gabriel asked. 'Unless... your foot? How is it now?'

She looked down and smiled. 'It feels a little bruised but it's already much better, and not nearly bad enough to hold me back from attending the party.' She looked so hopeful that he couldn't help being flattered. 'OK then. I suppose it's not like I have far to go if I decide to return to my room.'

'Good point,' Gabe said. 'Though I hope it doesn't come to that.'

She laughed. 'My foot's perfectly fine; I barely feel the bruising now. I'm only teasing you.'

'Great,' Luke agreed. 'This party should be so much fun that you'll be too busy enjoying yourself to worry about it.'

9

DAISY

Daisy stood at the front door of the hotel, unable to believe the thick veil of fog that had descended overnight.

'I hope this lifts by this afternoon,' she said to Fi. 'Most of the guests for the party are supposed to be flying in today.'

Fi chewed the top of the pencil she was using to annotate a text book. 'No chance.'

Daisy frowned and returned to her position behind the reception counter. 'What do you mean?'

Fi groaned and threw down her pencil in frustration. 'I'll never get this to stay in my head,' she said. 'I wish I didn't have to study it.'

Daisy pulled the textbook closer to her and saw that it was about learning French. 'I thought you all learnt French at school?'

Fi shrugged. 'We do, but I skived most of the lessons and now need to brush up on it.' When Daisy looked confused, Fi added, 'We get paid more if we're bilingual and working in the hospitality market.'

Daisy hadn't realised that, which didn't really matter because she couldn't speak anything other than English. 'The fog,' she said, wanting to know why Fi was so insistent that it wouldn't be lifting any time soon.

'What? Oh, yes.' Fi smiled knowingly. 'This sort of thing happens occasionally. The fog descends out of the blue and stays a few days.'

'Days?' Daisy was horrified. 'But what about the party? The guests need to get here.'

'Well, it *might* lift,' Fi said. 'I wouldn't really know, but I think they should make plans to take the ferry if they're travelling from England or France, just in case.'

'I agree,' Gabe said, coming up to them. 'This looks as if it's here for the next few days.'

'That's what I said.' Fi winked at Daisy.

'What shall we do?' Daisy asked Gabe, hoping he had a suggestion. 'I suppose you'll be getting in contact with as many of the guests as possible and suggest they make bookings for the ferry. Rather they arrive here late than not at all.'

'I will,' he said. 'And the sooner they book seats the better. It's a busy time of the year and they're not the only ones who'll be trying to get a place.'

'Can we do anything?' Daisy asked, as Gabriel walked to his office.

'Not really. If any guests phone, tell them about the boat and give them the number to make the booking.'

She nodded and gazed out at the pale grey view, stunned that it was so dense and at the lack of any breeze to move it away from the island. 'I've never seen anything quite this bad before,' she said, thinking how eerie it seemed.

'I remember a couple of years ago leaving college,' Fi said, staring out the window. 'I'd spent a gloriously sunny day sitting in a hot classroom and couldn't wait to get home and sunbathe by the pool. Seb drove me home and literally all I did was walk into the house, run to my bedroom, and change into my bikini. When I stepped outside moments later there was a sea mist, as thick as this, billowing around from the back of the house and I had to go inside to put on some clothes because the temperature had dropped so much.'

Daisy shivered at the thought. 'That must have been disappointing,' she said. 'How amazing, though, having your own pool. I wish we'd had one when I was growing up.'

'I guess,' Fi said, sounding less than impressed. 'What else did you wish for in your home back in England?'

'A front door,' Daisy said, recalling her disappointment when a maisonette her mother had found for them years before fell through and her dream of having their own front door that stepped from inside their house out to a garden vanished.

'Surely you must have had your own front door,' Fi said, pulling a face.

Daisy nodded. 'Yes, to our flat, but it always led to a corridor, never to our own front garden.'

Fi stared at her, eyes narrowed, as she thought about Daisy's comment. 'Seriously?'

Daisy nodded. 'It's fine,' she said. 'I suppose we've just grown up wishing for different things.'

'You can say that again,' Fi said. 'You're more than welcome to come and sunbathe at Seb's house with me if you like,' she added.

Daisy hoped she hadn't caused Fi to be embarrassed. 'Maybe one day,' she said. 'I really want to get on with my painting on my days off just now.' She rested her hand on Fi's arm and smiled at her. 'I wasn't having a go when I said what I did, you know?'

Fi returned her smile. 'I know. I just hadn't ever thought about something like a front garden before. Seb is always telling me how I should get out into the real world and experience other things, but then when I come up with ideas, he won't let me try any of them.'

'I'm sure he's only looking out for you,' Daisy said. 'He sounds really lovely.'

Fi leant in closer to Daisy as if she was about to confide something very confidential to her. 'He is,' she whispered, laughing. 'But I like winding him up. He can be a bit stuffy at times.'

Fi turned out to be correct with her prediction about the weather. The fog didn't move from the ground and Daisy could tell that Gabriel was beginning to worry about the party. When he came through to reception just before the end of her shift, she asked if he'd managed to contact everyone on the guest list.

'Most of them,' he said.

'What do we do if Bryn and Soraya can't make it to the island?' Fi asked. 'They are the hosts, after all. Do we get on with all the work we need to do to get the orangery ready for tomorrow evening?'

'We carry on as usual,' he said. 'Daisy, please call the girls from Lapins de Lune to check that they have everything they need to decorate the party room. Fi, you can call the musicians to make sure they'll be there on time, and I'll go and check that the kitchen and bar staff are ready for tomorrow.'

Daisy spotted her father hurrying down the corridor towards her. 'Damn,' she muttered under her breath.

'What's the matter?' Gabe said, turning to see who she was talking about. 'Ahh, do you want me to go and divert him?'

She shook her head. There was little point. She knew her father would find a way to come and talk to her if he wanted to, so she may as well get this over and done with. She checked her watch. 'Only five minutes until the end of my shift,' she said.

'Go on,' Gabe said. 'I'll stay here with Fi until the next shift takes over.'

Daisy got up and walked over to her father. 'I can tell by the determined look on your face that you want to speak to me.'

'Yes.' He glanced over his shoulder. 'It's not often I get a chance to speak to you without Stella being there and she's in the bath. So, I hoped you wouldn't mind giving me a couple of minutes to try and clear a few things up between us.'

'I'll need to go and change. I'll meet you out the back by the steps to the gardens in ten minutes. I doubt anyone will be out there in this weather.'

She hurried to her room and quickly pulled on a pair of jeans, a thin jumper, and a cotton jacket.

'That was fast,' he said, when she joined him shortly after. 'Shall we go this way?' He indicated a pathway that would take them to the edge of the grounds.

'Yes, sure,' Daisy said. They began walking. 'So, what did you want to talk to me about?'

'The thing is, Daisy, I don't want you to think that you aren't important to me.'

'I know that,' she admitted, stepping over one of the small geometric pools dotted down through the valley gardens. 'But it hurt when I met your wife and my half-brother and they had no idea I even existed.' She'd been dreading speaking to him, not certain if she could keep her anger under control, but now it was happening, she was relieved to be able to share the feelings that had been troubling her.

They arrived at a small clearing where a weathered wooden bench nestled. 'Let's sit here,' he suggested.

Daisy sat down and waited for him to do the same. 'I know you're in a difficult position, but it hurts to be someone's secret.'

He sighed heavily. 'I know and I'm sorry. Your mother and I were very much in love, but we were very young and I panicked and ran away. I'll never forgive myself for leaving her when she needed me most. I wasn't away long and did try to persuade her that we should be married once I'd come back, but she didn't trust me not to run off again.' He hesitated. 'I wouldn't have, you know?'

Daisy wanted to believe him. After all, he was the only family she had left, and hadn't he always remembered her birthdays and Christmas? Sometimes he'd even managed to pop in on those special days; sometimes, but not very often. 'Mum always said she didn't mind you marrying Clarissa so soon after I was born and I believed her for years.' She thought back to the time when she was in her teens that it occurred to her that her mother had only told her that so she didn't fret about her. 'She knew that I wouldn't have agreed to see you if I'd known how you'd hurt her, and she was right.'

'It was good of her,' he said. 'I was always grateful and it was why I tried to see you as often as I did.'

Daisy sighed. 'I understand you not mentioning me to your first wife,' she said, wondering how she would feel if she had discovered her husband had a whole part of his life that he hadn't shared with her. 'But why not tell Stella about me? She had a right to know I existed, surely?'

He nodded. 'You're right, I know you are, but I was frightened that she wouldn't agree to marry me if she discovered that I'd kept such a huge secret from Clarissa for all those years.'

'Then she doesn't know the real you, and she deserved to before making the decision to spend the rest of her life with you.'

He stood up and pushed both hands through his short hair. Daisy softened towards him when she could see how upset he was. Then it dawned on her that maybe this was how he acted whenever things got difficult for him with his wife, and her sympathy waned.

'Daisy, I know I've done wrong, but your mum didn't want to

share you with me most of the time. She liked the idea of me loving you and being there for you for birthdays and that sort of thing, but she was insistent that she was your only true parent.'

Daisy wanted to argue with him but could imagine her mother acting like that. Hadn't she made a point of living an almost hermit-like existence for most of Daisy's life?

'Yes, but that doesn't excuse your behaviour to Stella, or your son, does it?'

'No,' he said eventually. 'It doesn't.' He picked a daisy growing through a hole in between two stones making up the top of the wall and began pulling off the petals, one-by-one. Daisy cringed. It was as if he was pulling her apart because she'd appeared in his perfect second marriage and caused issues with his pretty young wife.

He stopped what he was doing and looked at her. Then glancing back down to the dismembered flower in his hand groaned. 'Oh, that must look bad.'

Daisy shook her head. 'Don't worry about it.' She stood up.

'Where are you going?' he asked.

'Back to my room; I've got things to do and you need to get back to Stella if you don't want her wondering where you've got to.' Daisy began walking along the path, relieved to be getting away from him.

He called after her, but she ignored him. Seconds later she heard his footsteps as he ran to catch up with her. 'Daisy,' he said from behind her. She stopped and turned to face him. 'Where do we go from here?' he asked.

She shrugged. 'I don't know,' she said honestly. 'Maybe you need to talk this through with Stella. I'm not a part of your life. Let's face it, I never really have been, and its fine,' she said, when he went to protest. 'I like being independent. You carry on and I'll do the same, and if we meet again we'll say hello and be civil.'

'But you're my daughter and I love you.'

Daisy closed her eyes, desperately trying to remain calm and not let him know now much this was taking out of her. 'But I don't really fit into your life any more, do I?' she said, wishing he'd leave her alone.

'You could, if you wanted to,' he argued, his voice quiet and strained.

'Let's leave it for now, shall we? I'm still recovering from Mum dying and trying to make a life for myself. Maybe in a couple of years we could give it another try.'

'But how will I know where to contact you?'

She thought for a moment. 'Write to me here. I'll make sure they have a forwarding address when I move on.'

'Peter!' someone called from higher up the pathway. He stiffened and Daisy realised it must be Stella.

'You'd better go,' she said. 'You don't want her to discover we've met up in secret.'

She watched him head off into the hotel, thinking that she had no intention of being second best any more. His wife and son now knew about her and she had no intention of meeting him behind their backs ever again. She would hate someone to do that to her.

The following morning Daisy woke before her alarm went off. Her first thought was the chaos that would be caused to the party guests if the fog hadn't dispersed. Willing the fog to have lifted, she got out of bed and took three strides to her bedroom window. She pulled back the curtains and winced. She could barely see a few feet ahead of her. Her heart sank as she wondered how the party was going to turn out when most of its important guests wouldn't be able to attend. She hurriedly showered and dressed and went to find Gabriel to see if there was anything she could do to help.

'Not good, is it?' he said, staring out of the front door of the hotel, his tanned arms crossed in front of his chest. 'I spoke to Bryn and Soraya last night and explained that this sometimes happens. I tried to persuade them to book the ferry for them and their family to come across today. It's the only way they're going to get here. I hope they did as I suggested.'

'Me too.'

'I saw the Lapins de Lune van on my way through here,' she said, recalling the two girls unloading their hampers with a tall fair man and two of the hotel bar staff. 'I thought they did chintzy weddings, or that's what Fi said anyway.'

'They do all sorts of events,' he said thoughtfully. 'Shall we go and see if we can lend them a hand?'

They walked to the car park at the rear of the hotel.

'They have vintage crockery with some nice Art Deco designs which they'll use here,' he said. 'Izzy and Jess have only been going a couple of years, but they helped my parents out after the fire and they're very hardworking girls,' he said.

Daisy loved the idea of having her own business one day and said so.

'What would you like to do?' he asked, holding open the back door and stepping back to let her pass.

'I'm not really sure. I'd love my own gallery, but I know that's expensive and out of my league.'

'You shouldn't ever doubt yourself.' He frowned. 'You can do whatever you wish, you know. You'll find a way, I'm sure of it.'

She smiled up at him. 'I wish I had as much faith in my abilities as you seem to,' she said, spotting the two girls still unloading their van and giggling with the men helping them.

'I know what you mean,' he said.

Confused by what he'd said, she stopped. 'What?'

He shook his head. 'Only that my grandmother was saying something similar to me the other day.'

She relaxed. She probably shouldn't be so defensive. She was aware that for some reason she always assumed someone was trying to put her down or was making a derogatory remark. Especially Gabriel, but he'd only ever been kind to her, she realised. She wondered if it had something to do with the way her mum had always looked at things. She hoped she wasn't becoming like her; it had been hard living with someone who only ever seemed to see the negative in things.

'Lydia's right; you should have more faith in yourself,' she said eventually.

'Ditto,' he said, giving her a brief hug. 'I think we could both learn a lot from her.'

'Hey, Izzy, Jess,' Gabriel called, taking Daisy by the hand and leading her over to the van to meet them. 'Meet Daisy. She's a friend of mine who's working here on reception for the summer. We've come to help unload your stuff.'

'We met at the Sunset Concert, remember?' Jess said, noticing Daisy's hand in his.

Daisy recognised her and pulled her hand away, embarrassed that he was being so friendly. After all, she had only met these people once and they'd been witness to her embarrassment when she'd met Bella for the first time. It hadn't been the best start to a friendship.

'We've got a lot to do in the next few hours,' Izzy said. 'We were hoping to come here and set up yesterday, but we're running a bit late.'

As Daisy helped the others unload the crockery and linen, she began to feel something she'd last enjoyed when with Gabriel in Vietnam: a kinship with others her own age. It was a comforting feeling and one she wanted to last.

She looked up at Gabriel carrying three heavy hampers, one on top of the other, as if they weighed nothing at all. He must have sensed her watching him, because he glanced at her and gave her a quick wink.

Daisy couldn't help smiling back at him, and noticed Izzy watching them. Gabriel took the hampers away and she bent to pick up a large bag containing linens when Jess whispered, 'We were wondering who the lucky girl would be who'd capture Gabriel's attention, but after the concert, well, we weren't sure.' She motioned her head to Izzy who immediately came over to join them.

'What's this?' Izzy asked, her voice quiet.

'You thought Gabriel was seeing Daisy.'

Daisy's eyes widened, horrified that they had got the wrong idea. 'No, it's not like that at all. We know each other from our travels, that's all.' Even to her own ears her insistence sounded forced.

'Yeah, yeah, we believe you.' Jess's voice dripped with sarcasm.

Daisy was about to tell them that they were wrong when she noticed Izzy pulling a face at Jess to get her to stop teasing. 'Oh, very funny,' she said, enjoying the banter. 'I thought you were being serious for a moment.'

'I did spot him winking at you though,' Izzy said, picking up a hamper and walking with Daisy around the back of the hotel to the orangery. 'He was looking at you before that too. I really do think he likes you, Daisy.'

Daisy felt her face reddening. She wasn't used to confiding in others and didn't want to have to admit to someone she'd only just met about their history together. 'He is lovely,' was all she'd say.

They arrived in the large room, with rounded windows on one side and a wall on the other. Daisy thought back to when she'd first arrived at the hotel and assumed this room must be a conservatory. She loved the plants growing up the back wall and the ceramic *jardinières* holding ferns that softened the sleek lines of the room. Fi had told her that even though this room was added only ten years ago, the light switches and chandeliers were authentic 1920s which Rick had sourced in a reclamation yard. The effect was stunning.

She watched as Jess and Izzy unpacked their stock then helped carry linen and crockery to where they indicated. A couple of hours later the room looked completely different and almost ready for the party to begin. It was like stepping into a scene from *The Great Gatsby*, but on a much smaller scale, with the abundance of pale pink hydrangeas brought inside from the garden in tall square planters, the old-fashioned champagne glasses placed in tiers for a waterfall of champagne to cascade down, and groups of silver and purple metallic balloons placed in different areas around the ceiling.

Gabriel had had to leave to go and sort out issues with guests who had been delayed by the weather, but sent through a bartender with a tray of lemonade for them to enjoy. The girls sat near the main door of the orangery and sipped at their cool drinks.

'Blimey, I'm hot,' Izzy said, fanning herself with a leftover napkin. 'How can it still be this temperature when there's fog sitting on the ground?'

'No idea,' Daisy said. 'It does seem very humid.' She relished the cool drink as the bubbles burst at the back of her throat. 'Gabriel told me you cater for vintage weddings and parties,' she said, wanting to know more about the girls and their business. 'Do you do many Art Deco themed ones?'

Jess shook her head. 'Not many, but we're doing more now.' She looked around the large room. 'You couldn't really do anything else in this place,' she said. 'It's very glamorous here, don't you think?'

Daisy nodded. 'It is. I'd never been inside such a beautiful building before coming to work here. I still can't get over the huge black and silver front doors each time I come into the hotel.'

'It is a very beautiful old building,' Izzy said. 'My mum remembers it from when she was a child. She said it was so out of character from the granite farmhouses and cottages in the area that it caused quite a lot of consternation with the nearby locals as it was being built. Then they got used to it, but after a while it was neglected and the building decayed. She said it looks better now since Rick and Francesca renovated it. Apparently it took them a couple of years to ensure that everything was exactly how it should be. They sent off the light switches, door handles and other bits to be re-chromed, so that they could keep as many of the original pieces from the building as possible.'

'It makes all the difference,' Daisy said. 'It's like going back in time when you walk into this place. I almost feel like I should be dressed up in a pretty frock when I come in to work.'

'What are Francesca and Rick like to work for?' Izzy asked. 'Fun I should think.'

Daisy thought about their slightly eccentric ways. She giggled. 'They're great to work for. They expect us to do our jobs well, which is only right, but they're kind and hardworking themselves.' She lowered her voice. 'I especially love working for Mrs Grey.'

Jess sighed. 'She's so beautiful. It's hard to imagine she's in her eighties.'

'My mum told me all about her and said I should look her up on the internet, which I did,' Izzy said. 'She was stunning when she was young, but I think she had quite a tough time of it when she disappeared.'

Daisy wasn't going to confide in them about Lydia's past. 'She's a lovely lady,' was all she'd say.

Jess finished her drink and placed her empty glass on the tray. 'Come along, we'd better keep going otherwise we won't be ready on time.'

Daisy couldn't imagine what still needed to be done to the room. Jess must have seen her confusion and said, 'Table decorations. Sit there and watch,' she said, looking very pleased with herself. 'We have three different decorations with us, so there's a variation to the settings.'

Daisy watched as Jess and Izzy took out square glass vases in assorted styles and placed them in the middle of the tables all around the room. In the taller vases they placed huge white feathers, three in each one. In the shorter ones, they placed cream-coloured candles, draped with golden strings of beads, and they filled the shortest vases with pearls of all sizes, pushing a small candle into the middle of the arrangement.

'Wow, that looks so impressive,' Daisy said, impressed with the transformation of the tables. 'I'm beginning to feel like I should be dressing up for this party.'

'We will be,' Jess said. She looked Daisy up and down. 'If you need to borrow a dress for tonight, just say so. We always dress up to fit into whatever occasion we're hosting and have several flapper dressers each. You're about the same size as Izzy so you'll probably be OK.'

Izzy clapped her hands. 'You can come back to our cottage with us, if you like. We can help you get ready.'

'We've got some gorgeous head-dresses you can choose from, too,' Jess added. She looked at Izzy. 'I think the black one with the peacock feather will look perfect with Daisy's hair. Although we'll need to tie your hair up, put it in a tight chignon at the back. I think it'll look very dramatic. What do you think, Iz?'

Izzy nodded. 'Yes. Daisy, you're going to look gorgeous.'

Daisy couldn't help getting excited at the prospect of dressing up in something so different to anything she'd ever worn before. 'OK,' she said. 'I'd love to.'

'Brilliant,' Izzy said. 'Now we'd better get on, otherwise we won't have time to go and change.'

Daisy, having seen what they'd done with the tables, helped them check that everything was exactly as it should be. She was distracted by a sound coming from the pathway to the side of the building, when she spotted Gabriel walking round, joined by the tall man that had arrived with the girls.

'That's Ed,' Izzy said quietly. 'Oh, you met him at the Sunset Concert too, didn't you?'

Jess leaned over to Daisy and whispered. 'It's like love's young dream with those two since they hooked up.'

'Hah,' Izzy said. 'You can talk. You and my brother drive me nuts with all your mooning about.' She turned to Daisy. 'One minute she's besotted with my brother, the next with Ed's. I think she just likes the attention from both of them.'

Daisy laughed. These girls were so much fun. She was loving being in their company and realised she was feeling happier than she had since Gabriel's revelation at the concert. 'What do you think they're carrying?' she asked.

The three girls stared out of the window and watched as brass stands were placed by the entrance of the orangery, five in a row, then a chain was linked to each one.

'Oh, wow, it's for a red carpet,' Jess laughed, as Gabriel unrolled one between the two linked rows. 'This is going to be a brilliant party.'

Daisy thought so too. She was so busy watching Gabriel and

Ed setting up the red carpet, she almost bumped into two waiters carrying through a huge cake. 'Oh, sorry,' she gasped, quickly moving out of their way as it teetered slightly on the tray they were carrying.

They set the three-tiered cake down on a circular table near to the back wall. Each tier was different. The top one was white and circular, the middle one silver and square and the largest one at the bottom square with rounded edges and gold with pearl beading. She'd never seen anything like it before.

Two bar staff carried in trays of glasses and arranged them in order on a table near to where the cake stood.

'I think we need to get out of here now,' said Izzy, studying the room. 'It looks like we've covered everything and they'll want to be bringing in the food and booze soon.' She checked her watch. 'Come on, Daisy, let's clear these hampers away into the van and go back to the cottage and make ourselves glamorous.'

'Here, we'll give you a hand,' Gabriel said, coming into the room and helping with their boxes and hampers. He took one of the hampers from Daisy's hands, his finger grazing her own, sending shockwaves through her body. She glanced up at him and for a few seconds everything was blanked out as they locked eyes and stared at each other.

'Er, you guys,' Ed said, shaking his head. 'We need to get a move on.'

Daisy could feel the blood rushing to her face. She looked away and hurriedly picked up another basket to carry. Everything was soon safely in the van.

'You're going?' Gabriel asked, when Daisy stepped up to the vehicle. He looked, Daisy thought, rather disappointed.

She told him about the cottage and the girls lending her an outfit for the party. He smiled. 'That's brilliant. I'll see you later then.'

As the van wended its way along the south coast, Daisy looked out at St Aubin's Bay with its wide curved beach and Elizabeth Castle sitting proudly in the middle of the sea. The sun sparkled on the almost still water and she wondered why she hadn't taken the time to come out and investigate more of this island by herself before now.

'We live in Rozel,' Izzy said. 'Have you been there yet?'

Daisy shook her head. 'No, I haven't seen much of the island at all so far. I only arrived a few weeks ago and have been working as many hours as I could since then to try and save up.'

'What are you saving for?' Jess asked, stretching her arm out of her own window and yawning.

Daisy had to admit that she wasn't certain yet. 'I want to go travelling again, but most of all I want to be able to rent my own place at some point.'

'Do you think you'll stay over here?' Ed asked.

She shrugged. 'I do like it here,' she said, thinking of Gabe. 'But there's so much I haven't seen yet. I was told that it's only an hour by boat to St Malo and there's a train there that can take me straight to Paris in only a couple of hours.'

'That's right,' Ed said. 'If ever you want somewhere to stay when you're travelling in France, let me know. My family have a home there.'

Jess and Izzy giggled at this comment, but Daisy wasn't sure why. She assumed it must be some standing joke between them.

'Thank you,' she said. 'I'll remember to do that.'

They drove past the town and up over Gorey Hill, past Mont Orgueil Castle, and up over another hill. 'I'll never find my way around this place,' she said. 'The roads are so narrow and windy it's hard to know where I am.'

'We get lost sometimes,' Jess said. 'Even though the island's not very large, they say that there's about two hundred miles of roads what with all the tiny lanes.'

'I can't see how that works,' Izzy said.

'Nor me,' Jess agreed.

The van turned right eventually and down a long hill, getting narrower at the bottom. Daisy spotted the sea only a slightly darker blue to the sky, and at the bottom a beautiful stone breakwater. 'Is this Rozel Harbour?' she asked, intrigued.

'It is,' Jess said. 'The cottage is right here,' she said, parking next to a tiny garden at the front of a pretty white building.

'Oh, it's beautiful. You live here?'

The girls nodded. 'It was my gran's home,' Jess said. 'She left it to me when she died and we live here and run our business from here too.'

Daisy followed them out of the van and stood silently at the entrance of the pretty cottage. 'You're so lucky.'

'We are,' Jess agreed, locking the van and waiting for Daisy. They walked inside and Jess waved Daisy into the little living room.

'Ed, will you get Daisy and yourself a drink while Jess and I go and fetch a couple of dresses for her to look at?'

Sitting down opposite Ed with a cool glass of orange juice, Daisy asked, 'Do you live here too?'

'No, when I'm in Jersey I have a place at the manor where I'm a groundsman. The rest of the time I live in France with my parents; they have a business there.'

'Oh, right,' she said.

The girls soon reappeared carrying several dresses each. They hung them all from the pelmet over the front window.

'Well, which one do you like best?' Jess asked, smiling. 'Take a couple upstairs and try them on if you'd prefer. You can shower too if you want.'

'What about you, Ed?' Izzy asked.

'I don't think they'll suit me,' he joked. Shaking his head, he added. 'I've left my suit upstairs. I'll go and change and leave you three to get ready.'

Daisy chose three fringed dresses: a gold one, a pink one, and a black one. After a quick shower she decided on the black dress and hurriedly put it on and headed downstairs, her curly hair still damp.

'You look stunning,' Jess said. 'Wait there while we go and change, and have a look in those boxes where you'll find the headdresses.'

She picked up each of the headbands, all decorated differently with an assortment of beads and feathers. Unable to wait, she tried on the peacock feather one she thought most suited her dress and, staring at her reflection in the mirror, couldn't help smiling. She looked so different, sophisticated somehow, and she loved it.

Someone walked into the room behind her. She turned to see Ed. 'Looks lovely,' he said. 'The girls will be delighted you've found one you like.'

Jess and Izzy followed him in moments later. 'Wow, you look fabulous,' Jess said. 'I knew these dresses would suit you.'

They lent her red lipstick and eyeliner to go with the outfit. The effect was startling.

'What do you think?' Izzy asked, when she didn't speak for a few seconds.

'I like it,' she said.

'You look very sophisticated,' Jess said. 'It really suits you.'

She thought it did too, but didn't like to say so. Maybe this summer in Jersey was going to be the time that her life truly did change for the better. 'You both look amazing,' she said, smiling at Jess in a red dress and Izzy in gold. 'I think this party is going to be great fun.'

'Me too,' Izzy agreed, linking arms with her and Jess. 'Come on, Ed, take a picture of us three. I want to post it on our website; it'll be good for advertising this style of party.'

Jess nodded. 'Good idea.'

Daisy hated having her photo taken, but didn't dare upset the girls by saying so. They'd been so generous to her and letting them take a picture of her was the least she could do.

Ed took his phone and waved for them to stand a little closer. 'Smile, girls,' he said, taking several pictures. He handed the phone to Jess.

'We look gorgeous,' she said.

Daisy and Izzy laughed. 'If you do say so yourself,' Izzy giggled.

Ed looked at his watch. 'We're going to have to get a move on if you girls don't want to be late.'

'Damn,' Jess said, seeing the time. 'We need to be there before everyone else,' she said, eyes filled with panic. 'We can't be late.'

'We won't be if we leave right now,' Izzy said, picking up her bag and the car keys. 'Come on.'

* * *

They arrived at the hotel and hurried into the orangery. The only person there was Gabriel, doing a last-minute check of the room. A trio were playing lively music in keeping with the era over in one corner of the room near a temporary dance floor. Daisy felt like her namesake in *The Great Gatsby* when Gabriel turned around and smiled at her.

Her stomach flipped over and her breath caught in her throat. He looked incredible. He'd slicked back his hair, showing his tanned face off to perfection, and wore a dinner jacket with a white shirt and bow tie. He walked over to join her. Daisy cleared her throat and tried to think of something coherent to say.

'You look incredible,' he said his voice catching. 'So...'

'Over the top?'

He laughed. 'I was going to say glamorous.'

'Oh,' she said, embarrassed by her instinctive reaction to be negative. Too many years being told she shouldn't forget who she was. She was beginning to realise that her mother had been wrong on many levels.

'Thank you,' she said, when he didn't say anything further. He didn't speak but stared at her. She was beginning to feel a little uncomfortable by his silence. 'Is anything wrong?' she asked. Maybe her lipstick had smudged or something.

He shook his head. 'No. I was just— Well, you look stunning.'

Daisy couldn't take her eyes away from his. She had no idea how long they stood like that. Seconds, minutes... it was only when she realised someone was tapping Gabriel on the shoulder and he looked away to see who it was that she became aware they were still in the middle of the orangery, which was now filling with guests.

He rested his hand on her bare shoulder. 'Sorry, I'll just have to go and deal with this,' he said. 'It seems our party hosts have arrived. I must greet them.'

'Of course,' she said.

She spotted Izzy and Jess, smiling and chatting to other staff members and several guests who were making their way into the room. The red carpet gave them all something to talk about as they walked in. She saw Luke arrive with his wife, Bea. He looked a little uncomfortable in his dinner suit.

'So, what do you think?' She looked up to see Ed holding out a glass of champagne to her. 'They know how to put on a party here, don't they?'

She nodded. 'The girls are very good at dressing a room. You must be very proud of them.'

He smiled. 'They certainly do.'

The room was filling fast and getting noisier. Daisy tilted her head in the direction of an exuberant couple who had just arrived and were holding up their glasses to a group of friends. 'They were in that period drama from last year,' she said, amazed at how different the couple looked without their powdered wigs.

'They're probably good friends with Francesca and Rick,' he said. 'In fact, I'm surprised those two haven't come back for tonight. Maybe they didn't have time to catch the ferry.'

Daisy looked out of the glazed wall overlooking the garden to the orange glow formed by the garden lights in the dense fog. 'It's still terrible out there. What a shame, when there's usually such an incredible view of the bay.'

'I think it looks eerie,' Izzy said, coming to stand next to them. 'As if tonight is part of a hazy dream, where anything's possible.'

Daisy could see what she meant. 'It's like we've been transported back in time to the twenties.' She liked the idea.

'Everything seems to be going fine here,' Izzy said, looking around the room.

They spoke for a little longer until raucous voices could be heard coming along the pathway towards the party. She saw a couple who she recognised from many films, walking hand in hand. Gabriel followed them, his head bent slightly as he said something amusing to his grandmother.

The glamorous couple stopped at the door, letting Gabriel and Lydia walk ahead of them into the room. Gabriel called out for everyone's attention.

When Daisy saw who was standing there she gasped, and turning to the woman standing next to her said, 'That's Brynmor Wensley Morgan, and his wife Soraya.' She was unable to believe that she was in the same room as the great actor she'd seen in so many films and had never been able to afford to watch at the theatre.

The woman looked at her strangely. 'I take it that you're new here, otherwise you'd have probably come across them both before. They're good friends of the family.'

Daisy shook her head. 'Yes, fairly new,' she whispered.

Gabriel held his hands up to quieten the excited chattering in the room. 'Dear friends, we're here tonight to celebrate fifty years in the business that is show, for this amazingly talented couple that all of us know and most of us are lucky to consider as close friends.' He held up his glass in a toast. 'I'd like you to join me in raising your glasses to our fabulous hosts, Bryn and his lovely wife, Soraya.'

The guests cheered and raised their glasses, chanting their hosts' names as the couple made their grand entrance into the packed room.

'Bryn would like to say a few words,' Gabriel said, stepping back to let the larger-than-life actor and his wife speak.

Daisy watched Gabriel. Living with his theatrical parents seemed to have given him a confidence she couldn't imagine possessing.

'And,' Bryn continued, bringing Daisy back to the present as his clipped, strong voice carried easily to everyone in the room, 'to celebrate half a century in the business that Soraya and I love so much—' he arched an eyebrow dramatically '—despite neither of us getting the merest sniff of an Oscar, Soraya and I would like to thank you all for travelling here tonight through the inclement weather to enjoy our special evening with us.'

The guests clapped and Bryn and Soraya took a bow, laughing and giving each other a quick peck on the lips.

Soraya clamped her free hand over Bryn's mouth as he opened it to speak, and said, 'I'd like to thank the Encore, and the girls from Lapins de Lune, and especially the divine Gabriel.' She lifted her hand in a mock whisper. 'Who really should have become an actor and delighted us all on the screen as well as in this hotel. You've all worked very hard to make tonight possible.'

Daisy joined in the applause. She beamed at Lydia who looked resplendent in her shiny dark grey dress and matching headdress with long opera pearls tied in a lose knot below her chest. Lydia spotted her and walked over.

'You look stunning, Daisy,' she said. 'How lovely to see you here tonight. I wasn't sure if you'd be on duty or not.'

Daisy shook her head. 'Not tonight; Fi's holding the fort but she'll join us later.'

Lydia looked at Gabriel. 'Is that elegant brother of hers coming tonight?' She looked back at Daisy. 'Young Sebastian Fielding caused something of an uproar here in the island last year. It was in all the papers, and not just the local one.' She lowered her voice. 'He can come across as a little fierce, but he's a hardworking man who only wants the best for his employees, and he's devoted to his younger sister.'

Daisy recalled Fi's chatter about the brother who bossed her around but spoiled her. 'She talks about him a lot.'

'Gabriel,' Lydia said, waving him over to join them. When he reached them, Lydia said, 'Why don't you relax for a moment and ask Daisy for a dance? You'd like to dance, wouldn't you?' she asked, her tone implying that a refusal would be out of the question.

Daisy smiled. 'I've got no idea how to Charleston,' she said, presuming that's what Bryn and Soraya and their guests were doing on the dance floor.

Lydia grabbed hold of Daisy's arm and one of Gabriel's, and pushed them towards the dance floor. 'Go on, you two.' She shook her head. 'In my day you never missed an opportunity to have fun.'

Gabriel took Daisy by the hand before she had a chance to argue and led her onto the wooden floor. 'Sorry about that,' he said. 'But she won't give up until we do. It can't be that hard, can it?' he said, watching the others for a second before beginning to do a vague impression of what they were doing.

Daisy laughed at his comedic attempts to copy the others. He was obviously more used to the water than the dance floor, but she decided that if he could have fun without worrying about making a fool of himself, then she could do the same.

'There you go,' he shouted, not attempting to hide his amusement at her. 'You've nearly got it.'

Two dances later and Daisy, out of breath but happy, took Gabriel's hand and led him over to one of the tables. 'Can we sit?' she asked, pulling out a chair and sitting down.

He turned his chair so that he was facing her a bit more and nodded at one of the bartenders, who immediately brought over a tray of drinks. Thanking him, Gabriel took two glasses from the tray and handed one to Daisy. 'That was fun.'

She laughed. 'It was. I'm a bit of a *Strictly* fan and love watching the different dances. I think the Charleston always looks great fun.'

'I'm so glad you came tonight, Daisy,' he said, before leaning forward and kissing her quickly on her lips.

Startled but pleased with what he'd just done, she smiled. 'So am I.'

'I want you to know that I'm doing everything in my power to sort out my divorce.'

Daisy's mood plummeted. She hated to be reminded of his situation and that they couldn't be a couple. 'Let's not talk about it tonight.'

He took her hand in his. 'Having met your father and learnt something of your past, I can understand the way you feel about my situation much more. I probably shouldn't have kissed you, but I want you to know how I feel about you. Our time together in Vietnam was special. It was like nothing I've ever experienced before.'

'And you don't think it was just because of the magic of the surroundings?'

'It helped, I suppose, but Vietnam was more mystical to me because I shared those experiences with you.'

She couldn't help agreeing with his sentiment. 'I know what you mean. I feel the same way about our time there.'

'I wish you'd answered my emails. We still could have spoken on the phone, or I could have come to Devon and spent time with you.' He looked so sincere. 'Maybe met your mother.'

She shook her head. Not wishing to discuss her issues with Aaron and unused to sharing her private life, she didn't like to admit that it had never occurred to her to introduce him to her mother. 'My mother had issues,' she said. 'She was intensely private and a little ashamed of her home.' She cleared her throat. 'It was quite rundown and she hated living there.'

'Didn't she invite anyone there at all?' he asked, looking stunned at the prospect. 'What about her friends, or your friends?'

Daisy sighed. 'I didn't have any, and neither did she.'

He stared at her for a moment and Daisy could have bitten her tongue for opening up so much to him. She wished she could take back what she'd just said. Now he was bound to see her in a different light. She'd done so well up until now at reinventing herself.

'Don't look so horrified,' he said, giving her hand a squeeze. 'None of our lives are exactly how we might wish them to be.' He tilted his head. 'Yes, I know I'm speaking as someone who has enjoyed a better life than most, but it can be quite hard when you're fourteen and your mum has acted a pretty risqué part in a movie.'

Daisy winced. 'I hadn't thought of that sort of thing.' She could see the hurt in his eyes.

'I love my mum,' he said, lowering his voice so only she could hear him speak. 'But I had to learn to stand up for myself at a young age. Not everyone's parents' lives are lived through the magazines. Some of the stories were... difficult to read knowing I had to go to school on the Monday morning and deal with some fool who thinks he's funny for sharing details with the rest of my class.'

Daisy couldn't help feeling sorry for him. 'We've had pretty opposite upbringings if you think about it,' she said, as it dawned on her that something halfway between the two was probably what most people experienced. 'I'm not sure which was the most enjoyable.'

His expression softened. 'Probably neither,' he said, smiling widely at her. 'At least we have that in common.'

Daisy smiled. He was right and for once she didn't feel so much of an outsider. To think that his childhood might have been as difficult as hers, albeit in a completely different way, was reassuring somehow. She was about so tell him how much better he'd made her feel when there was an upsurge in the volume in the room. Both of them turned their heads to see what all the commotion was about.

'Your parents – they're back!' she said, delighted to see they had been able to get to Jersey in time for the party.

He and Daisy stood up together. 'Come on, let's go and say hi to them,' he said, taking her by the hand.

It felt so natural that it was only when Francesca made a point of spotting their hand-holding and raised a perfectly threaded eyebrow in their direction that Daisy felt at all awkward and let go. She could feel Gabriel staring at her and hoped she hadn't hurt his feelings.

'Darling, so good to see you again,' Francesca cheered, giving Gabriel a hug. 'You look very handsome in all your finery.'

'Thanks, Mum. You look amazing as usual.' He smiled at his dad. 'Great to see you back again. Will you two be here for a while or is this a flying visit?'

'I'm flying out again first thing if this bloody fog lifts,' his father said. 'We had to get the ferry here. Still only three quarters of the way through my tour, so there's no chance of a break for me yet.'

'Yes, but you love it,' Francesca said putting her arm around Rick's waist. 'I'm back for a bit now. Filming wrapped yesterday.'

'That was quick,' Gabriel said.

Daisy had no idea how long it took to shoot a film, so didn't like to comment.

'Not really; I was only in the final scenes of the filming, so they didn't need me at the beginning. It was only a small part.' She smiled at various people in the room. 'Bryn and Soraya seem to be having a ball; they look like they've been dancing for ages. I'd better go and have a chat with them.' Before leaving she added, 'This all looks fabulous, darling, well done.'

Daisy and Gabriel watched his parents walking away, chatting to people as they made their way across the crowded room.

'Why is she so surprised that you've pulled this together so well?' Daisy couldn't help asking.

Gabriel smiled. 'Because she knows how I'd much prefer to spend my days down on the beach, or diving somewhere. Staying indoors for too long makes me restless.'

'Won't you ever want to settle down somewhere?' Daisy asked. 'I mean, have your own home, rather than being away on projects all the time and living out of a rucksack?'

He shrugged. 'Maybe, but right now I love what I do and can't see myself giving it up any time soon.'

Then we're really not suited, thought Daisy. However much she might wish his divorce to be finalised and to have a home of her own where she could put down roots and make a life for herself, Gabriel was obviously not the person with whom she could ever hope to achieve this dream.

Before she could say anything further there was a shriek followed by a loud crash as a large tray of glasses was knocked from the bar area onto the floor.

'Bryn, be careful,' Soraya shrieked, staring at the splintered glass all around their feet. 'You shouldn't be so exuberant.'

Bryn raised his hands. 'Not to worry, if someone will bring me a dustpan and brush I'll clear this mess in a jiffy. Just put the breakages on our bill.'

'Sorry,' Gabriel said. 'I'm going to have to go and sort this out.'

She nodded and took the opportunity to excuse herself and go to the ladies'. She was having a lot of fun, but couldn't help being sad that she and Gabriel wanted such different things for their futures.

Feeling a little more settled, she returned several minutes later to see someone sitting on her chair in deep conversation with Gabriel. Unsure whether to interrupt them she hesitated, then when the woman looked over at someone in the crowd, Daisy realised it was Bella. She decided this was her cue to leave.

10

GABRIEL

Gabriel was woken by his mobile ringing. 'Hello?' he said, checking his watch to see if he'd overslept, and noticing that it was just after seven in the morning.

'Gabriel? It's Fanshawe, your father's lawyer. Sorry if I've woken you but I'm on an early flight to London and don't have much time. I wanted to ask you if you got married in Jersey.'

'No, South Africa,' Gabe answered, pushing himself to a sitting position and rubbing his eyes with the back of his free hand. 'Why?'

'You might be able to arrange for a divorce or annulment in South Africa if that's where you were married.' There was a mumble and clatter in the background. 'Sorry, I have to go now but wanted you to know that this might be one way to sort things out.'

Gabe couldn't believe it. 'Thank you, that's great news.'

'I'm not promising anything, mind.'

'No, of course.' He took a breath to say more but realised that the call had been ended. Delighted with this unexpected news Gabe dropped his phone onto his duvet and got out of bed. He needed to speak to Bella as soon as possible, but first he wanted a shower to work out exactly how he was going to persuade her to do this for him.

Freshly showered and dressed he phoned Bella and asked her to meet him for breakfast at St Ouen's Bay.

'So,' she said, sipping at her latte. 'To what do I owe this pleasure? I can only imagine you'd bring me out to this beautiful bay and buy me breakfast if it was to break bad news to me about the project.'

'That's partly it, yes,' he admitted, going on to explain that the funding had been rescinded.

'Damn, that's lousy. Our findings were so positive, too. I suppose that means we'll have to watch while another company completes our work, then?'

'I haven't been told of anyone else taking over, just that with cuts that we won't be getting any further funding.'

'I thought we'd be fine since we'd discovered that new species of sea anemone,' she said, looking downcast.

'Me too.' He took a bite of his bacon roll and they ate in silence for a few minutes, both looking out at the rolling waves on the wide beach. 'I'm going out soon to close everything down. I'll take a few more samples of the algae and sea grasses in the area so we can test them, but other than that I'll just have to ensure our records are fully up to date and the lab reports on the new species we believe we've found are recorded.'

'Such a disappointment though,' she said. Looking up at him she narrowed her eyes. 'There's more though, isn't there? Why would you bring me here to tell me this when I'd already told you months ago that I'm taking a sabbatical from work?'

He explained about Daisy's reluctance to be involved with him romantically if he was still married.

'But that's ridiculous,' she said. 'We're not together any more.'

'She has her reasons,' he said, going on to explain about the phone call that morning from advocate Fanshawe. He waited while she absorbed what he'd just said.

'Bloody hell, Gabe, I won't do it. Just because your new girl-friend doesn't like our situation doesn't mean I have to traipse all the way to South Africa to get an annulment.' She shook her head. 'Especially when you don't even know that they'll grant us one.'

'I know, and I understand you being angry with me for even suggesting this to you.'

She stared at him for a few moments. 'Have you told her what you're planning?' He shook his head.

'No. I don't want to say anything until I'm sure it'll work out.' He was beginning to wonder why he'd thought this would be a good idea.

'Oh, fine. I'll do it for you. I'll come over and help you wrap everything up with the project and help you try and sort out this divorce. But if she gets upset about us travelling out there together then that's your problem, not mine.'

It was at times like this that he remembered why he'd always been so fond of Bella. She was strong and determined but you never knew what decision she'd make. 'Thanks, Bella. I owe you one.'

'No, you don't,' she said, her voice sombre. 'You've never let me down and it doesn't matter who you or I are with, you'll always hold a special place in my heart. Anyway, I was there at the beginning of the project and it's only right that I should be there at the end.'

He sighed. 'Thank you.'

She giggled. 'Don't thank me yet; you've still got to break this news to your girlfriend, or whatever she is.'

11

DAISY

It was Daisy's day off, and despite a nagging hangover she was feeling cheerful. The sun had begun to burn through the fog that morning and was now brightening up the day.

Deciding to make the most of the glorious weather she walked to Beauport headland and set up her easel. Daisy was delighted to have found a position that gave her a great view of the bay below without being in the way of the footpaths that two people and their dogs had already walked down.

She'd been looking forward to coming here since overhearing one of the guests talking about how magnificent the views were. They hadn't been exaggerating. Despite it only being seven-thirty in the morning, Daisy could see several yachts anchored in the bay and presumed they must have spent the night rolling on the gentle waves.

She breathed in the warm sea air and marvelled at the dew on the grassy mounds surrounding her pitch. The turquoise sea was calm and it seemed that nothing could possibly be wrong in a world where this sort of beauty existed. She chose several oils from her khaki bag and squeezed the colours onto her palette.

Gazing out at the one large rock rising from the sea between where she stood and the opposite headland, she let her mind wander and began to paint.

She was barely aware of the few passers-by who came her way or of the sun as it warmed her face and arms. She loved painting and losing herself in the emotion of the image she was recreating. It was only when someone stopped to ask if they could take her photo that she realised how long she'd been painting and how thirsty she was.

'You're an excellent artist,' the bearded middle-aged man said, as he stared over her shoulder at the painting.

'Thank you,' Daisy replied. It dawned on her that he didn't look like the usual tourist taking holiday snaps. 'Are you on holiday?'

He shook his head and held up his camera briefly. 'No, I work for *The Jersey Scene*, the local glossy mag. I'm doing a piece about outdoor activities for the next edition. Do you mind me using your picture for the magazine?'

She thought about his question, a niggling doubt creeping into her stomach. If it was a local magazine then who was going to ever see her picture on the mainland? It should be fine, surely. And she'd been fine with her photo going up on a local business's website yesterday. 'Well...' She considered his request a little further. 'This is a local magazine, you say?'

'It is.' He gave her a reassuring smile. 'I'll understand if you'd rather I didn't use your picture, but I was taken by your concentration while you painted that beautiful landscape of the bay. I was hoping for a picture within a picture, as it were.'

She was being over cautious. Aaron had probably moved on by now. She didn't want this stranger to think she was being ridiculous. If he wouldn't see the magazine, then what was there to worry about? 'No, it's fine,' she said, aware he'd been waiting patiently for her answer.

'Great, thanks.' He lifted his camera up to his face. 'If you just carry on with your painting and maybe look over the top of the canvas at the view, please.'

She did as he asked. Hearing the camera click several times, she continued to hold her pose.

'Perfect,' he said. She turned to face him, smiling. He reached into his back pocket and pulled out a business card. 'If you want a copy, please call this number and I can send one to you.'

'I might do that,' she said, reading his name and dropping the card into her canvas bag.

'Or if you like I could take your mobile number and let you know when the article is out?' he said, replacing the cap on his expensive-looking camera.

'I don't have a mobile,' she said, aware that this usually surprised people when they discovered it, but who did she have to call? It was pointless having something you didn't need, something that could be traced by a determined person.

'You don't have a phone?' He smiled. 'You really are an artist,' he laughed. 'More interested in your craft than keeping up with what people are doing, I guess.'

She hadn't ever thought about it like that before. 'I suppose you're right.'

He looked down at her partially completed painting and again at the view ahead. 'You really are very good. Are you a professional artist?'

She shook her head. 'No, but I hope to be someday.'

'Well, if your talent is anything to go by, I'm sure you'll end up achieving your ambition,' he said, holding out his hand. 'It was good to meet you.'

'You too,' she said, shaking his hand, then taking up her brush again as soon as he was out of sight.

About an hour later, Daisy sensed that she was being watched. Her heart pounded and she tried not to panic. She looked around slowly, trying to act as if she was surveying the view, but couldn't see anyone. She was being ridiculous. She was in Jersey now. She carried on painting until she was sure she'd heard someone say her name. The hairs stood up on her arms as she listened, but not hearing it again, decided that she'd been imagining things.

'There you are,' Gabriel said, as he came along the dusty footpath.

Daisy jumped, not expecting him to be here. So that's who she'd felt watching her. She was so relieved she couldn't help smiling widely at him. 'Gabriel,' she said, unused to seeing people she knew unexpectedly here on the island. It was a comforting feeling. 'How did you know where to find me?'

'Fi said you were coming here to paint for a few hours,' he said. 'I didn't like to disturb you, but it's lunchtime now, so I thought I'd bring you some food in case you were hungry.'

She looked down at the small hamper he was carrying and couldn't help smiling. 'You've bought me a picnic?'

She'd enjoyed so few picnics and the best one by far had been the one Gabriel had taken to the Sunset Concert, and that had been cut short. She was still upset with him, but at that moment her stomach growled, reminding her that she hadn't eaten since her supper the night before.

'You're obviously hungry,' he said, before she had a chance to refuse his kind offer.

She shrugged. 'I've never had a picnic before,' she admitted. 'Well, not actually *eaten* one.'

'We're not going to discuss my previous attempt at bringing you a picnic.'

'No, we're not,' she said, interested to see what goodies he'd packed for their al fresco lunch.

He looked happy to have pleased her. 'Then I hope this one lives up to your estimation.' He stepped closer to her easel, studied it, and then looked past it to the bay in the background.

Daisy hoped he liked what he saw. She knew art was subjective, but it gave her confidence when any of the few people she'd shown her paintings to had professed to liking her work. 'What do you think?'

He didn't speak for a few moments, staring at the painting, before saying, 'It's incredible. You're very talented.'

She smiled as he turned to face her. 'Thank you, I appreciate that.'

'I'm only being honest,' he said. He held up the hamper. 'Shall I help you carry your easel, or do you want to eat somewhere close by so you don't have to move it?'

She looked around at the gorse and grass to try and locate somewhere suitable for them to sit. 'There should be fine,' she said, pointing to a small area where the grass was shorter and there was a clear view of the bay. 'I can see my canvas from here, so there's no chance of anyone messing with it.'

Gabriel carried the hamper over to their designated area and put it down. He unrolled the plaid picnic rug he'd taken to the concert and motioned for her to take a seat.

Daisy couldn't hide her happiness as she settled down, closing her eyes briefly in the warm sunshine. When she opened them he was holding out a champagne glass for her to take.

'Isn't it a bit early?' she giggled, feeling deliciously carefree.

'Nope,' he smiled. 'My grandmother said it's never too early in the day for either chocolate or champagne.'

'Lydia's a wise woman,' Daisy said, taking the glass from him and holding it while he poured it half full. She watched as he took a small bottle of orange juice, unscrewed the lid, and topped off the drink with it. 'You see, you're not being totally indulgent – you're also getting one of your five a day.'

She waited for him to make up the same drink for himself, and when he held his glass up, he said, 'To you, lovely Daisy. Here's to a perfect summer in Jersey.'

'Hear, hear,' she agreed, taking a sip and relishing the taste of the Buck's Fizz in her mouth.

He drank from his glass and then, putting it down on a flat stone, unpacked plates, a baguette, a plate of Jersey butter, tomatoes, cold cooked Jersey Royals, a slab of brie, and some grapes. 'I hope you like all this,' he said, handing her a plate.

Daisy nodded. She placed her glass down carefully and then started selecting food. As they ate, she thought how perfect this all was. 'Thanks so much, Gabe.'

'My pleasure,' he said, smiling. 'I wasn't sure if you wanted to be left alone to paint, but thought you could always tell me to get lost and I'd have left you in peace.'

She laughed. 'I'd never do that,' she said.

'Really?'

'Not when you've come so well prepared to feed me,' she joked.

He hesitated and she wondered what he was refraining from saying to her. She didn't want him to bring up the subject of Bella, or anything that might sour their moment, so she quickly picked up her glass to toast him once more. 'To you. May your summer be as perfect as you hope it to be.'

He mirrored her actions and said, 'Thank you, Daisy.'

Several people wandered past them and one nosy dog sniffed around their food before being called away by its owner. She tried to implant the image of Gabriel sitting next to her on the rug into her mind so that she'd never forget it.

'Your painting really is very good,' he said eventually. 'You should try to sell them at one of the galleries, or maybe in a couple of the local shops. They're certainly good enough to make you some money.'

She hadn't dared hope that she could sell her work just yet, but liked the thought of earning extra cash to build up a nest-egg to support whatever she decided to do at the end of the summer season when the hotel closed for the winter. 'I'm not sure I'm ready to show them to too many people yet,' she said, doubting his confidence in her abilities.

'Why not? They're excellent.'

He looked sincere and she believed that he was telling her the truth, and for that she was grateful. She just didn't have the confidence in herself to ask anyone to hang them in their gallery or shop just yet. Maybe soon, she thought. 'There are so many beautiful locations here on the island, it's hard to choose where to start.'

He nodded. 'I'm the same with the bays. I loved exploring them as a kid but never seemed to have the time to try out every cove or beach here.'

She could imagine him as a teenager, inquisitive and desperate to discover new things in the island's waters. 'What was your favourite pastime apart from diving?'

He shrugged. 'Underwater photography, I suppose.'

She laughed. 'So, still under the water then?'

'Yes, I suppose it was,' he smiled. 'I've always been happier in the water, or so my mother always said. I used to run away on the beach whenever she took me there as a child, so she always make sure I was wearing bright swimming trunks. She was grateful that a lot of the locals recognised me as her son and kept an eye out for me whenever I took off in search of sea shells, or driftwood, or other treasures I could take back home to the hotel to keep in the secret stash under my bed.'

'And do you still have a secret stash?'

'I do,' he said, smiling at her, the skin around his dark eyes crinkling slightly.

Daisy sighed, soothed by Gabriel's jovial company and the glasses of Buck's Fizz. She relaxed and lay back on her elbows on the rug. 'This is bliss,' she said. 'I can't imagine ever wanting to leave this place. Everything seems close and it makes me feel cosseted somehow.'

'I suppose it helps that so many people know each other here,' Gabriel said. 'When I was a teenager I couldn't wait to leave and see the world, but I always enjoy coming home to Jersey. My parents feel the same way, although it's a pain having to take that extra flight to the mainland to connect with any other flight.'

'Worth it, though,' Daisy said, thinking that an extra flight to reach the outside world was even more of a reason to come and live here. She was beginning to feel safe for the first time since being so anonymous in Vietnam.

'I'm going to have to leave again soon,' Gabriel said quietly, staring out at the channel as if longing to be somewhere far away.

Daisy tried not to overreact. 'Your project?'

He finished his drink, and resting on one elbow smiled at her. He seemed sad. 'They held their meeting and still won't give us the sponsorship. So I'm going to have to travel back to try and find more backing.'

'What will you do?'

He reached out his hand and picked a blade of grass, curling it between two fingers as he stared miserably at it. 'I have to try to rescue what we've started. I'm going to need more sponsorship to carry on, but until I find it, I'm going to have to shut everything down. It's devastating for the others involved. Everyone in the team has put months of their lives into the research. It would be frustrating to think of it going to waste if we can't afford to finish our work.'

She hated to think of the Encore without Gabriel there greeting guests. She'd got used to seeing him in passing and didn't like the thought of him being far away, somewhere where she wouldn't have contact with him.

'I'll miss you,' she said honestly. 'It's not going to be the same without you.'

His lips drew back in a slow smile and he looked up from the blade of grass into her eyes. 'That's good to know. I'll miss you too.'

'Will you be away long?' She found she didn't care what he read from her questions.

'I'm not sure. It could be a few weeks or maybe months. We might be lucky enough to find more funding, and if that happens then I could stay away for a bit longer. I need to do the best I can for my team.'

She knew it was selfish of her to want him to stay, especially as she'd been so insistent that there could be nothing between them while he was still married to Bella. 'Your work is so important, Gabe. It must make you feel so satisfied at the end of each day to know you're doing something that could make such a difference to other people's lives.'

'I get as much joy out of helping them as they do with me and my team being there and working on everything.' He was quiet for a moment. 'Daisy, I have to tell you that Bella will be coming out with me. She's been a part of several of the projects I've been involved in and this is one of them. She didn't really want to come along this time but there's something I'm hoping she can help me with in South Africa. I'll tell you about it when I know it's worked, but however you feel about this you must know that it's important.'

She stared at him, stunned. She wanted to trust him. Wished she could more than anything, but she'd trusted in the past and ended up having to deal with the consequences. Sitting bolt upright and not caring that she'd knocked over her glass, Daisy glared at him. 'Is this the reason for the unexpected picnic, to soften me up before slamming me with that nugget of information?'

He reached out to take her arm. 'Daisy, listen to me, please. I need you to trust me on this.'

She shrugged him off. 'Look, you go and do what you have to do. I understand that you have commitments.' She made a pretence of checking her watch. She wasn't sure why but needed to do something. 'I need to get on with this painting.' She strode away, back to her paints and easel and picked up her brush and a tube of oil paint. She didn't hear Gabriel come up behind her. 'Daisy...' he said, touching her shoulder lightly, giving her a fright and causing her to spin round and squirt Azure Blue all over his grey T-shirt. Daisy gasped.

Gabriel's mouth dropped open in surprise. 'Sorry, I didn't mean to give you a fright,' he said. He stared down at the paint splashed across his top and then looked at Daisy and said, 'If you give me the brush I'll rescue some of that and put it on your palette. You don't want to waste it.'

Damn Aaron for making her so distrustful and nervous. 'It's not your fault,' she admitted, embarrassed by her reaction. He was right, though – the paints were expensive and she didn't have money to throw away by wasting half of her oils. 'Don't worry, I'll do it,' she said, not wishing to give in to anything he suggested too easily.

She put her hand inside his top, the back of her fingers

connecting with his stomach, which contracted on her touch. He gave a small intake of breath and without thinking she looked up at him to see him staring intently at her. Before she had time to think, his head had lowered and his lips connected with hers.

The taste of orange and champagne on his firm lips and the warm sun on her face took her back to them being together in Vietnam, and forgetting everything else she continued kissing him, one hand on the inside of his top, the other dropped to her side.

Someone cleared their throat behind her, causing Daisy to remember where she was. She spun round, taking Gabe with her as she pulled his top. An old man walking two Labradors was smiling at them.

'I'm so sorry,' she said, realising she and Gabe had been blocking the pathway.

He grinned at them with amusement and said, 'Don't you worry, lovely, it warms my heart to see two youngsters so in love. Now if I can just get past you both, I'll leave you to carry on.'

Daisy's face reddened. She opened her mouth to argue that he was mistaken, but Gabriel, taking her hand and extricating it from his top, pulled her gently back from the path. They stepped onto a slight mound to give the man and his dogs space to pass them.

'Thank you,' he said.

As soon as the man was out of earshot, Daisy faced Gabriel and glared at him. 'I don't know what came over me,' she said, furious with herself. She daren't let him think that she'd forgotten about his situation with Bella.

He took her by the shoulders. 'Daisy, really, Bella coming with me is not what it seems,' he said, as if he'd heard her thoughts. 'I wish you'd trust me.'

'I do trust you, Gabriel. I hope the two of you have a lovely time.' She stared at her painting intently, willing him to go away.

He sighed. 'Daisy, as I explained earlier, Bella and I worked on the project before. She was there right at the beginning and she's coming back to try and resolve a few issues. She's part of this team.'

She wanted to believe him but knew from past experience that her instincts where men had been concerned were off-kilter. 'Look,' she said, tired of thinking about it all. 'I wish your project all the luck in the world, but I need to get on with this painting before I lose the daylight.'

He frowned. 'Fine. I'll leave you to get on, but I wish you wouldn't judge me by other people, Daisy.'

She watched him walk off to collect the picnic hamper, his T-shirt smeared with paint. Realising that she must also be covered in the bright blue, she looked down to see her top now ruined with a reminder of that kiss. Daisy looked at the half-finished painting drying on her easel and couldn't help wishing things could be different between them. She wanted more than anything to trust him and to let herself go and get closer to him, but she wasn't going to end up like her mother had done, bitter and alone. She'd learnt the hard way that just because you want someone to be a certain way, it doesn't mean that they will be.

She picked up her paintbrush and pictured how happy her mother would be to see her standing here right now. Her last wish had been for Daisy to leave their home town and move away, start afresh somewhere new and build the life for herself that her mother hadn't managed to achieve. She felt her throat constricting as the knowledge that whatever she did make of her life would not be something that she'd ever be able to share with her mother.

Tired of feeling sorry for herself, she pulled a tissue out of her back pocket and blew her nose 'Right,' she said, clearing her throat. 'Time to finish this painting.' She focused her attention back to the spectacular view behind her easel. The one thing she could rely on was her ambition to see her paintings sold, but she needed to finish some first. 'Here goes.'

12

GABRIEL

'You must explain to Daisy why you're leaving,' Lydia insisted, as they walked along the beach early one morning a few days later. 'She needs to understand what you're trying to do to sort everything out.'

'Not yet,' he said, bending down to pick up a lump of green glass made opaque from years of roughening by the sea and sand. 'As far as she's concerned what we had is behind her.' He rubbed his thumb against the rough surface. 'I thought we could make a go of it, but she's adamant that she won't be in a relationship with a married man, and I can understand her decision. That's why I've persuaded Bella to come with me on this leg of the project so that we can try and get our marriage annulled while we're in South Africa. She was reluctant to go and says she needs a break from being away, but I've managed to explain to her how this will benefit us both. She's met someone new now, you know?'

'Good, I'm pleased, but I don't understand why you don't explain to Daisy exactly what you're doing?'

He wished he could. 'I would, but I don't want to give her any false hope. I daren't mention it to her yet.'

Lydia pulled her straw hat down further over her eyes. 'I do hope you two can resolve this matter. Maybe I'm an old romantic but I know life is really too short for these dramas. But if you're sure now is not the time to tell Daisy, then fine. I just hope you can sort this out when you're in South Africa.'

'So do I. I think Daisy believed me when I told her that Bella and I are no longer romantically linked in any way, but she's been badly hurt by her parents' choices, Nan. The next few weeks are going to be important in so many ways.'

'I can see that now, darling,' she said. 'And I'll be thinking of you the whole time.'

They walked on for a few minutes in silence. Gabe could tell his grandmother was concerned for him. She was obviously fond of Daisy and he could understand her irritation with the situation and hoped that he could resolve these issues once and for all.

'I have to admit something,' she said, placing her hand on his arm. They stopped and turned to face the gentle waves hitting the beach. 'I did wonder why you and Bella got married. After all, this isn't the fifties; you don't need to be married to have a baby.'

He knew that, only too well, now. 'I was wrapped up in the whole "doing the right thing" vibe. I was missing Daisy and was hurt by her ignoring me. I think I probably got carried away with the thought of having something to look forward to.' He pushed the toes of one foot into the soft, pale-gold sand. 'What can I say, I'm an idiot.'

Lydia gave him a brief hug. 'Darling, you're not an idiot. Maybe a little misdirected for a bit, but your intentions were good.' She walked on and Gabriel followed. 'So, what will you tell Daisy?'

'She knows the funding for my project has been rescinded and that I need to go and either find more backing, or wrap up the whole thing for the time being. It's not as if we can be together until I sort everything out with Bella anyway, and Daisy's busy here with the season building up.'

'It's going to be hard for you both,' Lydia said, waving to a neighbour who was throwing a ball for their Labrador on the beach.

'It's the only way I can think of to sort this mess out.'

'Then good luck to you.'

They carried on walking and chatting. It was a perfect early August morning and Gabriel wished he could stay and carry on enjoying the summer with Daisy working at the hotel. Who knew if she'd still be there next year, or even by the winter, he mused. He had to speak to her and hope she'd understand his reasons for leaving. He didn't even have the excuse that he was needed at the Encore now his mother was back from filming.

It dawned on him that he needed to have a chat with his mother too before he left.

* * *

Later that morning, Gabriel knocked on Francesca's office door and entered. 'Morning, Mum,' he said, going over to give her a kiss before sitting down opposite her at her desk. 'So, how was the shoot? I didn't get a chance to ask you at the party.'

'It was great fun,' she said. 'I'd still much rather play the gorgeous heroine than her mother, but those days have long gone, more's the pity.'

'You still look amazing, you know that.' He smiled at her, remembering how proud he'd always been when she'd collected him from school and always looked more glamorous than any of the other mothers.

'Thank you, sweetheart.' Her mobile pinged and she quickly replied to the message she'd received. 'There's probably going to be a sequel, so I should have more work from the franchise, which is great to know.'

'Good for you.' His mother was always much happier when she had filming work to look forward to. His parents might make a decent living from running the hotel, but he knew that both their loves remained in their respective entertainment careers. 'So, did you enjoy the party?'

'Yes, I thought you did an amazing job with everything, especially with the issue of the delays due to the damn fog. Your father was very pleased so many people made it and we took a huge amount at the bar, which is always good. Bryn and Soraya had a ball too and want to book us to host their next wedding anniversary do, so we're delighted with everything.' She narrowed her eyes and studied him for a moment.

Gabriel wasn't sure if she was about to discuss his looming trip, or Daisy. Gossip was always rife in this place among the staff.

'Go on,' he said. 'I know there's something you want to say to me.'

She smiled and leant forward, resting her elbows on the desk. 'I presume you've come here this morning to tell me that you're going away, and soon?'

He nodded. 'I am.' He explained about the funding of his project, but decided against mentioning Bella and the divorce.

'I thought so,' she said. 'I wish there was something I could do, but my money has been ear-marked for the work on the kitchen garden and your dad's tour money won't come in for a few months yet.'

He'd never accepted money from his parents before now and had no intention of taking from them when they worked so hard for everything they had. 'I know, Mum, and it's fine. I'll sort this out somehow.'

'I'd love to help you, Gabriel,' she said, looking miserable. 'I wish you didn't have to go again so soon. I haven't seen very much of you at all recently.'

He reached out and rested his palm on the back of her hand. 'I know, but I'll be back as soon as I can and we can catch up then.'

'You're going soon then, as in this week?'

'I have to,' he said. 'Tomorrow morning, first thing.'

'Oh, that is soon,' she said, looking disappointed.

He hated seeing her sad, especially as his father was still away, but it couldn't be helped. 'You and Nan can spend some quality time together until Dad returns,' he said.

'True. Have you told her you'll be going tomorrow?'

'Nan?'

She studied his face before saying, 'Of course. Who else could you think I meant?'

This was his cue to leave. If his mother didn't know already about him and Daisy, then he wasn't going to enlighten her.

'Gabriel,' she said. 'I noticed you holding young Daisy's hand at the party. Is there something you want to tell me?'

He would have loved to tell her that they were a couple, but there was no point leaving Daisy to have to cope with his mother's interference if he didn't manage to sort out a divorce.

'No,' he said, deciding that there would be plenty of time to explain everything about him and Daisy if they did get back together. He stood to leave. 'I'd better get on. I've got a few calls to make and emails to write to try and drum up funding before I go. I need to at least try and arrive with some encouraging news.'

He kissed her goodbye and left.

He was walking along the main corridor when Daisy's father, Peter, called out to him. Gabriel went to him. 'Hello, are you enjoying your stay?'

'We've had a wonderful time, thank you,' he said, moving from one foot to the other.

Gabriel waited for him to speak. He was sure Peter was trying to tell him something. He wished he'd hurry up; he was running out of time if he wanted to complete everything he needed to do today. 'Is there something you wish to speak to me about?'

Peter took a deep breath and exhaled sharply. 'Yes.' He glanced up and down the corridor to see if anyone was coming and waved Gabriel over to a small side room. Closing the door behind them, he said, 'I've heard on the grapevine that you're having problems with your sponsors for some conservation project you're involved with.'

Gabriel couldn't understand how he'd know this, but nodded. 'That's right,' he said, suspicious of the man's interest.

Peter cleared his throat. 'I want to offer you sponsorship of up to ten thousand pounds.'

Gabriel's eyes widened. 'Peter, that's incredibly generous,' he said, unable to keep a smile from his face. Maybe he wasn't such a bad guy after all, he thought. Perhaps Daisy had only seen her father through her mother's eyes.

Peter pushed his hands deep into his pockets. 'Ahh, but I want something in return.'

Gabriel frowned. He wasn't sure he was going to like what was coming next. 'Go on,' he said quietly, intrigued by what Peter could want from him.

'I need you to persuade Daisy to meet with me. She's refusing to have anything to do with me at the moment. I know she's feeling hurt that I never told her about Stella and our son before now, but it's complicated for me.'

And there it was, thought Gabriel, disappointed in his willingness to believe this man's motives over Daisy's insistence that he wasn't the kind man he appeared to be on the surface.

'No,' Gabriel said without hesitation.

Peter's bushy eyebrows shot up, giving him the look of a stunned gerbil.

'Why not? I think it's a pretty generous offer.' When Gabriel didn't reply, he added, 'Don't you care about your project?'

Gabriel felt his hackles rising. He studied Peter for a moment, trying not to show how angry he was with this man's attempt to force him into betraying Daisy's wishes. 'I care about it very much, but I'm not going to trade in Daisy's feelings for cash. Maybe if you thought about her in terms that didn't include your finances, then you might be able to build a relationship with her,' he said, not caring that he was being rude to a guest.

'You'll discover that life isn't all about love and romance, young man,' he said, looking annoyed to have failed in his endeavour. 'When it comes to women and children it is all about money. You'll discover that fact when you come to have your own family.'

Gabriel didn't care. He refused to be used in this way. 'Daisy is a beautiful person but she's been hurt by you. Instead of investing your money in shortcuts, why not try to invest your time getting to know her?'

'Haven't you noticed that she's not interested in me?' he hissed through clenched teeth.

Gabriel struggled to contain his irritation with this selfish man. 'Yes, but she feels this way after a lifetime of disappointments and coming second best in your affections. Her feelings towards you are not going to change overnight.'

Peter waved his hand in Gabriel's face. 'You're a fool,' he said, glaring at him before marching out of the room and slamming the door behind him.

Gabriel took a deep breath to calm his temper. No wonder Daisy's mum kept her daughter away from this short-sighted man. What he didn't understand was what Daisy's mother had ever seen in him in the first place. He slowly began to calm down. He wasn't interested in Daisy's parents and their mistakes, but he was concerned about her. From what he'd gleaned she'd been through a lot of heartache in her life and he wasn't going to be party to any further upsets.

Passing reception, he saw that Daisy wasn't there and Fi was working alone.

'She's not on until twelve,' she said, giving him a flirtatious wink.

'You're very cheeky, you know that?' he laughed.

'Sorry, I forgot myself again.'

'Its fine. Was there something else?'

She considered his question for a couple of seconds. 'Only that I'm pretty sure I'm right about how you two feel about each other, despite your denials.'

'Why, what does Daisy say?'

Fi raised her eyebrows, 'She's my friend and you're the bosses' son; you think my loyalties will lie with you?'

'No, of course not,' he said, amused by her retort and comforted that Daisy had such a loyal friend.

'I'm joking.' She pulled a face, leaning a little closer to him and checking that no one was nearby to hear what she was about to say. 'I can see the way she looks at you, but she insists there's nothing going on. I'd believe her if I didn't keep catching you both checking out each other. It's like you're both trying to hide your feelings and I've no idea why.'

He didn't like the thought of displaying his feelings so obviously, but Fi had a point. 'We have unresolved issues, that much I can tell you.'

Fi snorted. 'Well, that tells me nothing. I'd ask Daisy, but she's always telling me to mind my own business.'

Gabriel couldn't help liking this bubbly girl, even though she was at times a little noisy for someone working on reception, and she rarely remembered to keep her thoughts to herself. 'I'll pop back later when she's here. There's something I need to speak to her about.'

'OK, I'll tell her.'

'No, please don't say anything. I don't need her finding a way to keep busy elsewhere. I have to speak to her today.'

'Fine, I'll keep my mouth firmly shut.'

He doubted that was possible, but smiled and left her to deal with a guest who'd arrived with his wife and two small children.

He sat in his room in the Martello tower and spoke to four contacts, two of whom said they'd consider putting forward his funding request to the following month's board meetings. Then, Gabriel typed up several letters to other corporations and contacts, followed by emails to a few more. Finally, sealing the envelopes closed, he placed stamps on them and left his room to walk to the postbox down the road. He was on his way back past the terrace at the front of his grandmother's house when he thought he heard movement down at the end of the garden behind some bushes. He stopped walking and peered in the direction of the sound to try and see what it could be.

'Bloody thing.'

It was Daisy. His heart pounded to hear her voice so unexpectedly. He didn't relish what he was about to say to her but was relieved to be able to do it away from any of the staff and guests at the hotel. He went inside the house and poured two glasses of orange juice for them, then went back out to join her.

He watched silently for a few seconds, not wishing to give her a fright or interrupt her while she concentrated on her painting, like he had done at Beauport. Her eyes narrowed as she concentrated, her tongue poked out between her lips as her fine paintbrush made a line on the canvas. She stopped and turning her head, yelped.

'I didn't realise you were standing there,' she said. 'How long have you been watching me?'

'Sorry,' he said, holding out a glass of juice for her. 'Your work looked intricate and I didn't want to startle you.'

Her expression softened. 'It's driving me nuts,' she said. 'I can't seem to get this bit of shading right.'

He moved closer and studied the painting. 'It's stunning,' he said, seeing his grandmother's view of the beach below her home.

'Thanks, but it's not quite right yet.'

'It looks pretty good to me.' He took a sip of his drink and watched her do the same. 'Have you completed many paintings now?'

'A few, but not nearly enough for a collection.' She placed her brush down.

'Look, I wanted to apologise for the other day. It didn't quite turn out as I'd wanted it to.' He wasn't sure that had come out as he'd intended, either. 'That is...'

She smiled. 'It's fine, I know what you mean.' She finished her drink and passed him the empty glass. 'I should really get on as my shift starts at noon.'

He knew he had to speak to her now, before she discovered his departure from someone else. 'Daisy, can we take a brief walk, maybe on the beach?'

She frowned. 'Can't it wait? I really do want to get on with this while I can.'

He pictured his mother discussing him leaving the next day and knew that if he didn't want to ruin what friendship he still had with Daisy, he had to tell her now. 'Sorry, I know, but there's something I need to tell you and I'm afraid it really can't wait.'

'Fine, come on then.' She didn't look too pleased, but he was glad she'd agreed to listen to him.

They walked along the garden and he placed the two empty glasses on the garden wall before leading her down the concrete steps onto the beach below.

He didn't know how she was going to react so thought he'd just come out with it. 'I'm leaving tomorrow morning,' he said, not waiting for her to comment. 'I've tried to drum up as much interest in the project as possible and now I have to get back to South Africa and do what I can to keep it going.'

Daisy's step hesitated. 'Tomorrow?'

He was relieved to see she looked disappointed at his news. Maybe there was some hope for him after all.

'Yes. Mum is back now, so there's nothing keeping me here. I owe it to my team to get back there and do what I can.'

'Do you know how long you'll be away?' she asked, hesitating before adding, 'I only ask because I know that Lydia misses you when you're not here.'

'I know. But she loves having you coming to her garden to paint.'

'I suppose so.'

They walked on in silence for a bit.

Daisy cleared her throat. 'I really should be getting back to my painting,' she said. 'But good luck with your project, I hope you're able to rescue it.'

'Of course,' he said. 'I'm only telling you now because I didn't want you to hear it from someone else.'

She knitted her eyebrows together. 'Right. Well, thanks, that was thoughtful of you.'

She gave him a brief smile and turned to go back to the steps leading up to the garden. Gabriel watched her go. He saw her hesitate, but she didn't turn round, just stared up the beach towards where someone was standing at the water's edge. He couldn't tell who it was, but Daisy didn't wave at the person so she couldn't have known them. As the figure walked away it occurred to him that Daisy seemed a little rushed as she ran back up the steps, but then again he *had* taken her away from her work and she was obviously in a hurry to return to it.

13

DAISY

Daisy forced a smile on her face to greet the group of new arrivals entering the hotel. Gabe had been gone for over two weeks and she was still expecting to see him appearing around the hotel. Fi had just gone to fetch them both a coffee. It had been a busy morning, and she was glad not to have too much time to wallow.

She'd noticed that her father and his family had left a few days earlier than she'd expected. He hadn't said goodbye, but it was a relief not to have had to go through the charade of being nice to him in front of his wife and son.

When everyone was checked in and given cards to their rooms, the guests left her to accompany the porters up to their relevant floors. She noticed a lady, whom Daisy assumed must be nearly eighty years old, standing with a much younger man.

'Sorry for keeping you waiting,' she said. 'Can I help you?'

'Yes, I'm Dolores Mulroon,' the lady said. She had an American accent with a slight southern twang to it that Daisy loved. 'My friend and I have booked adjoining rooms for one week.'

Daisy was used to seeing older women with younger men, and vice versa, but this couple really did have a large age difference. She tapped the woman's name into the computer system and called up her details and then her friend's. 'Mr Swinton?' The man nodded. 'Yes, we have the rooms you requested, overlooking the garden at the west side of the hotel. Can I take a credit card and your passports, please?' She pushed two forms and pens towards them. 'And if you'd please fill these in and sign them.'

The lady handed Daisy her credit card. 'Thank you, Mrs Mulroon,' she said.

'Call me Dolores,' she said. 'Everyone does.'

'Thank you, Dolores,' Daisy said, taking the card.

All the formalities completed, Daisy nodded for the concierge to come and take over with their luggage and any restaurant bookings they might wish to make.

As soon as they'd gone into the lift, Fi arrived back at the desk carrying a tray with their coffees on it. 'Blimey, good for her,' she said.

Daisy frowned at her colleague. 'Stop making assumptions. They could simply be friends for all we know.'

Fi blew on her coffee. 'Surely you're not that innocent,' she said. 'Right, never mind them – I want to invite you to something.'

Daisy sat back down at her desk, intrigued. 'Go on then, what is it?'

'You know my brother's fiancé Paige is a shoe designer?'

'Yes, and?'

'Well, there's a fashion show being held at Elizabeth Castle next week. It's for charity and Paige's shoes are being featured. Seb has offered us tickets. What do you think? Want to come?'

Daisy didn't have to consider the offer; she'd never been to a fashion show before. 'I'd love to go, thanks.'

Fi smiled. 'Cool, I'll let him know.'

Daisy glanced at the calendar. She hadn't returned to Lydia's garden since seeing Gabe there the day before he'd left the island.

The thought of going there and knowing he'd gone didn't appeal to her. Thankfully the hotel was full, so she'd been able to work extra shifts and keep busy. Unfortunately her painting was a little behind because of her working hours and she needed to rectify that if she was to build up enough canvases to exhibit somewhere.

'Don't suppose you have any ideas for where I can go and paint?' she asked Fi.

'Um, millions of ideas,' Fi said. 'Like what sort of thing are you looking for? Beach views, landscapes, fit blokes jogging?' She giggled.

Daisy couldn't help smiling at her friend. 'Somewhere I haven't been before.' Daisy tried to be more specific. 'I was thinking of a wooded place, or somewhere with water.'

Fi laughed. 'Er, we're surrounded by water, or hadn't you noticed.'

Daisy picked up her notepad and swatted Fi with it. 'Are you going to be helpful, or not?' she teased.

'How about Queen's Valley?'

Daisy shrugged. 'What's it like there?'

Fi took a tentative sip of her coffee and sat back in her chair. 'If you ever watched *Bergerac* then you'll remember he had a farmhouse in a valley.'

'I've caught it on TV a couple of times.'

'Well, that farm was in Queen's Valley. In the late eighties, or maybe the early nineties, the authorities flooded the area to make a reservoir.'

Daisy was fascinated. 'So, is his farm still there? Could I visit it?'

Fi shook her head. 'No, it's underwater now, which I think is a shame. I sometimes see re-runs of the series and like to see how the island has changed since it was filmed. I'd have loved to go to that farm and have a nose about.'

Daisy agreed. 'There must be other locations to visit that are still around though,' she said. 'Maybe we could go and see a few of them when we're next off work together?'

Fi nodded. 'Great idea, I'd like that.' She thought for a moment. 'Francesca was telling me one day how people used to come here and try to find out where they were filming the series. I think she was in a couple of episodes and I know Rick sang in one or two of them.'

Daisy decided she should pay more attention to the programme when she next caught an episode on television. 'I suppose having worked here we might actually recognise some of the actors, or the extras, if we look really hard.'

Two more guests arrived and cut short their chat, but Daisy couldn't help thinking that her and Fi's friendship was probably going to get stronger. She liked the prospect of having a close female friend.

'Good morning, girls.' Lydia walked into the hotel, a smile on her face and a bunch of freesias in one hand. 'I thought these would smell lovely behind the counter on your desk.'

Daisy took the flowers and sniffed. 'What a gorgeous scent,' she said. 'Thank you.' It was good to see Lydia again and she immediately felt guilty not going up to see her at the house. All she'd thought about was missing Gabriel. It hadn't occurred to her to think of Lydia and how she'd feel without her grandson there to keep her company. 'I'm sorry I haven't been around lately.'

Lydia shook her head. 'Don't be silly. It would be lovely to see you painting in the garden again at some point though,' she said. She turned her attention to Fi. 'This young lady is an excellent artist. Did you know that?'

Fi shook her head. 'I knew she liked to paint, but I haven't seen any of her pictures yet,' she said, in a mildly accusatory tone. 'I thought we were friends.'

'We are, but I'm not so sure I'm happy enough with what I've done yet to show anyone.'

'Rubbish,' Lydia said. 'The problem is that your comfort zone is here.' She held her hand next to her own stomach. 'But in order to succeed you have to force yourself to work outside your comfort zone, here.' She moved her hand further away from her stomach. 'Trust in yourself and take a chance. After all, art is subjective. Not everyone will like your work, but having seen it, I can't imagine that many won't. It's excellent.'

Daisy could feel her face reddening at the compliments coming from Lydia. 'Thank you,' she said. 'Maybe I should take your advice and be a little bolder.'

'Of course you should,' Fi said. 'I've always thought that if someone doesn't like me, or something I've done, then it's their problem. You should feel the same way about your pictures.'

Lydia laughed. 'Yes, Fi. However, you've been blessed with an inordinate amount of self-confidence and not all of us are lucky enough to have that.'

'Maybe not,' Daisy said, taking in what the two women she liked best in the world had said to her. 'But I like the notion and think I'm going to start following both your advice, starting from now.'

The phone rang and Fi answered it. She began typing information into the computer system and Lydia leant closer to Daisy. 'Good,' she said smiling at her. She lowered her voice and added, 'You're growing more confident and with it, more lovely each day. It's wonderful to see.'

Daisy had never received such a heart-warming compliment

before and it felt wonderful. 'Thank you,' she said. 'That means a lot.'

Lydia smiled. 'I'd better get on; Francesca is waiting to talk to me about something. I have a feeling it's to do with Gabriel and his project.'

Her mood dropping, Daisy nodded. 'I hope he's able to find a way to sort things out.'

Lydia nodded and walked away to the door leading to the back of the hotel and Francesca's office.

Fi finished her call. 'What was that all about? Something to do with Gabriel?'

Daisy took a sip of her coffee. 'She's worried about him.'

'She's so lovely,' Fi said. 'I wish I had a grandmother as caring and as glamorous as Lydia.'

'So do I.'

They became lost in their own thoughts, drinking their coffee and making the most of a quiet period.

'Let's go to Queen's Valley this afternoon anyway,' Fi suggested. 'I can go for a run around the dam and you can paint. The reservoir is really picturesque. What do you say?'

'I'd love it,' Daisy said.

* * *

As they drove along the east coast towards Gorey, Fi told Daisy about her new boyfriend. 'Well, he's not a proper boyfriend, but we've been out a couple of times for a drink and once for a meal. He's not like my usual bloke, you know, always wanting to talk about himself. Phil is interested in what I'm doing and my job at the hotel,' she said, grinning. 'He's hot, too.'

Daisy opened her window a little further. It was so warm and the air did little to cool them. 'I'm pleased for you,' she said, enjoying seeing Fi so excited about this new relationship. 'He sounds lovely.'

'He is.' She took the sharp turning up Gorey Hill, turning left a minute or so later and left again at the end of the road. 'It's just down here,' she said, making yet another turn. 'I hope you'll be able to meet him soon.' She giggled. 'Hey, maybe he's got a brother or a friend for you.'

Daisy shook her head. 'No thank you,' she said, not wishing to be with anyone apart from Gabriel, even if he was unavailable. 'I'm quite happy as a singleton.'

'Suit yourself.'

Fi took another left and drove slowly into the Queen's Valley car park. 'Here we are,' she said, parking the car and getting out. 'I thought we could walk round until you found the best place to set up your easel, and I can have a run while you paint.'

'Brilliant.' Daisy unloaded her easel and paints from Fi's Golf and sighed. 'You drive like you're racing,' she said, glad to be out of the car after Fi's erratic driving through the narrow Jersey lanes. 'I think I'll get the bus back to the hotel afterwards,' she teased.

'You will, if you're not going to appreciate my driving!' Fi laughed. 'I'd love you to meet Phil though, Daisy,' she added. 'Seb is always such a misery when it comes to meeting men that I like.'

'He's probably only being protective,' Daisy said, struggling to lift her rucksack onto her shoulder when it caught on a beach bag in the back of Fi's car.

'Here, let me.' Fi picked up the easel and closed the car boot. 'Come on, it's this way. This is actually two dams joined together, I think. I'll also take you to Val de la Mare on the west side of the island some time; that's a beautiful dam with lots of trees and pathways to explore.'

They walked through the gate and along the pathway. Fi

hadn't been exaggerating – it was beautiful with the blue of the sky reflected in the dark expanse of water. The reservoir was larger than Daisy had expected and surrounded by trees and bushes. Daisy commented on how quiet it was on their walk.

Fi checked her watch. 'I think it's probably the school run at the moment so parents will be collecting their kids, but it'll probably be a bit busier later when they come out to walk their dogs. I've nearly tripped over quite a few of them when I've been out here running.'

They'd been walking about twenty minutes when Daisy stopped. 'I think I'll set up here,' she said, taking in the view across the dam. 'You go for your run.'

'I was going to show you round a little further,' Fi said.

'No, this is fine. You get on, then maybe later we can go and have a better look around.'

Fi put down the easel and stretched her legs a little more. 'Great. I'll see you in twenty minutes or so. I can come back for you later if you'd like to stay on.'

Daisy had been painting for a few minutes when she sensed she was being watched. Surely no one could know she was here? It wasn't as if they'd been followed, she was certain of that. She surreptitiously surveyed the area across from where she was standing but couldn't see anyone at all. Then checking behind her, she spotted an elderly couple walking their Jack Russell on a lead.

'Paranoid,' she said to herself. She was standing right out in the open, on the wide walkway, so it wasn't as if anyone could creep up on her. She shook her head to dispel the ridiculous thoughts coursing through her head. She needed a few early nights then maybe this paranoia would go away.

She took a deep breath and continued with the first touches

of her painting. Within what seemed like seconds, Fi jogged up to her, only slightly out of breath.

'How's it going?' she asked. 'Phil's just called me on my mobile and asked if I could meet him down at Gorey for an ice cream. You can come too, if you like, or I could collect you in about an hour. It's up to you.'

Daisy didn't want to intrude on Fi's unexpected meeting with her new man and was perfectly happy working on her painting. 'No, I'm fine here. I can meet you back at the gate in about an hour, or whatever suits you best.'

Fi narrowed her eyes. 'I don't have your mobile number. If you give it to me, I'll call you when I'm leaving and that'll give you a chance to walk back to the car park to meet me.'

Daisy grimaced. 'Sorry, I don't have one.'

Fi laughed. 'Who doesn't have a mobile now? That's so odd, Daisy.'

'I did have one, but I lost it,' she said, not wishing to continue with the conversation.

'I had a friend who was standing outside a café down in Rozel when a seagull took her phone out of her hand, I think it thought she was holding up a piece of bread or something. She screamed but it dropped it in the sea and she never got it back. Bloody birds.'

Daisy smiled, unsure what to suggest. 'I can always catch a bus back to the hotel, rather than you coming back to fetch me,' she suggested.

Fi shook her head. 'No, it's fine. I'll go to meet him and jog back here to fetch you when I'm done. The exercise will do me good.'

'That's perfect, thanks,' Daisy said, grateful for the extra time to continue with what she was doing. 'I'll see you when you get back.'

'Great,' Fi said, turning to leave and texting as she walked away.

Daisy pushed a stray strand of hair away from her face and began working on her painting once again.

Sometime later while taking a break, she put her hand up to the back of her neck when suddenly another hand rested itself on top of hers. Daisy shrieked and spun round, horrified to see the one man she'd been avoiding for the past two years. He was standing so close to her she could feel his warm breath on her face.

'So this is where you've been hiding,' he said. 'You ran away from me once, to Vietnam of all places. I told you then that you wouldn't get away from me twice. You did try though, didn't you?'

She could barely catch her breath, the shock of seeing him standing in front of her was so great. It was like being in a nightmare. 'Aaron, I...'

'You what, Daisy?' he asked, breathing heavily, his voice calm yet with a suppressed rage she knew only too well could be unleashed at any second. 'You were looking for me here? You hoped I'd find you?' He raised a thick dark eyebrow. 'You thought you'd hide here away from me, didn't you? Admit it.'

She didn't know how to react. If only she'd agreed to go with Fi instead of standing here by herself. Why hadn't she listened to her instincts and not stayed out here where she could be watched?

'Even your hair's different,' he said. 'All those years dying it and cutting it short. Look at you now with your long, curly blonde hair.' He moved even closer, so his nose was almost touching hers. 'I'd recognise you anywhere, though.'

She swallowed in an attempt to moisten her dry mouth. Summoning up her courage, she braced herself. She was determined to brazen out this confrontation, however much she wanted to cover her face with her hands and cry. Hopefully someone would come by here soon, she thought. Hadn't Fi said that after the school run people would be bringing their dogs here?

Bolstered by that thought, she cleared her throat. 'We agreed things weren't working between us, Aaron,' she said, trying to keep her voice as strong and adamant as possible. Even saying his name out loud made her want to throw up. Everything he represented frightened her. So much for starting a brand-new life in Jersey.

The beautifully shaped lips she'd once found so attractive pulled back in a slow sardonic smile that chilled her to her core.

'I told you before your mother died that our relationship was over when *I* said it was, and not before.'

'You knew she died?' Daisy couldn't understand how. It wasn't as if her mother's death had been recorded in the local papers.

'I was at her funeral,' he said. 'Didn't you see me?'

She shivered. Thinking back to the rainy day when only a handful of kindly neighbours and her mother's nurse had attended the brief service before her body was cremated, she realised he must have been watching her then, too.

She stifled a cry. 'No, I didn't,' she admitted, wishing she could believe he was bluffing. The day had been a mixture of emotions with Daisy's heartache, and yet at the same time the relief that her mother was no longer suffering.

It dawned on her that he was waiting for her to say something, but what could she say? He always liked to think he was so clever, she mused, aware that she was trembling. Then it dawned on her. 'How did you know I was in Jersey?' she asked, unable to help feeling intrigued as well as terrified. If she was going to find a way to be rid of him then she needed to discover how he worked.

He tapped the side of his nose with one of his fingers. 'Now that would be telling,' he said, smiling. 'So, aren't you going to give your childhood sweetheart a kiss? Or is there someone else who you've been snogging behind my back?'

She moved her hand to behind her where her palette knife rested in her back pocket and touched the handle for comfort. 'I'm not seeing anyone and I'm not giving you a kiss,' she said, summoning up all her bravery to stand up to him. 'You might not like to think that our relationship is over, but it is. You shouldn't have raised your hand to me and now Mum's dead there's no one you can threaten to make me keep seeing you.'

'You came back from your jaunt to the east when you found out I'd been in touch with her though, didn't you?'

'You might have frightened Mum with your antics, but you don't scare me any more,' she lied, unable to hide her irritation with him for manipulating her sick mother.

'We both know that's crap,' he said looking smug. 'You soon came running back when your mother's neighbour asked you to, didn't you?'

'Yes,' she said, sickened at the triumphant tone in his voice. 'But only because I suspected she'd taken a turn for the worse, which she had, thanks to your threats. Now why don't you leave me alone and find someone who suits you far better than I ever did.'

'You loved me once, you can love me again.'

'Before you became controlling and tried to dictate everything about how I should behave,' she said, forgetting what he was capable of for a moment.

He touched her face with the tips of his fingers. She recoiled without thinking.

Aaron narrowed his eyes and stared at her. He bent his head, resting it hard against her forehead, and whispered, 'You're lucky

I've got to leave now, but don't think you can tell me what I will and won't feel about you. You're mine. You always were, and don't you forget it.' He stepped back. 'I'll see you again, but right now I'm supposed to be buying ice creams.'

He turned and walked away, laughing. Amused by his own actions as always, Daisy thought, nausea rising. How was she ever going to be truly rid of him? she wondered, panic-stricken. Spots danced in front of her eyes and her head pounded. For a moment she thought she was going to pass out.

She put her paintbrush down on her easel and went to sit on a nearby grassy verge. She bent forward and lowered her head between her knees. How had he found her here? She took a few deep breaths and wondered if maybe Jersey was too small a place for her to lose herself. She needed to go somewhere huge. A big city, perhaps? Wherever she chose it would have to be a busy place and somewhere he'd never think of looking for her.

Two women with small boys and a dog each walked up to her. 'You OK, love?' one of them asked, looking concerned.

Daisy forced a smile onto her face. 'Yes, thank you. Just a bit overtired maybe.'

'We've got a bottle of water if you need a drink,' offered the other woman.

'No, thank you. I've got a bottle in my bag,' Daisy said. She stood up as if to reassure them that she was fine, and satisfied they both continued with their walk.

Checking around her to see that Aaron wasn't coming back again, she picked up her paintbrush and palette and set to work on her picture. She didn't want anyone knowing what had happened. It was far too humiliating. She decided that the best thing to do was to carry on with her painting, so that she could have something to show for her time here when Fi did return to collect her.

Her hand was shaking, so she took a few deep breaths to try and calm down so that she could have control over her movements on the canvas. Why couldn't he just leave her alone and move on? she wondered. Hadn't they endured enough dramas together for one lifetime? She swallowed the lump forming in her throat and tried not to give in to the despair that seeing him once again had made her feel.

She focused on the view ahead and her half-painted canvas and it seemed like no time at all when Fi ran up, causing her to jump and drop her paintbrush on the grassy pathway.

'Oh, sorry, Daisy,' Fi said. 'I didn't mean to give you a fright. You must have been concentrating hard not to hear me calling you.'

The thought that she'd not heard bothered Daisy. If only she could manage to paint and stay remotely in the present to be able to hear what was going on around her, she thought. 'Sorry, I tend to become so involved in what I'm painting that I have no idea what's going on nearby,' she said, noticing how radiant Fi looked. 'You obviously had a lovely time with your new man.'

Fi nodded. 'I did,' she giggled. 'He's so hot and very naughty. We had an ice cream.'

Daisy wiped her brush on a piece of paper towelling, amused by her friend's enthusiasm. 'Getting an ice cream doesn't sound that naughty to me,' she said, unable to help smiling.

Fi winked at her, helping her pack up her things. 'I can't wait for you to meet him, he's gorgeous.'

They arrived back at the hotel and Fi dropped Daisy off and left to return to her brother's home. 'Don't forget you said you'd come to the fashion show tomorrow,' she said.

'Won't you want to take Phil instead of me?'

Fi shook her head. 'No, I can meet him afterwards,' she said. 'I doubt he'd appreciate the fashion as much as you would. Anyway

I want to chat about Paige's designs with you afterwards. I'm thinking of asking her to make me a bespoke pair.'

'How can I help?' Daisy asked, lifting her easel box and rucksack from the back of the car. 'I don't have any upmarket shoes.'

'Maybe not,' Fi said, glancing down at Daisy's flip flops. 'But you're creative and know colours, so you should be able to help me put together some ideas before I speak to Paige.'

Daisy liked the idea. 'Great, I'd love that,' she said. 'Right, I'll catch you later. I'd better take this painting to my room and let it dry if I'm not going to smudge it,' she said, relieved to have some time alone in her room where she could sit quietly and muse over her confrontation with Aaron.

She unlocked her bedroom door and entered, almost slipping on a note that had been pushed underneath her door. Daisy put away her paint things and rested the wet canvas against the small inbuilt dressing table before bending down to retrieve the piece of folded paper. Opening the note, she read, *I hope your friend was able to find you.* It was signed by one of the receptionists who'd been on duty.

Daisy sat heavily on her bed. She was sure they weren't supposed to give out staff details. She re-read the note, irritated that one of her colleagues had been careless enough to give a complete stranger details of her whereabouts, and decided to have a word with her when she next saw her. Now though, she needed time to gather herself and come to terms with the fact that Aaron had found her again. If he'd phoned here, then he knew she was living and working at the hotel. He was charming enough to glean information from the savviest of people, and Daisy decided that if she was going to get away from him, then she would need to find a way to do it that freed her from him forever.

14

DAISY

Refusing to let her new colleagues discover anything about her difficult past, Daisy put on a brave face and tried to push the image of Aaron threatening her at the dam to the back of her mind. The following evening, she was determined to enjoy the fashion show as she and Fi took their seats in the front row.

'I didn't expect to have tickets to sit here,' she whispered, as they placed their bags on the floor under their chairs. 'This is amazing.'

'I know, it's so cool.' Fi giggled. 'Paige is fabulous. She's the only one who manages to keep Seb in his place, and I can always rely on her to put my side of an argument across if he and I have fallen out about something.'

'Has he met Phil yet?' Daisy hoped Fi's brother didn't take a dislike to the man she was so besotted with.

Fi shook her head. 'Not yet, thankfully. Seb has been away and I'm trying to keep them apart for as long as possible. I don't need him to come down on me all serious and bossy.'

'I know he's probably annoying at times,' Daisy said, 'but I'd love to have an older brother to look out for me.' More than anything right now, she thought, but refrained from adding.

'Yes, you're right, but he forgets that I'm not a kid any more. I can make my own decisions.'

'I know, and he'll understand that one day.'

'You think?' Fi joked. 'Ooh look, I think they're about to start the show.'

The lights dimmed in the hall and lit up the runway. The chilled music changed to something far more dramatic and the show began.

Daisy was entranced. She hadn't expected such a small island to put on something as professional as she'd seen in magazines. The tall, angular models strutted down the runway, their bodies showing off the local designs, their feet encased in the most gorgeous shoes she'd ever seen. She noticed that each heel had a letter P embossed on it.

'Wow, those shoes are to die for,' she cooed, aware that she'd probably never have money to purchase a pair, never mind having anywhere to go to wear them. 'I can't wait to see the shoes she designs for you.'

'Me neither,' Fi said. 'Look at that jacket.' She pointed to a fuchsia pink cotton jacket being worn by one of the models. 'I can see me in that, can't you?'

Daisy smiled. 'Yes, I can,' she said, able to imagine her elegantly tall friend in almost every outfit she'd seen being shown.

A chill ran down her neck and Daisy glanced across the hall, thinking she'd seen someone who looked very much like Aaron amongst the seated crowd. She peered to get a better view, but realised she must have been imagining it. She hoped she wasn't going to start thinking she could see him everywhere she went. She loved this new home of hers and wanted to be able to explore all its beaches and walks, but knowing he could be around any corner was very unnerving.

The show ended and everyone stood to applaud the designers. Daisy watched as Paige walked down the runway, hand-in-hand with the clothes designer, both bowing at the end and smiling to their appreciative audience.

'She's great, isn't she?' Fi said, clapping harder as Paige walked past, giving her a wink when she spotted her and Daisy standing next to the runway.

'Do you want to try and go backstage to see the outfits?' Fi asked.

'You have to ask?' Daisy waited for Fi to go first and followed her, both trying to walk against the crowd as they slowly left the hall.

Eventually they made their way backstage, to be stopped by a burly guard. 'Sorry, ladies,' he said. 'Only those with passes are allowed back here.'

'It's OK,' Paige shouted, hurrying towards them. 'These two are family,' she said, hugging Fi and shaking Daisy's hand. 'You must be Daisy,' she said. 'Fi has told me so much about you. Didn't we meet briefly at the Encore party?'

'Yes, that's right,' Daisy said, pleased that Paige remembered her.

'Follow me and you can come and try on a few pairs of shoes. You'll need to get to them before my sister does; she's determined to persuade me to give her at least one pair.'

Daisy couldn't wait to try them on. She gasped in delight when they arrived at the selection of shoes and picking up a red patent pair, she examined them in awe.

'Try them on,' Paige said. 'See how they feel to walk in. I like to think that my shoes feel as good as they look.'

Daisy slipped off her sandals and stepped into the skyscraper heels. She so rarely wore high heels that at first it felt slightly surreal to be so tall. She was almost eye to eye with Fi who had yet to choose a pair.

'Well?' Paige asked. 'How are they?'

Daisy beamed at her. 'They're heavenly,' she said. 'I love how they're cushioned, especially at the ball of my foot.'

'Good, I'm glad. They suit you, too,' Paige said, staring down and admiring Daisy's slim feet in her heels. 'You'd make a great foot model.'

* * *

Buoyed by the fun she'd had at the fashion show, Daisy decided to put Aaron to the back of her mind and concentrate on her painting. She was also determined not to give Aaron another chance to surprise her and spent the rest of August making the most of Lydia's garden where she felt completely safe. She found new vantage points from which she could reproduce unusual and colourful views, and not once was she disturbed by anyone other than Lydia's gardener, or Lydia herself, asking her if she wanted to join her for lunch, a walk on the beach, or simply a chat.

She hadn't seen Fi for a few days, but was happy to accept her friend's invitation for her to spend an afternoon off sunbathing at her brother's house. She'd put on her bikini in preparation.

'He's away again for a few days,' Fi said, throwing towels onto three sunbeds and then straightening them out neatly. 'Take any one you like. I'll fetch some drinks.'

Daisy wasn't sure who else would be joining them and not wishing to lie in between friends, she took the sunbed furthest from the large doors into the living room. She stepped out of her shorts and T-shirt and lay down. 'This is wonderful,' she said to herself, looking around the white walls and pale cream tiled area surrounding the large rectangular pool. Taking the lid off a tube of sun cream, she began smoothing it over her skin.

Fi came back outside a short time later carrying a tray with a glass jug of Pimm's and three glasses. 'Phil wants to meet you,' Fi said. 'I've told him to come here and say hi. You don't mind, do you?'

Daisy shook her head. 'Of course not,' she said, excited to finally be meeting this mystery man Fi thought so much about.

Fi nudged her in the ribs. 'When your man comes back, you'll have him to drool over.'

Daisy wished Fi didn't presume that Gabriel was her anything; it only made her daydream and refresh the hope she had that one day they'd find a way to be together. 'Gabriel is not my man. Please don't ever say that sort of thing at the hotel, people might get the wrong idea.'

'I won't, don't worry,' she said, pouring two glasses of the dark amber liquid and popping a strawberry from the jug into each glass. 'Here you go, drama queen.'

Daisy took her glass and smiled. 'I'm not. Do you think Francesca would be happy if she thought I liked Gabriel?'

Fi sat down on the sunbed next to Daisy and took a sip of her drink.

'Yum. Listen, Gabriel is a grown man and I shouldn't think he's taken his mother's advice for years. And as far as Francesca's concerned, I think she'd be delighted if anyone managed to persuade her son to stay in Jersey. She doesn't show it too much, but I suspect she misses him just as much as Lydia does. What do you think?'

Daisy knew how much she missed him. 'Probably. She is his mother, after all.' She noticed Fi glancing at her watch. 'What time are you expecting Phil to arrive?'

'Any time now,' Fi said. 'Do you think I look OK in this bikini?'

she asked, staring down at her perfectly toned stomach. 'Or maybe I should wear one that doesn't show off quite so much of me.'

Daisy shrugged. 'I think you look great, but if you'll feel happier in something else then change.'

Fi considered her reply and stood up, placing her glass down on the small table between them. 'I'll be back in a couple of secs,' she said, running inside the house.

Daisy closed her eyes and dozed. She spent all her spare time painting and for once it felt good to simply lie in the sun and do nothing at all. She heard a sound next to her and smiled. 'You were quick.'

'I presume you mean someone else,' said a familiar deep voice, the sound of which made the tiny hairs on her arms stand to attention and her heart drop to the pit of her stomach.

Daisy opened her eyes and had to cover her mouth to stifle a scream. 'What are you doing here?' she asked Aaron, seeing him sitting on Fi's sun lounger, his feet up and hands resting behind his head as he lay back. 'You can't just waltz into people's homes whenever you choose,' she said, recalling how he had done just that at her mother's small flat on several occasions, frightening them both. His uninvited visits had ended up with her mother insisting Daisy travel to Vietnam to try and stay away from him until he lost interest in her. She'd only agreed to go away because it was so out of character for her mother to want her to do something like that. Her heart ached at the thought that this obsessive fool, who she'd once thought to love, could still be chasing her so long after she'd ended their relationship.

'I've been invited, just like you, sweet Daisy,' he said, his voice so soft and loving it made her blood run cold. 'Aren't you pleased to see me here?' Confused, Daisy opened her mouth to retaliate but Fi stepped outside. Instead of her looking shocked to see this stranger in her brother's home, she beamed and ran over to greet him. 'Phil, you're here,' Fi shrieked.

He lifted her up and swung her around, winking at Daisy as she crossed his line of vision. 'I've just been making friends with Daisy here,' he said. 'You never told me she was this pretty.'

Daisy couldn't believe it.

He put Fi back down and instantly Daisy noticed that her friend's expression had changed. Why is she glaring at me like that, Daisy wondered?

He took Fi's hand and led her over to the bar area. 'This is delicious,' he said. 'Can I have a glass?'

Fi smiled at him, though Daisy noticed it seemed forced. She was pouring the liquid into the spare glass when he added, 'Daisy kindly let me have a sip of hers. It's delicious.'

'What?' Daisy couldn't believe his cheek. He was so obviously trying to cause friction between them, but she hoped Fi knew her well enough to see through his nastiness. He gave her a sly smile over the rim of his glass when he took a mouthful of his drink, and to Daisy's horror Fi noticed and glared at her.

Unsure what to do next and aware that he was well-practised when it came to being calculating, she tried to think of the best way to counteract his plan. Failing and hating the way Fi was being upset by his actions, Daisy stood up.

'Fi, this man you know as "Phil" is actually an ex of mine. His real name is Aaron and he's been stalking me for three years.'

Aaron shook his head, his eyebrows knitted together and his mouth dropped open momentarily. 'Seriously? Are you quite all right, um, Daisy, is it?'

She pushed passed him and stood facing Fi. 'Can we have a quiet chat, just the two of us?' she pleaded, desperate to stop this nonsense before they were drawn more deeply into it.

Fi stared at her as if she'd never seen her before. 'Why are you doing this, Daisy?' she asked, her voice cracking with emotion and her eyes filling with tears.

Aaron walked up to stand at Fi's side. 'Maybe Daisy is a little jealous,' he said, giving her a pitiful look. Daisy wanted to slap his smug face but didn't have the courage, and knew from experience that he was far stronger than she was. She clenched her fists in an attempt to restrain herself from doing anything that could incite the situation further. Why wasn't Fi listening to her? Surely she didn't believe the nonsense Aaron was saying?

'Shut up, Aaron,' Daisy snapped. 'I know your nasty little games.' She focused her attention on Fi. 'He's making this up,' she said, reaching out to place her hand on Fi's shoulder.

Fi shied away from her touch. 'I think you should go, don't you?' she said. 'I'm not sure why you're acting so crazily, but I won't stand here and let you cause trouble between me and my boyfriend.'

Daisy sighed. 'OK, I'll go,' she said, going to put on her T-shirt and shorts and slipping her feet into her flip flops. She picked up her sun cream. 'But I'm telling you, I know him as Aaron. We were childhood sweethearts until his unreasonable behaviour pushed me to the brink. He's far nastier than he seems, I promise you. He did things to me that left me no option but to get away from him.' She could see Fi wasn't convinced. 'Fi, he might seem gentle and kind to you, and he was to me, too, at one time, but he's also hit me.'

Fi glared at Aaron. 'Is this true?'

He shook his head. 'Fi, darling, how well do you know this woman? Seriously. You can choose to believe her if you want, but you know me well enough to trust me, surely?'

He looked and sounded so convincing, Daisy could see Fi was shocked and unsure who to trust. He was right, Fi didn't know her well. 'Listen,' Daisy said. 'I know it sounds obnoxious, but he's only seeing you to get closer to me, to pay me back for leaving him.'

Fi gasped. 'Stop it, Daisy!' she shouted. 'I don't know why you're doing this to me. Can't you be pleased that I've found someone I like?' She turned her head away, staring out onto the wooded garden. Aaron put his arm around her shoulder and gave Daisy a smile that was so chilling in its confidence she knew she would have to find a way to help Fi discover the depths of his cruelty for herself.

Daisy reached the door to go back into the house and turned to Fi. 'I wish I could convince you to trust me. Please though, don't trust anything he says,' she said, before walking into the house and out of the front door. When she was sure she was far enough away from the house, she fell back to rest against the granite wall and cried.

Gathering herself, she decided to walk back to the hotel, hoping it wasn't too far. She needed time to think things through. Hadn't Aaron managed to tarnish too many years of her life already? She liked Fi, and despite her friend's reticence to believe what she'd told her about him, Daisy couldn't bear to think of him using her friend to get back at her. She had to do something, but what?

By the time she walked up the hotel driveway and around the back of the building to the staff quarters over an hour later, Daisy was so furious that she hadn't come up with a reasonable solution she failed to notice the person standing by the doorway. She marched inside and up the hallway stopping in front of her bedroom door to find the key lurking deep in her bag.

'Daisy?' a deep voice said. 'Are you all right?'

It took a second to register that Gabriel had just spoken to her. She spun round to face him. He opened his mouth to add something, but overcome with delight at seeing him standing there so unexpectedly, she bounded towards him and hugged him tightly. Resting her head against his chest, she sighed heavily.

'I'm so glad to see you,' she murmured, as his arms tightened around her back.

They stood silently for a few moments. She could feel his heart pounding rapidly and it dawned on her that her welcome was a little out of character and might have seemed a bit odd. She dropped her arms away from him and stood back.

'Sorry about that,' she said, clearing her throat. 'I'm just so pleased to see you.'

'Is everything OK?' he asked, frowning. 'You seem a little, erm, overwrought.'

Remembering where she was, she motioned for him to follow her. 'Please come into my room for a moment, there's something I need to tell you.'

He didn't reply but waited for her to unlock her door and followed her into her room.

'Sit down,' she said, indicating the only chair in the room. 'I'm afraid I've only got water to drink.'

'It's fine,' he said. 'I don't need anything.' He peered over across the room to where her canvasses were stacked against the wall in two batches. 'Are those your paintings?'

She could see even he thought that was a silly question and smiled. 'No, they're my shoe collection.'

He pulled a face at her. 'Could I have a look at them, do you think?'

She frowned. She wasn't ready to share them. They were far too personal to her and anyway, she mused, what if he hated what he saw?

'Stop thinking up reasons why not and say yes,' he said, waiting patiently.

'Fine, go on then.' She took a few strands of hair and twisted them through her fingers as he silently pulled back one, then another and finally all of her paintings.

He lifted two paintings and laid them on the bed. 'Would you mind if I took some photos of them?'

'What for?' She stood up, ready to retrieve them from him, but he stared at her. 'What?'

'Daisy, you're an excellent artist but you're shy. Who knows when I'll ever get another chance to see these again? I'd like pictures of them so that I can look at them again later. Would you mind if I showed my grandmother?'

She thought back to the times Lydia had come up to chat to her and look at her canvases while she painted. 'No, I don't mind you showing her.'

'Let me photograph more of them,' he said, replacing the two he'd extracted and replacing them with others.

She watched his broad shoulders as he bent down over her canvases. She felt so safe with him around. It dawned on her that the only other time she'd ever felt this relaxed was when they were on the other side of the world.

'There, that should do it,' he said.

'You must have photographed them all,' she said, waiting for him to sit back down again.

'Damn, what's wrong with me?' he said. 'I come here because something's the matter and end up taking photos of your paintings.' He stared at her. 'You wanted to tell me something,' he said, frowning. 'What's happened and how I can help?'

She sat down on the edge of her bed. She needed to share her fears with someone. He listened with intent silence as she told him all about Aaron; how they'd met at school and how he'd changed from a loving, caring boyfriend into a paranoid stalker.

'His behaviour worsened the more my art took off. I had a few pieces in the local papers. He kept putting it down, saying things like they were only writing about me because there was nothing else to feature in the paper, that I shouldn't take any notice because what the hell did they know about art, and so on.' She shivered at the memory of what she was about to share next. 'At first we'd argue and I'd stand up for myself, but then he started to hit me.' She heard Gabe groan, but continued. 'I didn't dare argue with him after that. He began turning up at Mum's place at odd times late at night or very early in the morning on some bizarre pretext that he didn't even try to make plausible. I was terrified of Mum working out what was going on. I didn't know how to make him stop and I couldn't let her see me with bruises. She had enough to contend with, what with her being so unwell.'

'Daisy, that's horrific,' he said, moving towards her.

She shook her head. 'Please, just listen. If I stop telling you I might be too embarrassed to start again.'

He sat down and waited silently for her to continue.

'I know I sound pathetic.'

'You don't.'

She closed her eyes briefly. 'It all came to a head when I was offered my own exhibition. Aaron tried to persuade me that I'd humiliate myself if I put my paintings on display, but I'd painted my whole life and this was what I'd wanted more than anything. We rowed, he hit me, but this time I decided that I was going to stand up for myself and go through with the exhibition. It meant too much to me not to.' She shrugged. 'And anyway, Mum would never have understood if I'd turned down such a dream offer.' She could see he was shocked by the things she was confiding in him but had to hope that he believed her more than Fi had done.

'Go on,' he said, his voice gentle.

'Well, the day of the exhibition came and Aaron initially refused to go, which had been a relief. Even Mum managed to make it along with her carer who kindly brought her along in a wheelchair.' Her voice wavered at the thought of her mother's proud face as the mayor gave a speech about her being a future star of the art world. She coughed to clear her throat. 'The man who'd arranged the exhibition then said a few words, ending with an announcement that he was offering to exhibit my art at his showroom in London later that year. I didn't realise that Aaron had come to the exhibition but just as the announcement was made he began shouting about how ridiculous it all was, how my paintings were amateurish and how I'd only go and let the guy down by not coming up with the paintings he'd need for the London exhibition.' She hesitated. 'Which in the end I did, by running away. Everyone was stunned by Aaron's outburst and my mother's perfect evening was ruined. The mayor shouted for him to leave, but Aaron raced up to me before anyone could stop him and took hold of one of my wrists, squeezing so hard I thought he'd break it.' She rubbed her wrist recalling the intense pain he's caused that night.

'He smiled at me and whispered that I'd better run, and run fast if I didn't want him to do something that would ruin my life and that of my mother's, and that if he thought I'd caused trouble that night I hadn't seen anything yet. Two guests who also knew him and thought he'd either gone mad or was drunk, grabbed hold of him and took him home. I believed what he'd told me though, and when I turned to look at my mum I could see that she'd been harbouring her own suspicions about him. We spoke later at home. We were both scared. She told me to leave and so I did.'

Daisy continued, telling Gabe about thinking she'd seen Aaron the last time they'd spoken on the beach near Lydia's house and how he'd confronted her at Queen's Valley. Then she added, 'My mum was terrified of him and his unexpected appearances at our flat. She was the one who insisted I go travelling in the vain hope that he'd tire of following me and move on. He didn't, of course. Now he's set his sights on Fi. She's obviously got close to him in the last few weeks and although it hurt when she believed him over me, I suppose she doesn't really know me or that I'd never do the things he was accusing me of. I just don't know what to do next, but I do know that she needs to get away from him. He seems even more crazy now than he did before and it frightens me,' she said, waiting for Gabriel to answer her.

He stared at her thoughtfully. She could see the muscles working in his jaw and could tell he was enraged on her behalf. As he sat there, she calmed down. It had been good to share her troubles with someone who believed her, someone she could trust.

'I'm so sorry you've had to deal with this by yourself, Daisy,' he said. 'But you're not alone now. I think the first thing we need to do is tip off her brother. I don't know Sebastian Fielding well, but I do know how protective he is of his sister and there's no way he'd let this sly bastard use her to get back at someone else.'

Daisy agreed, relief flooding through her to have him backing her. 'Yes, but what if Fi can't see through him?'

'We'll have to make sure she does, somehow.' He rubbed his unshaven chin. 'Don't fret, Daisy, we'll resolve this. Let me think about this for a bit.'

'Thanks, Gabe,' she said, grateful to him for believing her so willingly. It dawned on her that she hadn't asked him about his project. 'How is everything with you? Were you able to source finance to continue with your work?'

'A little, but only enough to finish the first stage, which we've now done. I've had to wrap everything up for now though, so I'm back here for a bit.'

'I'm sorry it didn't work out as you'd hoped,' she said, feeling guilty for being so pleased to see him.

'Not everything was a dead loss though,' he said. 'I was hoping you and I could go out for a walk later. There's something I want to tell you.'

'Can't you tell me now?'

He smiled and shook his head. 'Not yet. Shall we meet at the front of the hotel at, say, five?'

She nodded. 'I'd like that,' she said, delighted that her upsetting afternoon was turning into a much happier day than she'd expected.

He stood up and held out his arms. 'Can I give you another hug?'

Daisy couldn't help smiling as she stepped into his outstretched arms. 'Of course.'

It felt so good to be held by him once again. An image of Bella began forming in her mind, but she pushed it away. She wasn't doing anything wrong and right now she barely cared.

He put a finger under her chin and lifted her face to smile at her. 'It's good to see you again, Daisy.'

'It's good to see you, too,' she said.

'And you mustn't worry. We'll find a way to sort this out, I promise you. I'll go and give Sebastian a call, see what he says.'

15

GABRIEL

Gabriel was aware he was probably crossing the line by calling Fi's brother. His parents probably wouldn't approve, but he felt responsible for a young member of his staff and didn't wish to ask anything further of Daisy until she'd had a chance to come to terms with everything that had happened. He went to his office, closed the door and sat down to call Sebastian. The mobile number rang for a while and he was about to cut off the call when he heard a voice say, 'Sebastian Fielding, hold on one minute please.'

Gabriel waited while Sebastian spoke to someone.

'Sorry about that,' he said. 'I was just filling up with petrol.'

'I don't mean to interrupt you. I can call back if you're driving,' Gabriel said.

'No, not at all, I've come up from the South of France and am almost at the end of this drive, so I could do with something else to think about. Anyway, I've got the phone on hands free, so please carry on.'

'It's Gabriel Wilson here, your sister Fi works on the reception at my parents' hotel.' Gabriel heard Sebastian clear his throat.

'Is my sister all right?' he asked, the panic obvious in his tone.

'Yes, she's fine,' Gabriel said hurriedly, not wishing to worry him unnecessarily. 'But there's something I think you'd want to know.' He hesitated. 'Look wouldn't you rather call me back when you're not driving?'

'No, please continue.'

Sebastian explained about Aaron and how he'd stalked and threatened Daisy and how he was now using Fi to get back at her for leaving him. 'He hasn't done anything to Fi as yet, but I thought you'd want to know that he's hanging around and Fi seems to be getting quite close to him.' He spoke in more detail, filling Sebastian in on the things Daisy had told him about the man.

There was a brief silence. 'Thank you for telling me. I'll call my butler now – he'll know what to do and he'll ensure nothing untoward happens to my sister. And Gabriel?'

'Yes?'

'Thank you for taking the time to call me. I appreciate it.'

'No problem. Daisy will be relieved to know that I've been able to contact you.'

'I'm just outside Dinard now, so will be home in about two hours. I'd appreciate it if you have a chat with my sister as soon as you can; she needs to be put in the picture about this idiot. You can tell her I know and I'll sort this out as soon as I get back.'

Gabriel ended the call and rubbed his face with his hands. It was a relief that Sebastian had listened so readily to what he had to tell him. Not wishing to alert Fi to anything before she was in his office, he gave her a call at reception and asked her to come through as soon as possible.

She entered the room a short while later and took the proffered seat on the other side of the desk, looking a little concerned. 'This feels a little official,' she said, forcing a smile.

'Don't worry, it's not about the hotel.'

Her perfectly shaped eyebrows knitted together. 'What is it about then?' she asked. Then narrowing her eyes, added. 'It's about Phil, isn't it? Daisy's been saying things.' She went to stand up.

'Sit down, Fi,' Gabe snapped, tired of her blaming Daisy for something she wasn't guilty of. 'I've just got off the phone with your brother.'

'Why?' she asked nervously, but remaining seated. 'What have I done?'

'It's not you,' Gabe said, his voice gentle once more. 'It's Phil. He's not who he says he is. He's Daisy's ex-boyfriend Aaron who's trying to pay her back for leaving him when he got a bit too...' He tried to think what to say without frightening her. 'Intense.'

'Intense?' she glared at him. 'What's that supposed to mean? He's been caring and interested in what I've been doing, but that's because he likes me. I wouldn't call that intense.'

Gabe wished he didn't have to go into detail about Daisy's past, but needed Fi to listen and grasp what sort of guy she was getting herself involved with. He contemplated for a few seconds how much he should say next. 'I don't know what Daisy has told you about her reasons for leaving Devon, but they have a lot to do with Aaron.'

Fi narrowed her eyes. 'You mean Phil. Go on.'

'His real name is Aaron, whatever you choose to believe,' he said, becoming exasperated at her determination not to take in what he was trying to tell her. 'He and Daisy had known each other since they were teenagers but had been seeing each other as a couple. Daisy had been gaining more recognition for her paintings and eventually was given her own exhibition.' He wished he didn't have to go on and hoped that Daisy would understand why he was confiding so much in Fi.

'Go on,' she said, nibbling at one of her fingernails.

Relieved to finally have her full attention but not daring to go any further with Daisy's story, he said, 'Put it this way, he ended up becoming violent and did some things that made it impossible for her to stay in her hometown. Her mother felt the same way and persuaded Daisy to leave without him knowing.'

'Violent? What did he do?' Fi frowned.

'You'll need to ask her, but he eventually made a spectacle of himself in front of a room full of others at an exhibition, not just in front of Daisy, so it isn't just her word against his. I'm afraid you're going to have to ask her the rest. It's her story to tell and I think I've said enough. I just need you to listen to me and be warned about this guy.'

Fi sighed. 'I suppose if you've been speaking to my brother about this then you really are concerned about me.'

He nodded. 'I didn't mean to go behind your back but I was worried that unless someone intervened you could get hurt.'

Fi nodded. Her shoulders drooped and she crossed her legs, resting her elbows on her knees. 'If I'm perfectly honest I think I knew deep down that he was too good to be true, but didn't want to hear it. I feel stupid for not believing Daisy.' She looked up at him. 'Daisy isn't a liar. I should have accepted what she told me instead of listening to that creep.'

He stood up, walked around to her side and rested his hand on her shoulders. 'Don't be too hard on yourself. Daisy said he was very convincing when he wanted to be. She doesn't feel badly towards you, just concerned that he'll push things too far and you'll get hurt.'

Fi shook her head. 'I feel such a fool.'

'Don't. We're just relieved you're listening and are now aware of what he's up to.'

She stood up and gave him a brief hug. 'Thanks, Gabe, I really appreciate you bothering enough about me to contact my brother and speak to me like this.'

'No problem at all.' He stepped away from her and held open the office door. 'Now you'd better get back to reception and let Daisy know you're aware about Phil, or Aaron, or whatever he's calling himself now.'

'I'm a little nervous,' she said. 'He knows I'm working a shift now and might come here to find me.'

'It's fine. Once you've spoken to Daisy I'll give you a lift home. He won't expect you to be there and you can lock yourself in until your brother returns. I'm only down the road and a phone call away, and can come over at any time if you need me to.'

16

DAISY

Later, Daisy greeted Gabriel with a kiss on his cheek. He took her hand, and not wishing to appear uptight she forgot about the staff and let him lead her away from the hotel. They walked down the drive and along the road, crossing a short while later to the headland with the beach below.

'Fi phoned from her brother's home to let me know she was OK. Did you get hold of Sebastian?' she asked, intrigued to discover what had been said.

'I did, eventually. He's travelling back from the South of France and wasn't impressed with what I had to tell him.' They walked down several steps onto the fine golden sand. Daisy and Gabriel took off their shoes and left them behind a rock.

'Will he be returning here soon?' she asked, concerned at the thought of Fi being alone in the house with Aaron out there somewhere.

'Sebastian said he was just outside of Dinard, so near to the ferry. He should be back soon and said he'd come straight here. Apparently he has a butler at the house who'll keep an eye on Fi, so we shouldn't worry too much.' Gabriel looked down at her and gave her a reassuring smile. 'I got the impression the butler might be getting on a bit, but that he's more than capable of handling most situations.'

Daisy sighed with relief. 'Good, because I can't imagine her letting me back into the house. She really was disappointed in me, Gabe. It was horrible.'

'If you think I should pop round there and check up on her, tell me and I will.' He gave her hand a gentle squeeze. 'Sebastian did reassure me though. I spoke to Fi a little earlier at the hotel and she's tougher than you think, despite believing that slimy boyfriend of hers up until now.'

'Do you mean you told her all about him and she believed you?'

He nodded. 'She was a little embarrassed too, so be prepared for her being a tad uncomfortable around you for a bit.'

Daisy, feeling much better now that Sebastian was on his way back and that he and Gabriel weren't too worried, relaxed slightly.

They rounded a corner and Gabriel pulled at her hand, making her run with him into the mouth of a cave.

'Where are we?' she giggled, surprised.

'We're alone and now I can tell you something.'

'Go on,' she said, barely able to contain herself. 'What is so important that you couldn't tell me earlier?'

He took out a folded piece of paper from his back pocket. 'This is a certificate,' he said, unfolding it and handing it to her.

She studied it, frowning in confusion when she read his and Bella's names. She didn't want to read it but he'd been so good to listen to her and to speak to Sebastian that she thought it was the least she could do for him.

'But this looks like a... well, a marriage certificate. Why are you showing this to me?' She scowled at him and handed the certificate back.

'It's divorce papers. Bella and I managed to get a divorce,' he said, smiling widely at her. His handsome face seemed to be lit from inside somehow and it took Daisy a few seconds to register what he was telling her.

'But I thought you told me that you had to be married for three years in Jersey before getting a divorce.'

'That's right,' he grinned.

'So what's changed?' She was getting a little annoyed by his cheerfulness. 'They can't have updated the law to suit us in the last few weeks.'

He shook his head. 'No, but my lawyer reminded me that we weren't married here, but in South Africa. So when I went back to the project, I stopped over in Durban with Bella, and we saw a lawyer who set the papers in motion, and now we're officially divorced.'

'Seriously?' she asked, snatching back the certificate to have a better look at what it said. Gabriel and Bella were divorced. 'You're a single man?'

He laughed and pulled her into his arms. 'Yes, I am. So, Daisy Woods, can you now agree to come out with me, so that we can rekindle the amazing relationship we shared in Vietnam?'

She couldn't help smiling up at him. Daisy reached up and pulled his head down so that she could kiss him. 'Abso-bloody-lutely,' she said, kissing him again, astounded that he'd gone to such lengths to make her happy.

When they stopped to take a breath, Gabriel said, 'I've missed you so much. It's nearly driven me mad being so close to you but not being able to be with you.'

'Me too,' she admitted, stunned that her day had gone from one extreme to the other.

'Bella's coming to the hotel this evening to speak to you,' he said, as they held each other.

'Why?' She didn't have anything against Bella, but didn't see why they should meet for a chat.

'I asked her to, in case you didn't believe what I was telling you now.'

She loved that he wanted to make sure she understood how things could now stand between them. 'Fine, I'll see her,' she said.

They began walking back along the beach, hand in hand. She opened her mouth to tell him how happy she was when she spotted Aaron waiting for them by the rock where they'd left their shoes. She could see he had picked up hers.

'What are you doing here?' she asked, her happiness evaporating as he grinned at them. 'Haven't you caused enough trouble for one day?'

'Who's this?' Aaron asked rudely, standing up to sneer at Gabriel.

Gabriel let go of Daisy's hand and put an arm protectively around her shoulders. 'I'm Gabriel, Daisy's boyfriend.'

Any pretence at friendliness vanished from Aaron's face. 'How come I haven't seen you around then?'

Gabriel frowned. 'Not that it's any of your business, but I've been away. However, I'm back now and I'm not going anywhere, so if you've got an issue with that, or with Daisy, then speak to me. Daisy's told me all about you and your... fascination with her. Things have changed now and you can move on.'

'Don't you come all high and mighty with me.' Aaron hesitated. 'I don't suppose Daisy told you about our incident earlier today. She made a bit of a fool of herself over me at Fi's home.'

Daisy went to argue, but Gabriel tightened his hold slightly. Comforted, she relaxed a little.

'She told me what happened,' Gabriel said. 'But unsurprisingly her version is different to yours. I'm inclined to believe my girlfriend. So, if you don't mind, we'll take our shoes and get on.'

He took Daisy's shoes from Aaron and passed them to her before leaning past him and picking up his own shoes.

'I don't expect to see you hanging around her again,' Gabriel added, stopping to give Aaron a threatening glare.

Typical bully, thought Daisy as they walked off arm in arm. Can't help trying to terrorise someone smaller than him, but when Gabriel comes along he stands there looking all pathetic. She resisted looking back at her ex and put her arm around Gabe's waist.

'Goodbye, Aaron,' she said. 'If I see you again I'll report you to the police. Enough people have met you now to know what you look like, so it won't be difficult to trace you here.'

'She makes a good point,' Gabriel said. 'This is a small island where everyone knows everyone else and their business, so you'd be wise to consider that fact before coming back here again.'

They began walking. Daisy's legs felt like lead and she was sure that it was only Gabriel helping her that enabled her to move.

'I hope he does keep away,' she said, once they'd walked about a hundred yards away from him. Then a frightening thought struck her. 'What about Fi?'

'I'm sure Sebastian will have a few things to say to him if he bothers her again,' Gabe said, giving her a gentle squeeze. 'If not, then we'll have to think of something else.'

'Thank you,' she said, hating that she couldn't manage to sort Aaron out by herself.

'It's fine. Sometimes we all need to ask for help, even though we don't like to.'

She could tell he was referring to his project. 'What are you going to do?'

'I'm not sure,' he said quietly. 'But I'll work it out somehow. Right now, I just want to be certain you're OK and that he doesn't bother you again.'

She glanced over her shoulder, relieved to see no sign of Aaron. Then focusing her attention back on Gabriel, Daisy had to resist suggesting he ask Lydia for a loan. She sensed that she was the last person Gabriel would accept money from though, so said nothing. His parents worked to keep their hotel going. She wished she could think of a way to help him.

Playing over what Gabriel had said to Aaron, Daisy asked, 'Did you mean what you said back there?' They began walking up the stairs to his grandmother's garden. 'About everyone in the island knowing everything about everyone's business?'

He shook his head and laughed. 'It is hard to keep a secret here sometimes,' he said, pulling her to him in a soothing hug. 'But no, there are approximately ninety-nine thousand people living here and we couldn't all possibly know what everyone is doing. I should think it was probably like that in the earlier part of the twentieth century though. Then there were people who didn't leave their parish. It was a much closer community and I doubt you could get away with much. They'd certainly notice a stranger.'

'So how will we know if Aaron does come back?'

He kissed the top of her head. 'You're not the only one who knows what he looks like now, or how he behaves. You're safe here, Daisy.'

The relief of having someone on her side, who she didn't have to look out for, or protect against Aaron, was immense. 'Thank you. I used to have trust in my abilities to control my privacy, but he somehow manages to get close to me whenever he wants and I can't seem to find a way to stop him.'

'You're not on your own now though, Daisy,' Gabe said. 'It's time for you to relax and enjoy being here on this lovely island. You're one of us now, Daisy, and we look after our own.'

Daisy was trying to find a way to get Fi to speak to her. The atmosphere since their shift had begun was making them both miserable and she'd had enough. She opened her mouth to speak, but upon hearing footsteps she looked up to see a tall, dark man in a grey suit walking with an air of confidence into the hotel.

'Hello, Sebastian,' she said, thinking how immaculate he always appeared.

He stopped in front of the reception desk. He smiled at his sister and then looked at Daisy. 'Good to see you again, Daisy. I wanted to pop in and thank you for helping Fi.'

Daisy didn't look at Fi. She might have been proved right to accuse Aaron like she had, but she sensed that Fi was still a little crushed by the whole episode and knew better than most how it felt to have been humiliated by his web of lies.

'Is Gabriel around?' Sebastian asked. 'I was hoping to speak to him personally and thank him for phoning me and letting me know what was going on.'

'Do you have to do that now?' Fi asked, blushing. 'I'm sure he's busy.'

'He is,' Daisy agreed. 'He'll be in a meeting for the next half an hour or so.'

Fi looked around the hallway and leant forward. Lowering her voice, she added, 'He's trying to raise funds to keep his project going, and I don't think he's having much luck.'

'Project?' Sebastian frowned. 'Why don't you tell me a little about it?'

Not sure how much Gabriel would want them to say, Daisy decided that he needed help and if Sebastian Fielding could possibly help then she was willing to take Gabriel's irritation if she ended up inadvertently saying too much.

'If you come around here quickly,' Fi said, waving him to the other side of the reception desk, 'I'll show you Gabriel's website. It's fascinating. He's done so much stuff. Have you seen any of this yet, Daisy?' she asked, addressing Daisy for the first time that day.

'No,' Daisy said, relieved that Fi was being friendly once again. She wondered why she'd never thought to look up Gabriel's website for herself. Seeing it now, Daisy couldn't believe how impressive Gabriel's work was. No wonder he was devoted to it. He'd really done a lot to help others, she noted. As well as his current programme there were volunteer researcher and conservation posts for students and others wishing to gain experience and internships. 'This is much bigger than I'd expected,' she whispered.

Fi clicked on the page showing Gabriel's previous expeditions and projects. 'Look, he's pretty well-known.'

He was. Daisy couldn't take it in. She wasn't sure what she'd expected to see, but it was nothing of this scale. She could see Sebastian's interest had been piqued and said, 'He really is passionate about what he does, and it's so worthwhile, too.'

Sebastian didn't say anything. He rested his palms on the desk next to his sister and studied each page as Fi moved through them.

'Click on the present and future projects,' he said. 'Let's have a look at those.'

After reading through all the pages on Gabriel's website, they had a brief chat and Sebastian handed Daisy a business card.

'Please give this to Gabriel and ask him to give me a call. I've got a proposition for him.'

Daisy nodded and took the card, concentrating on not letting her excitement show. She barely dared to hope that Sebastian would offer Gabriel sponsorship for his project. 'Thank you, I will.'

They watched him leave. Daisy read his card and put it on her desk so that she wouldn't forget to pass it to Gabriel when he came through reception.

'Thanks, Daisy,' Fi said quietly.

Daisy knew this was the moment they needed to discuss what had happened between them. Part of her dreaded it, but she also wanted to clear the air between them and get back to how they'd been before Aaron's arrival in Jersey.

'I'm so sorry you had to get caught up in his snide mind games,' she said. 'I don't even think he fancies me any more. I suspect it's more that he's so used to following me and tormenting me that he didn't know how to stop.'

'I've no idea what Seb said to him,' Fi said, pulling a face. 'But I know that the shock of him arriving home a day earlier than we'd expected and catching Aaron with his hand around my throat probably wasn't the best way for them to meet.'

'Oh Fi, that's horrible,' Daisy said, shocked to hear this news. 'He was probably taking Gabriel's put-down on the beach out on you. I'm so sorry.'

Fi absent-mindedly rubbed her throat, around which she'd loosely tied a scarf. 'It's fine now. He's gone and I have a feeling he won't be back in a hurry. The fact that he used to bother you and your mum only tells me that he picks on those he considers weaker than himself. Now he's met Gabriel and Sebastian, I can't imagine he'll be bothering either of us again in too much of a hurry.'

Daisy didn't care that they were on duty. She stepped closer to

Fi and gave her a tight hug. 'I'm so relieved we're friends again; I hated it when we fell out.'

'Thanks to the guys it wasn't for long,' Fi said. 'I feel such an idiot for believing some moron over you. I think I was a bit jealous by the things he was saying about you.' She sighed. 'I'm never going to believe a bloke over a friend again.'

They sat back down at the counter. 'Seb showed me the magazine that Aaron had in his rucksack after Sebastian had his driver take him to the airport and put him on a plane,' Fi said.

'Why? What was in the magazine?' Daisy had seen a few copies of *The Jersey Scene* since her arrival but couldn't understand how that might have got into Aaron's hands.

Fi lowered her voice. 'Apparently there was a write-up in one of the English newspapers about Jersey being the place to visit, great local seafood, loads of brilliant restaurants, that sort of thing. There was a picture of you in it. You were painting at Beauport and someone had taken your picture. They didn't put your name but Aaron noticed you. He was boasting about contacting the journalist who did the write-up and how he persuaded him to give him the photographer's email address. The guy probably had to listen to one of his convincing stories and eventually told him where you'd been painting. I suppose it was a process of elimination knowing you'd been a receptionist at a hotel before and tracking you down from that. After all, Beauport isn't far from here and it was somewhere you could walk to paint.'

'Sly bastard,' Daisy said, stunned at his resourcefulness. 'Mind you,' she said. 'If him coming here meant he's now been deterred from following me ever again, then it was probably worth it.'

'Too right,' Fi said. 'I still can't believe I was taking in by all his crap.'

Daisy sympathised completely. 'I've been where you are, so

don't feel guilty. Aaron is very plausible. He's good looking and can be so kind and funny. It's a shame he has this other, darker side.' She gave Fi a nudge. 'You're lucky your brother and Gabriel warned him off; I've had a nightmare with him for the last few years.'

She thought back to the times he'd barged his way into their flat, watching her as she tried to remain calm in front of her mother.

'He's sick,' Fi said. 'By the sounds of it I've had a close call with him.'

'You have,' Daisy said, relieved. 'I'm sure we've seen the back of him now.' She willed it to be the case. She couldn't bear the thought of having to keep watching over her shoulder any more.

'He's gone now,' Fi said, a concerned look on her face. 'But it must have been frightening having him turn up here and then lie like he did about you.'

'It was as if I'd fallen back into a nightmare,' she admitted, shivering at the thought of him.

'It must have been,' Fi agreed. 'He really is good looking,' she added thoughtfully.

'Who is?' Gabriel asked coming out of the hallway at the side of the reception area.

'Not you,' Daisy joked. 'Well, you are of course, but we weren't talking about you.'

'Oh, thanks.'

'Daisy, where's that thing?' Fi asked. She looked at Gabriel. 'You've just missed my brother. He was looking for you.'

'He was?' Gabriel asked, looking disappointed. 'That's a shame.'

Daisy held up the business card. 'He wanted me to give this to you and asked if you could call him. There's something he wants to discuss with you.'

Gabriel looked intrigued. 'OK, I'll call him now.'

The girls waited impatiently for him to speak to Sebastian.

'I saw your dad checked out earlier than expected,' Fi said. 'Did he say goodbye to you before he left?'

Daisy shook her head. 'No, but that's pretty typical of him. I don't think he was very pleased with my lack of interest in playing the dutiful daughter. I've never really spent much time with him and I don't really need to find a new parent at my age. Mum was the only parent I was ever close to and I'm happy with that.'

'You're lucky... I never knew my mum.'

Daisy opened her mouth to speak, but it took a few seconds for her to think what to say. 'Oh, Fi, I never knew that. Can I ask why?'

'She died just after I was born. My dad and then my uncle pretty much brought me up. With Seb's help, of course.'

Daisy was stunned. She'd assumed that Fi's life had always been fun and carefree. 'That's so sad.'

Fi gave her a vague smile. 'I suppose it's not as if I knew her to miss her, but I did envy my friends for their closeness with their mothers. You, for example – I know you said your mum was unwell but it must have been incredible to be everything to someone.'

Daisy thought back to the intensity of her relationship with her mother and smiled. 'I miss my mum, but living with her could feel suffocating a lot of the time,' she admitted.

'I suppose so,' Fi said. She thought for a moment. 'I didn't ever miss out on attention because I was always spoilt and loved by those around me. Even Harwood, Seb's butler, has always looked out for me. It would have been nice to have experienced having a mother, though.'

'Yes, I can imagine it would have been,' Daisy agreed.

Gabriel came off the phone from speaking to Sebastian.

'You'll never guess what Sebastian's offering to do,' he said, his eyes lighting up with excitement.

Daisy couldn't help laughing, relieved for the change in subject. 'Going by the look on your face, I think I can take a pretty good guess.'

'He's going to sponsor the rest of the project,' he said, shaking his head in amazement. 'He said he's always been interested in conservation, but up until now hasn't made the time to actually get involved.'

'I'm so thrilled for you,' Daisy said, delighted to see him so happy.

'Me too,' Fi said. 'I told you I had a wonderful brother.'

'Thanks, girls,' he said, giving Fi a kiss on the forehead and Daisy a kiss on the mouth. 'Things can get underway again.'

Daisy was thrilled for him, but a little saddened that she would have to say goodbye to him once again.

He must have noticed her expression change because he added, 'You're coming with me, I hope.'

'I can't,' she said. 'I have to finish the season here at the Encore.'

He leant over the reception desk and cupped her chin in his hand. 'I know, but the project won't get underway again until the end of September, so you'll be able to fly out with me. If you want to, that is.'

She squealed, forgetting where she was. 'Of course I want to come with you.'

'Good, then that's settled.'

'I'm so pleased for you both,' Fi said quietly behind them.

Daisy and Gabriel let go of each other and turned to face her.

'I'm sorry, Fi,' Gabe said. 'You're welcome to come out and visit any time you like, you do know that, right?'

Her face lit up. 'I'd love to.'

'Sebastian said he'd come out and see what we're doing and how it all works, so you could travel out with him. It'll be fun to meet up again. I'll be able to show you what I've been working towards.'

'How long will we be out there?' Daisy asked, unable to hide her rising excitement.

'For most of the winter months,' Gabe said. 'We should be back here in the spring, so if you want to work another season here at the hotel, you'll be back in time.'

Daisy couldn't believe how well everything was turning out. 'Perfect.'

Gabriel kissed her quickly, then frowned and stepped away after spotting someone over by the door. 'Here, sir,' he said to a grey-haired gentleman struggling with a large leather suitcase. 'Let me help you with that.'

Daisy returned to her desk and moved her mouse to light up the computer screen, ready to check the guest into the hotel.

Gabriel followed him the few steps to the reception counter. 'I'll leave your case here for you and go and let the porter know you've arrived,' he said, walking away.

'Good afternoon,' Daisy said. 'Welcome to the Encore. Do you have a reservation?'

'No,' he said. 'I, er, wish to book in.'

Daisy smiled at him. 'One moment, sir.' She quickly checked the availability. 'We have a twin room at the rear of the hotel overlooking the valley, and a double at the front of the hotel overlooking the pool and gardens.'

'I take the room at the back,' he said.

She had just watched the old man follow the porter to the lift when Gabriel returned to the reception. He smiled at Fi who was busily typing a letter. 'All right if I step outside with Daisy for a few minutes?'

'Um, of course,' she said, looking taken aback at the request.

Gabriel ignored Daisy's quizzical look and waited for her to join him at the front door. They walked outside towards the rose garden.

'What is it?' Daisy asked. 'Is everything OK?'

'Yes, it's fine,' he said, checking they were alone. 'Over here,' he said, indicating the row of huge pine trees planted years ago along the wall near the road.

They reached the middle pine tree and Gabriel stopped and faced her.

'What time do you finish your shift?'

Daisy checked her watch, wondering why he couldn't have asked her that inside the hotel. 'In twenty minutes.'

'Right, I'll phone Nan now and tell her that I'll be bringing you and Mum to her house because I've got something I want to tell you all. I'll then go and chat to Mum and tell her I'll come and get her shortly and then when you're finished meet me at the back of the hotel.'

'Won't they think it strange that I'm going to be there?'

He stared at her, his dark eyes intent. 'No,' he said, his tone insistent. 'I'll be telling them about Sebastian's funding of the project and about us planning a future together.'

'We are?' she asked, stepping up to him and hugging him tightly around his waist before he had time to answer.

Gabriel held her close to him, laughing. 'Yes. We've wasted enough time with all this messing around. I want to be with you and I'm fairly sure you feel the same. So, from now on we plan things that will allow us to spend time together.' He kissed the top of her head. 'They'll need something to cheer them up when I tell them about my return to South Africa.'

She nodded and let go of him. 'I'd better get back to reception before Fi thinks I've left already,' she giggled.

17

GABRIEL

It took a bit of persuasion to get Gabriel's mother to agree to leave the hotel earlier than she'd intended and go with him and Daisy to his grandmother's house, but she'd given in eventually.

'I don't know why this couldn't have been done over the phone,' she grumbled, giving Daisy an over the shoulder glance as if it was her fault Francesca had to leave her office.

He parked the car at his grandmother's and walked around to open the passenger door for his mother. 'I wanted you all here together. Surely that isn't so dreadful?'

She groaned, holding up a spreadsheet in one hand and a yellow highlighter pen in the other. 'No, of course not, darling. I'm just busy and I have a lot to do with your father away touring.'

They arrived at the house. Gabriel smiled at Daisy.

'Come along, then. Let's find Nan and get this over with.'

As they walked around the side of the house, he spotted Lydia sitting down at the metal garden table reading a magazine. Gabriel poured them all a refreshing glass of homemade lemonade from the jug on the table and sat down.

'Thanks for the hurried gathering,' he said, smiling at Daisy.

He noticed she looked concerned. He understood how his mother could make people feel a little intimidated, with her booming voice and extrovert personality. She needed to overcome any fear she had of his mother and this was going to be a bit of a baptism of fire, but he wanted Daisy here to witness him telling his mother and grandmother about them being a couple and to see first-hand that she was now part of his family unit.

'You all know that the funding of my project was rescinded unexpectedly,' he began.

'Yes, darling,' his mother said. 'I wish your father and I were in a position to help you in some way. We both know how important this is to you and how hard you've worked on this.'

'It's fine, Mum,' he said. 'I want you both to know that earlier today, Fi's brother, Sebastian Fielding, offered to sponsor the project.'

'Oh, darling!' Lydia clapped her hands together. 'That's splendid news. I knew his father and uncle when I was younger,' she said. 'We mixed in the same circles in the sixties and seventies.'

His mother beamed at him, as he knew she would on hearing this news. 'I'm delighted for you. You deserve his support. Well done, you.'

'Thanks, Mum.' He drank some of the tart lemonade, relishing its coolness. 'I don't know if you knew,' he said, glancing at his mother and grandmother. 'But on my recent trip to South Africa, Bella joined me and while we were there we got a divorce.' He heard his grandmother's sigh of relief and suspected she knew what was coming next.

'It seems a bit of a drama bothering to go to South Africa to do it.' Francesca said. 'Why didn't you just wait until you could be divorced over here?'

He thought she might react in this way. 'Neither of us really wanted to stay married, but couldn't divorce in Jersey until we'd been married three years. We both also needed to go there to check the situation with the project, and as both of us wanted this divorce as much as the other we made a point of sorting it out. We were married there so it wasn't too difficult.' He focused his attention solely on his mother.

'I still think it was a bit unnecessary to rush it like that, Gabriel,' his mother argued.

'I did it because I want to be with Daisy.'

'Daisy?'

His mother scowled at the woman he loved, and not wishing Daisy to feel uncomfortable, he added, 'Yes. We met in Vietnam when I was travelling. She knew about me coming from Jersey, but not where I lived, or that my family ran a hotel, so it was a coincidence when she ended up working for you.'

His mother didn't look too convinced. 'Really?' she asked, looking doubtfully at Daisy.

Daisy smiled. 'I'm sure this is all a bit of a shock,' she said. 'But I can assure you I had no idea about Gabriel's connection to the Encore when I applied to work there. I know him as Gabriel Wilson. You and your husband have different last names, so how could I connect him?'

He watched his mother considering this question and then shrugging. 'I can see how that's possible,' she said eventually. 'But I still don't see the urgency for a divorce.' She hesitated and then narrowed her eyes first in Daisy's direction and then Gabriel's. 'Unless, of course, there's a reason you haven't shared with us?'

It took a moment for him to register what she meant. Knowing how she wasn't ready to be a grandmother, he knew that she wasn't making this assumption with any joy in her heart. He glared at her. 'There's only one reason: I'm in love with Daisy and want to be with her.'

'Do leave the boy alone, Francesca,' Lydia said. She turned her attention back to Gabriel and Daisy. 'I'm very happy for you both.' She smiled at Daisy. 'We've become quite close since you began working at the Encore and I'm delighted that my grandson has found someone as perfect as you to be with. I hope you'll both be very happy together.'

'Well, so do I,' his mother relented. 'I was merely being curious.'

Before his mother and grandmother could descend into an argument, he held up his hand to get their attention.

'Would you two mind if Daisy and I went for a walk on the beach?' He hoped Daisy didn't mind him taking her away from the table, but wanted to give his mother a chance to speak privately with Lydia. They could discuss his relationship with Daisy without her having to witness any nastiness from his mother, and he knew Lydia would defend Daisy in any way necessary. He also wanted to spend some time alone with Daisy while she wasn't working and they had a chance to be alone.

'Good idea,' his mother said. 'You two go and spend some time together.'

If her tone hadn't been so gentle, Gabriel would have worried that his mother had an agenda, but although she was a talented actress, he knew her too well for her to fool him. Aware that his grandmother wouldn't mind him leaving them alone to muse over his recent announcement, he stood up.

'Shall we?' he asked.

'That would be lovely,' Daisy said, giving him a smile.

They walked hand in hand across the manicured lawn, past the long rose bed towards the steps where jasmine grew entwined with passionflower up over the granite wall. The delicate scent filled the air and he wondered if he could ever feel this happy again.

Daisy breathed in deeply. 'For some reason this place reminds me of that hostel in Hội An that we stayed in briefly,' she said. 'I think it's the pungent smell of these flowers.'

'I had that feeling too,' he admitted. The scents might be different, but being with Daisy again, on a warm evening and in love, took him back to those precious times where nothing else mattered.

He waited for her to go ahead of him down the steps and onto the soft sand. They kicked off their shoes and Gabriel placed them down on the sand. As they walked each stared out at the almost glass-like sea.

'Poor Lydia.' Daisy sighed. The sound was so heartfelt, so filled with emotion.

'What's the matter?' It was extraordinary to see someone care so much for his grandmother. Usually it was only he who noticed how special she was.

'Don't you wonder about Lydia and Lorenzo wasting a lifetime of love by their falling out in the fifties? It's tragic.'

He thought so too. 'Who knows what they went through, or why neither of them tried to reconcile years ago. Maybe the hurt was too deep for her ever to forgive him properly.' He stopped walking and held her from carrying on any further along the beach.

She turned to him, a frown on her pretty face. 'What's the matter?'

'I think that if nothing else you and I need to learn from Nan and Lorenzo. Nan has had a happy life, but it's been filled with making others happy. I want us to live our lives. I don't want to spend a second longer than I have to without you next to me.'

She smiled up at him, making words unnecessary. She wrapped her arms around his neck, pulled his head down towards her and kissed him.

Gabriel held her tightly, losing himself in the sensation of her mouth on his. He wanted her so badly, but needed to take things slowly. He'd let her down and now he had to work hard to ensure she never had a reason to leave him again.

Something wet and cold brushed passed his leg, but he ignored it until Daisy shrieked and jumped back. He looked down to see a black Labrador shaking the sandy seawater from its coat.

'Carson, come here!' shouted an angry voice. Gabriel and Daisy looked at the red-faced man carrying a tennis ball. 'Sorry about that,' he called to them. 'Didn't mean to disturb you.'

Gabriel bent down and patted the dog. 'No problem,' he said, wanting to reassure the man.

Daisy slipped her arm around Gabriel's waist. 'Lovely dog,' she said. 'Wet, though.'

The man laughed. 'We'll leave you to get on,' he said, throwing the tennis ball in the opposite direction to distract the dog, who immediately bounded off across the beach in hot pursuit.

'It seems we're never going to get any privacy,' Daisy said. 'There's always someone around.'

He was relieved to hear a need in her voice that matched his own. 'Stay with me tonight,' he said, before remembering that he was going to take things slowly. 'We don't have to do anything, I just want to sleep with you next to me again. I've missed the nights in Vietnam when we shared a bed.'

'So have I,' she said, looking up at him, a distinct glint in her blue eyes. 'Although I hope you don't have a small bed like those back then.'

'Does that mean you will?' he asked, barely daring to believe she'd agreed.

'Yes,' she said, pinching his waist lightly.

They walked a little further, each in their own thoughts. Gabriel wanted nothing more than to take her immediately back to his tower, lock the door and the rest of the world outside and lie with her in his arms. They had to return to his family first though and see how things were getting on between his mother and grandmother.

'Won't Lydia mind me staying overnight?' she asked, a pink glow coming to her cheeks.

'No. She never comes into the tower and has always respected my privacy. I'd have to rent my own place if she didn't.'

Daisy considered what he'd said and seemed to relax a little. 'We'd better go and see how they're getting on,' Daisy said eventually.

They arrived back at the garden, where they could see Lydia and Francesca still talking quietly. 'They're looking pretty civil,' Gabriel joked, as he pushed his feet into his shoes. 'Although they're all actors, so they could be putting on a good show for our benefit.'

'Don't be mean,' Daisy said, putting on her own shoes as she held onto his arm for support.

'You never did have very good balance, did you?' he teased. He tickled her waist and she screamed and writhed away from him. 'Stop it,' she said, pushing her hand through her dishevelled hair. 'I'm supposed to be acting like a lady. Your mother's my boss, don't forget.'

'She's not going to be worried by you having a little fun,' he said, tickling her again. When she'd stopped laughing, he grabbed her and holding her tightly against him, stepped back behind a tall cluster of palm trees and kissed her.

Eventually, she broke the kiss and pushed him gently away. 'Come on, we need to go back and join them. I hope they didn't see you pull me into the bushes.'

He laughed. 'They're not bushes, and I doubt they saw anything from where they're sitting – they're too involved with their own conversation.'

'Good.' She straightened her top and tidied up her hair. She looked up at him, studied him briefly and reached up to smooth down his unruly mop. She took a deep breath. 'Right, now we can go back and behave like sensible adults.'

'If you insist,' he said, raising an eyebrow and making her laugh.

They reached the table and the conversation stopped. Lydia studied them briefly and smiled.

'Good walk?' she asked. They nodded. 'Sit down and we'll let you know what we've been saying.'

'This sounds serious,' Gabriel said, concerned. He held out Daisy's chair for her to sit before taking his own next to her. 'Is everything OK?'

'It is, darling,' his mum said.

Lydia took a sip from her almost empty glass. 'Stupid pride,' Lydia said. She turned her attention to Daisy and added, 'Which is why I was so determined you should give Gabriel a chance to put things right over his marriage to Bella. I couldn't bear to see two young people making the same mistake Lorenzo and I made. We were headstrong and very foolish and have wasted far too many years by ourselves when we could have enjoyed a life together.'

'Are you saying you've never been happy?' Francesca asked her mother, leaning forward and resting her chin in her cupped hands.

Lydia smiled. 'No. I've been very happy with my family and friends. I've had a delightful life, but not when it came to love. I've been lonely a lot of the time, but it was of my own making.'

'Mum,' Francesca said, shocked.

'Just listen and stop arguing, Mum,' Gabriel said, resting his hand on his mother's arm to comfort her.

Their meal finished, Francesca stood up. 'Right, I think it's time I left. There's a lot going on at the moment.' She looked from Gabriel to Daisy. 'I have a lot to mull over. For now though, I'm tired.'

Gabriel nodded. 'I'll give you a lift home,' he said. 'I'll leave Daisy here to chat to you, Nan, if that's OK?'

His grandmother took Daisy's hand in both of hers. 'Of course it is. We have much to discuss.'

Gabriel waited for his mother to kiss Lydia goodnight and the two of them walked across the lawn to his car. He held the door open for his mother to get in and looked up to see Daisy and his grandmother watching them in silence. The evening had gone better than he'd expected. He just wished his father was back from his tour to be able to hear his news.

The last thing he needed to do now that everything seemed to be going so well was to push Daisy away. He'd have to tell her what he'd done, and sooner rather than later.

18

DAISY

Daisy was content to stay with Lydia at her home while Gabriel dropped off his mother. No one seemed to think it odd that he'd left her here. I'm being paranoid again, she mused, deciding to make a concerted effort to worry less about what others thought of her. She wasn't her mother and she'd seen how poisonous it could be to focus too much of negative thoughts. Above all, it was a waste of energy.

Lydia stared out across the garden towards the beach before she began to speak again. 'I think I realised for the first time since running away from Lorenzo with Francesca how much long-term damage his infidelity had caused me, when I watched you and Gabriel coping with your relationship. I knew it deep down, of course, which is why I've been so determined to see you and Gabriel find a way to work through your issues,' Lydia said.

Daisy swallowed the lump forming in her throat. She couldn't help thinking of her own mother and her wasted life waiting for Peter who was never free to be with her. 'So many wasted lives,' she said quietly. 'Why do people make choices to spite themselves, do you think?' she asked, aware she'd almost done exactly the same thing.

'I have no idea,' Lydia said. 'Foolish pride, most probably. None of us want to lose face or be humiliated.'

Daisy watched the beautiful lady she'd come to love and wished she could erase the hurt she'd suffered for far too long. 'Thank you for being so bossy with me and making me at least give Gabriel the chance to put things right.'

'Bossy?' Lydia laughed. 'I supposed I can be, but you're both well-suited. I could tell the instant I saw you together that you felt about each other the same way Lorenzo and I had done when we were young. I couldn't bear to sit back and watch two people I was fond of make an unnecessary mistake. You and Gabriel didn't deserve to suffer because of a bad choice he'd made, and any preconceived ideas where you were concerned.'

'You're right,' Daisy said thoughtfully. 'I've spent too many years watching Mum suffering because of her choices with my dad after he walked out on her that time. I didn't want to have to go through the same thing.'

'And that's completely understandable,' Lydia said, giving her a hug. 'But you're clever enough to listen to advice and act on it.'

They sat in silence for a while, each lost in their own thoughts.

'Gabriel showed me the pictures he'd taken of your paintings,' Lydia said. 'They're exceptionally good, you know.'

Daisy couldn't help smiling gratefully. 'Thank you. I wasn't sure I should have let him take the pictures,' she said. 'But he was so insistent and I do know that I have to step out of my comfort zone if I want to eventually have the confidence to exhibit them somewhere.'

'You were right to let him take the pictures,' she said. 'Others should be allowed to appreciate your work. It would be a dreadful waste for them to be kept languishing in your room at the back of the hotel.'

They heard the low roar of Gabriel's Triumph Stag. Daisy's heart contracted.

'He's back quickly,' Lydia said, unable to hide her amusement. 'I suppose he didn't want to waste any of the time he could spend alone here with you.'

Daisy could feel the heat rising through her cheeks.

Lydia smiled. 'I shouldn't tease. I enjoy the fact that two young people who I care so much about seem to be falling in love with each other. It brings out the romantic in me.'

In love? She didn't doubt for a second that her feelings towards Gabriel were exactly that, but could she dare to believe that he could feel as strongly towards her? She didn't have time to mull over the idea because seconds later Gabriel called out to them both and joined them back at the table.

Lydia smiled. 'I think you gave your mother a lot to think about tonight, Gabriel,' she said.

Gabriel frowned. 'Do you think I should check if she's OK?' he asked.

He looked at Daisy while his grandmother mulled over this suggestion.

'No, darling,' Lydia said. 'I think *I* should call your mother. I need to have a quick word with her anyway. Why don't you to enjoy the rest of this beautiful evening and I'll catch up with you both in the morning?' Without waiting for them to reply, she stood up, blew them both a kiss and headed back inside.

Neither of them spoke until Lydia had disappeared, then Gabriel smiled at Daisy and said, 'Did you get the impression she was trying to be subtle just then?'

Daisy giggled. 'Just a little.' She wasn't sure what to say next.

The thought of an entire evening ahead alone with Gabriel caused her stomach to flip over. Stay calm, she told herself.

He looked a little uncertain. 'What would you rather do?' he asked, leaning towards her slightly over the table, his eyes narrowed. 'We could go for a walk again. The tide is fairly high, but it should be quiet at this time of night.'

'Sounds lovely,' she said, picturing their stroll.

'Or I could show you round the tower?'

She could see he was trying to keep from smiling, but didn't quite manage to achieve a serious expression.

She pretended to consider her options. 'The beach,' she said eventually, standing up. 'It's a glorious evening and we should make the most of this hot weather.'

She noticed his expression slip very slightly for a split-second, only for him to smile and stand to take her hand. 'Great idea,' he said.

Daisy enjoyed him being disappointed in her choice, but didn't want to appear too keen. They might have spent glorious nights together when they were in Asia, but they were on his home turf now and she didn't want his grandmother to discover that she'd gone with him to the tower as soon as she'd turned her back.

She breathed in the warm salty air, enjoying the scent of tea roses and jasmine that she'd become to associate with this beautiful place. 'I love it here so much,' she said, not meaning to voice her thoughts aloud.

He gave her hand a gentle squeeze and looked down at her, smiling. 'I'm so pleased you're happy here,' he said. 'I want you to stay here, with me.'

He led her down the steps onto the beach where the sand was warm and the lowering sun coloured the sky in the brightest oranges and golds Daisy thought she'd ever seen.

'With you? I...'

He looked out across the gently rolling waves. 'I probably shouldn't have said anything.'

She was glad he had.

They came to the end of the small beach and turned a slight corner past a large rock. Daisy spotted an opening and without giving herself time to think, pulled him with her into the dark recess. He opened his mouth to speak, but she reached up and pulled his head down so his lips met hers in a kiss.

Gabriel let go of her hand and pulled her into his arms. Holding her tightly he kissed her with a passion she'd fantasised about since leaving him behind in Asia. Daisy's heart pounded against his firm chest. He held her so tightly her body was almost crushed against his. She hoped she wouldn't wake up and discover that these delicious sensations were something from a dream.

Unable to resist, she let one hand travel down his back, over his gorgeously tight bum. Gabriel froze for a second and she thought he was holding his breath. Neither spoke. She drew her hand around between them and ran her fingers down the front of his trousers.

'I don't want you to stop,' he whispered hoarsely, 'but if I have to walk back to the tower without being reported for indecency, then I think you'll have to.'

She moved back lightly and looked down to where her hand was resting on him. 'Sorry,' she fibbed. 'I couldn't help myself.'

He cleared his throat. 'Don't apologise. I'd love for you to carry on, but maybe we should do so somewhere a little more private.'

She let her hand drop. 'I thought this was private, sort of.'

He kissed her cheek and lowered his voice. 'It is, to a degree.' He motioned his head so she looked up over her left shoulder.

'But I don't want to give my Nan's elderly neighbour too much excitement for one evening.'

Daisy couldn't see anything apart from the edge of a house. 'What do you mean?'

He bent his knees so he was her height and pointed a little further to the left. 'The sun room, can you see it?'

She gasped. Sitting at the window staring out to sea was a wizened old man. 'You don't think he saw anything, do you?' she asked, horrified.

'Put it this way,' Gabriel said trying not to laugh. 'When I spotted him a few moments ago, he wasn't as interested in the horizon as he now seems to be.'

Mortified, Daisy turned away. 'I'm so embarrassed.'

Gabriel hugged her tightly to him. 'Don't be silly,' he soothed.

She looked down at the bulge in his trousers. 'Maybe I should walk slightly in front of you,' she said, unable to help laughing. 'Come along, I don't want to give that old guy anything more to think about.'

They made their way towards Lydia's garden as the sun set down behind the hills towards the west of the island. Just as they reached the steps Gabriel hesitated.

'What's the matter?' Daisy asked, noticing his troubled expression.

'I need to tell you something,' he said.

Her heart pounded. It had been such an exciting evening so far, she didn't think she could bear for him to disappoint her by confiding something that would ruin everything between them. 'Go on then,' she said.

He stared at her and then down at the sand for a few seconds. Then taking a deep breath, he said, 'I showed the photos I took of your paintings to my grandmother.'

Was that it? Daisy smiled, relieved. 'I know, she told me. She was very complimentary too, which was lovely.'

He narrowed his eyes. 'I also showed my mother.'

She could sense there was more. 'Go on,' she said warily.

'She loved them too,' he said.

'She did? And what else, because I can tell there's more.'

'They've both agreed to hold an exhibition of your paintings at the hotel.' He stared at her as she thought about this unexpected turn of events.

She could see he was concerned about her reaction, but how could she be angry with someone who was making a dream of hers come true?

'Seriously?' She almost held her breath, unable to believe what he'd just told her, picturing how her paintings would look hung on the pristine walls of the Encore.

Gabriel's mouth drew back in a wide smile. 'Yes, of course seriously,' he laughed. 'How do you feel about it?'

She shrugged, trying to gauge how this news made her feel. 'Scared that people will see what an amateur I am, embarrassed that they're not more professional...' She tried to think of other things to add. 'Um...'

'But you don't mind?'

She squealed and jumped up and down a couple of times. 'Why would I mind? I'm delighted.' She grabbed hold of him and kissed him.

He took her in his arms and kissed her back with such force she wondered if her lips would bruise – not that she cared if they did. He kissed so beautifully and she would happily spend the rest of her life wrapped in his arms with her lips pressed against his.

He let go of her and took hold of her hand. 'I'm relieved you're not angry with me for being so presumptuous,' he said, as they ran up the stairs.

They slowed to a walk as they crossed the lawn and took the pathway towards his front door. 'It's open,' he said, motioning for her to go inside. 'Welcome to my humble abode.'

'I feel like Rapunzel,' she giggled, as he poured them both a drink and showed her the way up to the roof terrace.

'Well, I hope no one comes here to rescue you from *this* particular tower,' he teased, handing her a drink. 'I want you all to myself tonight.'

She pretended to peek around looking for something. 'No more nosy neighbours lurking anywhere then?'

'Better not be,' he said.

They sat down on the bench and Gabriel put one arm around Daisy's shoulders. 'I've imagined you sitting up here with me many times,' he said.

'I've imagined being with you, too,' she admitted. 'But it never occurred to me to picture us up on top of a granite tower staring out to sea like this.'

He bent down and kissed her. 'I'm glad you came to work at the Encore.'

'So am I.'

They leant back and slowly drank from their glasses, each lost in their own thoughts and memories.

'Remember getting up really early and going to the river bank to sit and watch the boats go by?' he asked eventually.

She didn't like to admit that she thought about it far more than was probably good for her. She nodded. 'I do.' She shivered involuntarily and he mistook her reaction for the coolness of the evening.

'It's amazing how the temperature drops here when the sun goes in,' he said.

Daisy nodded.

'Shall we go inside? It's more comfortable there anyway.'

'OK.' She let him take her glass so that she could climb back down the ladder to his room below. Somehow he managed to hold both glasses while following her down.

'I also recall being on that train journey when you insisted we could fit in the same bunk together,' she giggled. 'I had a bruise on my hips for weeks from when I fell out.'

He winced. 'Yes, I still feel guilty about not catching you that night.' He glanced down at her hip. 'Is it all right now?' he asked, touching it lightly with the side of his finger, a glint in his dark eyes.

She put her hands on her hips and tilted her head to one side. 'If it isn't then I've got a problem.'

They stared at each other in silence for a few seconds and Daisy wasn't sure where to look, especially as his double bed covered with its stark white sheets seemed like some sort of beacon.

'Would you rather we go downstairs?' he asked.

She thought about his offer, and realising that she'd waited for almost two years for this moment, shook her head. He seemed surprised by her reaction, then placing the glasses on his bedside table, he sat down on the bed.

She stared at him, not quite knowing what to do next.

He leaned towards her on the white sheets. 'Are you going to join me?' His eyes narrowed slightly. 'If you'd rather not stay in the tower with me tonight I can always ask Nan if you can sleep in one of her spare rooms. She wouldn't mind.'

'Would you?'

'What, mind?' He shrugged one shoulder. 'Of course not. I want you to be comfortable with me.'

She couldn't help feeling a little disappointed by his answer.

He smiled and his dark brown eyes twinkled mischievously. 'But if you mean would I mind not making love to you tonight, I can't lie. I'd mind very much. I've waited a long time to lie next to your beautiful body.'

She wasn't going to hold back from him any longer. Hadn't he proved how much he wanted to be with her? Hadn't he done all that she'd asked? She couldn't help smiling as she stepped forward and onto the bed next to him.

Gabriel smiled a long lazy smile. 'Hello again,' he said, when she lay down. He bent down so his lips connected with hers in a kiss that was so perfect she never wanted it to end.

'I've missed you so much,' he said, kissing her neck, moving down to her breasts and then her stomach.

Daisy gasped and covered her mouth with one hand. She didn't want to distract him, this was too delicious.

He peeked up at her. 'You're so beautiful,' he murmured as he moved lower. 'But these need to come off.' He undid the fastening on the side of her skirt. 'Lift your hips,' he murmured.

She did as he asked.

He slipped her skirt down past her thighs and dropped it on the floor, leaving her in her knickers. 'These too?' he asked, that familiar twinkle in his dark eyes.

She nodded. 'Go on then,' she said, barely able to force the words from her mouth as she looked down at his broad shoulders.

He kissed the insides of her thighs and slowly inched higher, each step causing her to catch her breath in delight. His tongue began doing things to her that she remembered from their time away, and Daisy was beginning to think that she couldn't take much more when Gabriel looked up at her and smiled.

Kissing his way back up her stomach, then her breasts, he smiled at her. 'Yes?' he whispered.

'Yes,' she replied impatiently.

Gabriel finally entered her, kissing her as he did so. Daisy didn't want to close her eyes. She'd imagined this moment so many times. Watching his beautiful face as they made love was like living a dream. Unable to think clearly, she closed her eyes, climaxing just before he did. Gabriel whispered something she couldn't hear, holding her to him as her mind splintered and she knew nothing could ever be this perfect again.

* * *

Daisy woke slowly the following morning.

'I love you,' she heard him say, so quietly she wasn't sure she'd dreamt it. She opened her eyes and stared through the small window at the rolling waves as they hit the sandy beach. Had she imagined those words? She squeezed her eyes shut, willing her memories of the previous night to be real. She'd dreamt so many times of hearing him saying exactly what she'd just heard, or thought she'd heard.

'Did you hear me?' he whispered, kissing her bare shoulder.

'I'm not sure,' she teased. 'What did you say?'

'I said I love you.'

She turned to face him and snuggled up against his chest, loving him more at that moment than she could ever have thought possible. 'I love you too.'

His hand glided down over the small of her back, stopping at her bottom. 'You're my very own Jersey Bombshell,' he laughed, his eyes soft with love.

She pushed him onto his back and sat astride him. 'Say it again.'

ACKNOWLEDGEMENTS

To all the women in my life who make every day so much more fun, especially my mother, Tess Jackson; aunts Maggie Reynolds and Gerry T; sisters Kate Goddard and Rachael Troy; cousin Jane le Lievre; and sister-in-law Sabine Troy.

To the brilliant Boldwood Books team, especially my editor Rachel Faulkner-Wilcox, and my copyeditor Gary Jukes.

To Christina Jones for her continued support and for insisting many years ago that I would be published. I didn't believe her at the time.

And most of all to you, lovely reader, for choosing to read this book, I hope you enjoyed it.

ABOUT THE AUTHOR

Georgina Troy writes bestselling uplifting romantic escapes and sets her novels on the island of Jersey, where she was born and has lived for most of her life.

Sign up to Georgina Troy's mailing list for news, competitions and updates on future books.

Visit Georgina's website: https://deborahcarr.org/my-books/georgina-troy-books/

Follow Georgina on social media here:

facebook.com/GeorginaTroyAuthor

x.com/GeorginaTroy

instagram.com/ajerseywriter

bookbub.com/authors/georgina-troy

ALSO BY GEORGINA TROY

The Sunshine Island Series

Finding Love on Sunshine Island

A Secret Escape to Sunshine Island

Chasing Dreams on Sunshine Island

The Golden Sands Bay Series

Summer Sundaes at Golden Sands Bay

Love Begins at Golden Sands Bay

Winter Whimsy at Golden Sands Bay

Sunny Days at Golden Sands Bay

Snow Angels at Golden Sands Bay

Sunflower Cliffs Series

New Beginnings by the Sunflower Cliffs

Secrets and Sunshine by the Sunflower Cliffs

Wedding Bells by the Sunflower Cliffs

Coming Home to the Sunflower Cliffs

Hollyhock Farm Series

Welcome to Hollyhock Farm

LOVE NOTES

LOVE IN EVERY CHAPTER

WHERE ALL YOUR ROMANCE
DREAMS COME TRUE!

THE HOME OF BESTSELLING
ROMANCE AND WOMEN'S
FICTION

 WARNING:
MAY CONTAIN SPICE

SIGN UP TO OUR
NEWSLETTER

https://bit.ly/Lovenotesnews

Boldwood

Boldwood Books is an award-winning fiction publishing company seeking out the best stories from around the world.

Find out more at www.boldwoodbooks.com

Join our reader community for brilliant books, competitions and offers!

Follow us
@BoldwoodBooks
@TheBoldBookClub

Sign up to our weekly
deals newsletter

https://bit.ly/BoldwoodBNewsletter

Printed in Great Britain
by Amazon

41955160R00152